GOLD
The

ANTHOLOGY:

AWARD WINNING PIECES
FROM THE JCDC LITERARY FESTIVAL
(1999-2006)

Jamaica Cultural Development Commission (JCDC)
An Agency of the Ministry of Youth & Culture

ANTHOLOGY:

AWARD WINNING PIECES
FROM THE JCDC LITERARY FESTIVAL
1999 2006

PELICAN PUBLISHERS LIMITED
Kingston, Jamaica W.I.

First published in Jamaica 2013, Pelican Publishers Limited

44 Lady Musgrave Road
Kingston 10, Jamaica, W.I
Tel: (876) 978-8377 | Fax: (876) 978-0048
Email: pelicanpublishers@gmail.com
Website: pelicanpublishers.com.jm

Cover Art courtesy of The Fuller Art Collection. Artist: Richard Hall

NATIONAL LIBRARY OF JAMAICA CATALOGUING IN PUBLICATION DATA

The gold anthology: award winning pieces from the JCDC Literary Festival 1999 - 2006 / Jamaica Cultural Development Commission

p. ; cm.

ISBN 978-976-8240-11-8 (pbk)

1. Short stories, Jamaican
2. Jamaican fiction
3. Literature – Jamaica – Collections

I. Jamaica Cultural Development Commission

808.83   dc 23

TABLE OF CONTENTS

PUBLISHER'S NOTE

The Jamaica Cultural Development Commission (JCDC) has as its mission, the enhancement of national development through cultural practices aimed at creating opportunities that unearth, develop, preserve and promote creative talents and expressions of the Jamaican people. *The Gold Anthology* is evidence of the fulfillment of this mandate and enjoys a timely release during the JCDC's fiftieth anniversary. This long-awaited work is an impressive collection highlighting the rich talent that abounds on the Jamaican cultural landscape.

Pelican Publishers is pleased to facilitate the sharing of these works and joins in celebrating the cultural excellence of Jamaicans at home and abroad. This publication ties directly into our mandate to not only communicate with creativity but to foster the creative spirit. It is our intention to nurture this relationship with the JCDC to publish future anthologies and to also broaden the scope of work by including other genres. Congratulations to the contributors who deserve the highest commendation for their efforts.

Latoya West-Blackwood

FOREWORD

In 1987, on the occasion of the twenty-fifth anniversary of Jamaica's Independence, the JCDC published *Festival Literary Anthology*, a selection of gold and silver medal-winning short stories from the competitions spanning the period 1967 to 1983. In their 'Editors' Note,' Kim Robinson and Leeta Hearne expressed the 'hope that future volumes will be able to supplement this first effort, not only by filling in whatever gaps exist within this collection but also by featuring other categories ....'

The present anthology is the first to have appeared since then. Given the overlong delay, its appearance is all the more welcome, and achieves a kind of symmetry by occurring just after the fiftieth anniversary of independence. To win a medal, especially gold, in the Festival literary competition is crucial recognition and encouragement. However, the value of the work is virtually lost if it is never subsequently published, because that value really lies in the response of readers and, through that response, in furthering the benefit of literature to society.

What is more, a publication such as this may well have a ripple effect, in causing other publishers to be open to publishing other work by the writers represented. We cannot expect the JCDC to be routinely both organizer of the competition and publisher of the outstanding work elicited by the competition. That they have been able to publish these two anthologies is to their credit. The publication of an anthology such as this one is also of benefit to the JCDC itself, in that it is 'black and white' evidence of the important contribution of the competition, thereby helping to underpin the status of the competition. This publication, like its precursor, also provides model and encouragement to would-be entrants, and so helps to ensure the healthy continuity of the competition.

The stories in this collection afford much pleasure, even as they engage the mind and the imagination. They cover an appreciable range of subject matter, craft and tone. Humour complements and carries seriousness. There are levels of achievement among them, but a few are superlative. We may find ourselves asking of their authors, 'Where have these people been? Why have we not heard of them before? What else have they written?' They deserve to be recognized in any reasonably full account of the Jamaican short story.

The gaps in the first anthology that were mentioned by its editors are no longer likely to be ever filled, and perhaps there are also gaps in the new anthology. Besides, we are still to see an anthology that features any genre other than the short story. We live in hope, even as we rejoice.

Edward Baugh
February 4, 2013

PREFACE

Though many years have passed since *Festival Literary Anthology* was first published (1987), this time around we have captured some of the best gold-winning stories awarded in our annual competition. We are eager to get out writers published and thus their works exposed to the widest possible market. This 'brand Jamaica' product is of great quality and will stay with us for a very long time. Jamaican literary treasures are often hidden in the creative tapestry of our people. Jamaicans are noted for excellence in various fields of endeavour; writing is an area of great creative force. We are only on the surface, but as we tap into our creative source our potential is limitless. This feast of gold awarded works will provide new material for leisure reading, for academics and schools of all levels, as well as provide Jamaica with a billboard of creative works which may be considered for film or such other creative outlets. To discover more about Jamaica and her people, the lives of inner city to rural folk readers will find within this anthology male and female perspectives which are exposed in the superb stories enlisted.

Apart from my mandate to manage the three areas of responsibility, Literary Arts, Drama and Speech with distinction, it remains a pleasure for me witnessing the judge's ability to scrutinize the entries, pick them apart as they in assessment adjudicate and at ceremony learn who the winners are. I am thrilled when gold medallists are named. Our skilled panel of judges though unquestioned in their ability to determine winners are often criticized for their critical marking. This is natural with all competitions. Judges are often surprised when they learn who the winners are, since they mark words with pseudonyms and not the writers' real names. It is always a joy to see the reaction of the judges when they discover on the evening of the award ceremony who the winning writers really are. Many Jamaican writers of note have benefited from the JCDC's competition by entering, being recognized and eventually becoming well-known. All the creative works contained herein redound to the history of Jamaica, and the perpetuity of the works gives credence to the publication and its importance to exposing talent and enriching the literary landscape for all Jamaica.

Andrew Brodber
Specialist – Speech, Drama and Literary Arts

ACKNOWLEDGEMENTS

This book is dedicated to all the Jamaica Creative Writing Competition winners of the JCDC.

Thanks to Bena Nakawuki and Andrew Brodber for editing and Tracey-Ann Campbell of JCDC for administrative assistance. Without the help of these individuals the production of this anthology would not have been possible.

Special thanks to Pelican Publishers Limited without whose funding this publication would not be possible. However, the most important thanks and appreciation goes to our writers, all of whom are gold medallists, whose work has made this anthology and our competition possible.

MEETING SAM SHARPE

BY DIONNE JACKSON MILLER

2004

"David! Deborah! Come here right now!" Their mother's voice rang out across the spacious yard, easily reaching the children, who sat under the spreading tamarind tree.

"I bet you Mommy has some more boxes for us to unpack," David said unhappily.

The twins had been working hard all day, helping their parents move house, and had escaped outside to take a break. So at first they showed no sign of moving, until their mother appeared in the doorway, with hands akimbo. They jumped up guiltily, but before she could say a word, Deborah ran over and hugged her.

"Mommy, don't get vexed. We're just tired from working all day."

Her mother held her at arm's length and looked at her. "You think you're smart, Deborah Andrina Johnson. I tell you what, finish unpacking the suitcases in your rooms and you can take a break."

Sighing, Deborah looked back at David and they both dragged themselves reluctantly into the house.

"Somebody can tell me why Mommy and Daddy decided to move in the Christmas holidays," David grumbled. "By the time we're finished unpacking, the holidays will be finished!"

He was lying sprawled across Deborah's bed in her upstairs room in the spacious house they had moved into only yesterday.

"You're talking about holidays? What about homework? My problem is that essay we're to write about slavery for history class. You finish yours yet?" she asked.

"Finish? I haven't started! But we still have two more weeks of holiday. I can't worry about that yet."

The move was a big pain, but at least they weren't changing schools, David thought. They had just moved from a tiny, cramped house in Westgreen, a community in Montego Bay, to a district in the hills of St. James, because their father had just fulfilled his life-long dream of buying a farm and wanted to live closer to the property. Since they were still living in the same parish, they wouldn't be changing schools, just travelling further in the mornings. The move meant that they were miles away from all their friends, though, which they had both complained about bitterly. But when parents decided to do anything, children seemed to have no say in the matter.

Even though David and Deborah were twins, David often thought how different they were. Rolling over, he stared out the window, thinking about the essay Deborah had mentioned. Who could seriously think about homework in the middle of the holidays? That was something you did the weekend before school started, when you knew time had run out so you had to come up with something. Plus, he hated history. He just couldn't get excited about all those people who died years ago and who nobody cared about anyway. He couldn't understand why people still got so worked up about slavery. It had happened so long ago it wasn't even worth thinking about!

"Aren't you going to finish unpacking so we can get out of here?" Deborah asked, her face hidden by the lid of a suitcase.

"Don't believe Mommy. We're never going to get out of here. She just told us that to hold us."

Deborah moved across to the large cupboard to inspect it. "David, come and look at this."

"What?" he asked without moving.

"Come, nuh. There's something on the top shelf in here, but I can't reach it."

"Something like what?" he asked, still uninterested. Their house wasn't a new one, and the previous owners had left behind a fair amount of junk that had to be thrown out during the unpacking and cleaning.

"David, get up and look nuh!"

Reluctantly, he slipped off the bed, and moved across to Deborah who stood peering up into the darkness. Then he saw what she was talking about. It looked like a small barrel. His interest was piqued. He ran to get an old chair and climbed up, grabbing the object with both hands. It was larger than he had thought, and he had to balance carefully to make sure that he didn't drop it. He lifted it down and his eyes widened.

"It's a drum! Look at this, Deborah. It's a drum! And it looks so old!"

The drum was about two feet high, made of dark brown wood, with strange carvings around the base and just beneath the skin. David gave it an experimental tap, and sneezed as a layer of dust rose up into his nostrils. Deborah laughed, then went to get a damp dust cloth and threw it to him. He wiped off the drum reverently, anxious to try it out. But not in the house. Mommy and Daddy would hear, and who knows, might take it away from them.

"Come on, let's go outside and try it out."

"But what about the work?"

"Trust me man, just trust me."

He ran downstairs to get one of the cardboard boxes that had already been emptied and hiding the drum inside, headed outside. As he expected, his mother's voice came again.

"David, where you going? What did I tell you?"

"Mommy, the dust is really bothering us. We have to get some fresh air."

His mother looked at him skeptically, but didn't object any further, and Deborah ran out behind him.

Under the tamarind tree, he settled down with a feeling of excitement, the drum between his knees. It was late evening, and the breeze blew coolly across his skin. The coloured streaks that announced the approach of night were starting to colour the sky with their indigo and deep rose hues.

"Come on! Hurry up nuh!" Deborah urged him.

David pulled the drum closer to himself, and imagining that he was a member of a famous reggae band, he started to beat it slowly and tentatively. He beat the drum faster. His hands seeming almost as though they were controlled by something or someone else; the beat moved beyond him and swirled around him, as the rhythm stirred his blood and made him want to shout out in joy.

Suddenly, he heard Deborah cry out. Startled, he opened his eyes. Disoriented, he saw everything swirling around him. The place had gone darker. It seemed that there were no lights at all, and he could hardly see. He wondered wildly if a tornado had hit Jamaica, although he had never heard of such a thing happening before. He tried to stop drumming, but it was as if his hands had taken on a life of their own, and the heavy beat continued. He could feel Deborah clutching his shirt in fright. Finally, the dizzying turning stopped, and he was able to drop the drum. He reached out for Deborah's hand.

"Man, what was that!"

His head was spinning and he could see from the way that Deborah pulled away her hand and held her head that she probably felt the same way. Then he looked beyond Deborah and his mouth fell open.

"Deborah," he tried to say, but the word came out as little more than a squeak and she didn't even look up.

He cleared his throat and tried again.

"Deborah." This time he got her name out, but even to him, his voice sounded strained and hoarse.

"What happen?"

Unable to put into words what he was seeing, he merely pointed, and she looked up. Her eyes widened. Their house had disappeared. It just wasn't there anymore. The streetlights had also vanished. What they could see in the semi-darkness was a row of rooms that looked like shacks, and a little way off, with their backs turned, a small group of people. In the distance, he could see some large buildings. David couldn't think why he hadn't noticed the changes at once, but maybe it was because he had been so dizzy.

The children sat for a few minutes, looking at each other in disbelief. Then David got to his feet.

"Come on, we have to find out what's going on."

They crept closer to the group of about fifty people, who were all gathered around a tall, dark skinned man, who was addressing them.

"That's why we have to take our freedom! The massas don't want to give us. The Queen freed us long time ago, and you see they still have us living here in slavery. We have to take our freedom."

"Take it? How you mean Joshua?"

The question came from a woman near David. He glanced at her and suffered yet another shock. He had never seen anyone dressed like that before. She was wearing a head tie and a long full skirt with an apron over it, and had bare feet. He glanced around. Everyone in the group had bare feet, and all their clothes seemed old, threadbare and faded. In the old clothes in which they had been cleaning the house, he and Deborah almost fit in.

"That's why Daddy Sharpe says we must stop working till they give us our freedom," the man called Joshua continued.

"Stop work? All of you must be mad. Yes, you and Daddy Sharpe too!" shouted another man. "Either of you going to come here and take the whipping for me when they decide to kill me?"

Murmurs of agreement came from a few of the people there.

"We have to stand together, Isaiah. They can't do anything to us if we all stand together. Look how many of us, and look how few of them," Joshua said.

"How many of us? But who has the guns, eh? Tell me that? Who has the guns, Joshua?"

"Isaiah, hush you mouth. You talking like you want to stay a slave all you life. Let Mr. Joshua talk!" another woman shouted.

Suddenly a little boy ran up, breathing heavily. "Overseer coming, overseer coming!"

"So you see, you have to accept Jesus Christ!" shouted Joshua suddenly, startling David.

"Do you accept Jesus?"

"Yes!" shouted the crowd.

"Do you know that things will be better over yonder?"

"Yes!"

"Well, then, come and join me and sing of the Lord's love for you." And the group broke into a fervent chorus.

Deborah nudged her brother.

"Act like you singing or they'll notice us," she whispered.

David started clapping and pretending to sing, although he didn't know the words. He heard the drumming of a horse's hooves and to his right, saw a white man approaching on a horse. He wore a broad hat, and was much better dressed than anyone there. He said nothing to the group, but sat there watching them sing. They seemed to pay no attention to him, but as the women sang and twirled and the men clapped their hands loudly, David got the strange feeling that they were putting on a show.

The man sat there, for about ten minutes, scowling at the group, but saying nothing, and then just as suddenly as he had come, turned the horse and left. The group continued to sing for a while, and then broke off again. Deborah leaned over to him.

"David something really weird is going on. Are you listening to them?"

"Yes, but I don't understand what's happening."

"You didn't hear them talk about Daddy Sharpe? Don't you know who that is?"

David looked at her blankly. Deborah sighed.

"Oh, I forgot how you're always sleeping in history class. Daddy Sharpe is Sam Sharpe, the national hero. And they're talking about what happened during the Christmas rebellion, when the slaves stopped working because they thought England had already abolished slavery, but the slave owners weren't telling them! David, we've gone back in time!"

David looked at her, and burst out laughing.

"Right!" he said.

"Aright then. You tell me what is going on. Where is our house? What are those shacks there? Who are these people? Why are they talking about slavery as if it still exists? And who was that white man on the horse?"

David looked at her. Deborah must be crazy. All those books she read and all those history classes must have driven her mad! He looked over at Joshua again, who was still talking intensely to the crowd.

"Well? They doing it tonight. We joining them or not?"

"Yes," shouted most of the group.

David saw one young woman near to him clutch a baby closer to her. The little girl was about two years old, and was sleeping on her mother's shoulder. David saw the young woman slip away from the group. Curious, he watched her until she entered one of the rooms a few yards away and closed the door quietly behind her. He supposed she didn't want to be a part of whatever was going to happen. He leaned over to Deborah.

"Ok. Let me get this straight. You're trying to tell me that we've gone back a million years in time, and this is now slavery time."

"1831," Deborah said helpfully.

"1831, why does that sound so wrong?"

"You don't think the Christmas rebellion happened in 1831?"

"Deborah. I never knew anything about the Christmas rebellion, so I have no idea when it happened. What is wrong is our being here!"

"It must be something to do with the drum, so you better hold on to it."

Grabbing it up from where it had fallen a few feet away, David saw that the crowd was dispersing, but not with the languor of people heading home after a long meeting, more with the energy of people moving on to something else.

One man ran past him and shouted out, "I tired of all this talk! Things going to happen tonight! Plantation burning down tonight!"

"No, we're doing this peacefully!" Joshua shouted, but the man paid no attention to him.

David and Deborah stood frightened, holding hands. David was clutching the drum under his free arm, and wondering what to do next.

Suddenly, someone called to him. "You with the drum! Come on!"

David hesitated, and the man said impatiently, "What you waiting for? I said come on!"

He followed the man, jogging to keep up, with Deborah right behind him. They passed some long, dark, buildings, saw some donkeys tied up in a yard and then came to a smaller building set a little apart. A group of other men was gathered around it, but then, one dark-skinned, scowling man shouted at them to stand back. Everybody shuffled back, as he held aloft a burning branch, before throwing it into the building, shouting "Freedom!" The building caught fire, slowly and the fire started to spread.

"Start playing!" the man who had led them there whispered to him urgently.

"What?" David asked, startled.

"Start playing. Send the word."

With no idea what he was doing, David again started to beat the old drum. But again his hands took over, and this time the beat was slow, and insistent, its sound echoing out into the countryside.

"Keep going," the man shouted, and ran off again.

David played long enough to see the men run off, all holding burning torches aloft, and in a few minutes fires started to spring up all over.

"What happened?" he asked Deborah.

"To whom?"

"What happened during the Christmas rebellion? And Christmas not gone anyway?"

"It really happened after Christmas. But like I said, the slaves believed that the slave owners didn't want to free them. Sam Sharpe was trying to get them to go on strike, but the slaves started burning down the plantations, and it started a rebellion, and the English soldiers ended up hanging a lot of people."

David stopped drumming abruptly.

"Hanging people? They hanged people? You have me standing here like an idiot drumming and they're going to be hanging people soon. Come on!"

"To where?"

"Away from where they hang people!" He said taking off.

In the distance they could see a group of men galloping towards the building. Their pale faces shone in the light from the fire as they shouted inaudibly to each other. The children ran past all the factory buildings. The doors to a few had been broken open by the men, and David could glimpse huge cauldrons in one, and in another smaller shed, an assortment of tools.

As they slowed down panting, the young woman David had seen earlier ran up to them screaming for help. "What happen?" David asked frightened, as he tugged on his arm. "My baby, my baby in the room and the fire coming! I put her down to sleep and went to see what was happening, and look, the building catch fire!"

David and Deborah looked up aghast, seeing the fire licking its way along the rickety porches in front of the room. "The rooms not on fire yet," David called. 'We can still get her."

"But we can't get through the verandah," the woman protested. "We can get in from the back," David called.

Without explaining further he ran back to the tool shed he had passed earlier, and looking around wildly, saw an assortment of machetes, hoes and some axes. Heaving one of the axes over his shoulder he ran back to the rooms, where the woman was now huddled in a heap on the ground crying. Deborah leaned over, trying to comfort her.

David paid them no attention and instead, ran around to the back of the flimsy board house and began hacking at the wall. It was hard work even though the wood appeared rotten. It seemed to take him an eternity to yank the heavy axe back out of the wood it had splintered and heave it again.

Out of the corner of his eye he saw two men running towards him, both carrying axes as well. With their help, the work went a lot faster. And soon there was a hole in the wall. They were trying to make it even bigger, when they heard the little girl scream.

"Stop, stop!" he shouted. "I have to go for her.

"You will dead!" one of the men shouted back.

"Nobody else is small enough to go through the hole," he said quickly, and not waiting to argue any more, started to climb through the hole.

The child was huddled into a corner near him, but the flames were very near, and the room tiny. Grabbing her up, he could feel the heat from the burning wood, which put up no resistance at all to the approaching flames. The child screamed again, and without bothering to take the time to comfort her, he ran back towards the hole, shoving her through. He felt someone take the child from him, and then grab his arms and haul him back out.

As he slipped through the hole, he felt the heat of the fire and tumbled on to the ground in his hurry to get away.

Outside, the woman was crying noisily and clutching the baby so tightly the child was crying out in protest. As soon as David tumbled on to the ground, she grabbed on to him.

"You saved my baby. You saved my baby!" She repeated over and over, embarrassing David, who was trying to gently extricate himself from her grip.

"That's alright," he said awkwardly.

Deborah punched him gently on his arm. "That was great!" She whispered.

"That was really great!"

Just as the fuss was getting to be embarrassing, a man ran by shouting, "Daddy Sharpe come, Daddy Sharpe come!"

Instantly, the people who were gathered around ran off.

The baby's mother stayed long enough to hug David one last time, her eyes brimming with gratitude, then she too ran off. David looked at Deborah and shrugged.

"Come on, let's see what's happening!"

They followed the stragglers until they saw the crowd gathered around a tall, thin, black man on a horse. They crept near to the front of the crowd, close enough to see the man's face in the light of the torches being held aloft by several of the men. Even with all that was happening, David noted that the man held himself on the horse erectly, with assurance and although his brow was creased with worry, he still appeared calm and authoritative.

"This is not what we wanted," he was saying to Joshua. "The plantations are burning all over St. James, and there is word that the white men have sent for the soldiers."

"But we can't back away now, Daddy Sharpe!" Joshua said.

"No," Daddy Sharpe agreed. "Try to keep the women and children safe, and try not to shed more blood than we need. Remember, we are acting in God's name, and he is not a God of murder."

Then he was gone, his horse's hooves pounding through the night. Long after David could no longer see him, he still seemed to hear the hooves pounding rhythmically. He strained his eyes through the night trying to catch another glimpse of Sam Sharpe, but feeling Deborah tugging at his arm, he looked around to see a young boy pounding on the drum, which he had put down nearby. That was the pounding he had heard, the familiar rhythm of the drum. Running over, he grabbed the drum away, hearing the boy's angry exclamation, but ignoring him.

Feeling the earth beginning to swing around him, he shouted out to Deborah, not seeing her. Suppose Deborah was left behind. He stared wildly around, looking for his sister, while the echoes of the drumbeats combined with the gently swinging landscape made him dizzy. Desperate now, he hit the drum hard, once, and shouted, "Stop!"

Amazingly, the spinning began to slow down, until he could make out once again the astonished faces of the young boy he had grabbed the drum from, and the men and women around him.

"Deborah," he shouted anxiously, not caring what they thought. But while he was looking about him wildly, he saw her running over to him crying.

"I thought you were leaving me!" she cried out. As she grabbed on to him, he started drumming, surely and strongly this time, and felt the now familiar sensation of dizziness.

After what seemed to be a very long time, the world settled down, and he opened his eyes, to find Deborah staring at him, under the tamarind tree. He looked around cautiously, almost afraid of what they would find, but he needn't have worried. He could see the light from their house spilling into the yard, beyond the house the streetlights gleamed reassuringly, and the sound of a television assured him. He could see the gleam of tears on Deborah's cheeks, and still frightened at the thought of how close he had come to leaving her behind, he wordlessly grabbed her hand and squeezed. Then, after hiding the drum once again in the cardboard box, he sprinted into the house.

"Wait! Where you going?" Deborah shouted after him, but David had gone.

By the time she caught up with him, he was lying on his stomach on her bed, deep in her history textbook.

"I wanted to see what happened after we left," he said without looking up. Deborah sat at the edge of the bed and waited.

"Listen to this Deborah: *The English called in reinforcements to quell the uprising, and arrested over three hundred slaves, including Sam Sharpe, the leader of the revolution. Sharpe and many others were hanged in the town square.*"

"They hanged him Deborah! They hanged him, and he wasn't even the one who wanted it to be violent!"

David read on.

"The Christmas rebellion, as it came to be known, hastened the end of slavery, and was one of the most important and final uprisings in the country. It reassured Sam Sharpe's place in history and his later status as one of Jamaica's national heroes."

Shutting the textbook, he sat up and looked at Deborah.

"You know how I always said that history is boring and irrelevant?" His sister nodded.

"It seems real when you realise that all these things happened to people like us. I wonder what happened to Joshua, and that little baby I saved?"

Looking off into the distance, he was silent for a while, and then looked over to Deborah and grinned.

"Do you think we can go back?"

"What are you, crazy?"

Deborah stared at him, and then slowly began to smile.

"Maybe. But not yet. I still have to recover from this trip!"

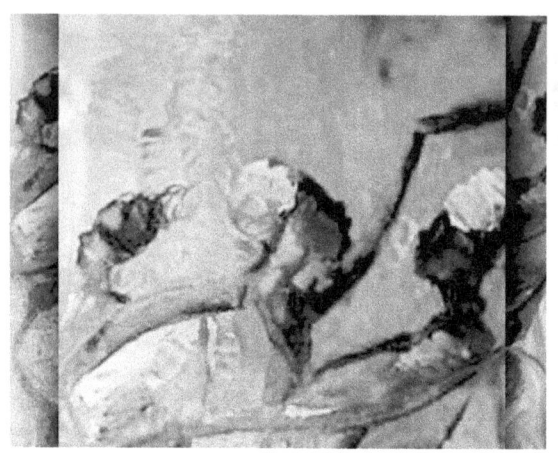

FI-WI MANGO DEM

BY CLAUDETTE BECKFORD-BRADY

2006

Wi nuh drink caafi-tea, mango time;

Care how nice it may be, mango time;

At di height-a di mango crop,

When di fruit dem a ripe an' drop,

Wash yu pat, tun dem dung, mango time.

The loud, off-key strains of the Jamaican folk song shattered the golden silence of the shimmering, early-June, Sunday afternoon. Prior to the assault on the silence, the only sounds that had graced the ears of Miss May had been the chirping and chattering of the birds that socialised in the orange tree outside her living room window.

Miss May leaned her head to one side to listen better. If she didn't know differently, she would swear that the singing was coming from right inside her front yard. But of course it couldn't be. She lived alone, and today was not the gardener's day, and besides, the gardener was a taciturn old man who never smiled, and rarely spoke – never mind sing.

Miss May got up from the day-bed she had been lounging on, and went to the window to look out into her front yard. The singer, whoever he was, had heard her unspoken plea, and the singing had stopped. The orange tree was devoid of birds; the strident tones of the singer had obviously scared them away, but the absence of the birds was compensated for by the snowy-white blossoms which sent a heavenly scent wafting through the open window and into the living room.

The garden looked serene in the golden glow of the late afternoon sun. The bougainvillea along the front wall ran a riot of colours; from pale pink through to the deepest reds and purples, and from rose through to burnt orange, all accessorised by the snowiness of the white variety. The border on one side of the driveway boasted many-hued crotons, and red and white hibiscus, or 'shoe-black' as they are commonly known. Several patches of Impatiens, locally known as 'Impatience,' and Coleus, known as 'Joseph Coat,' grew in the shade of tall Anthurium Lilies, while baskets of orchids hung from the limbs of various trees.

Miss May smiled as her eyes and heart revelled in the beauty of her garden. Her eyes continued their journey around the yard, passing over the St Julian and the East Indian mango trees, which were laden with ripe and turning fruit, past the patch of peppermint and fever (lemon) grass under the sweet-sop tree, and came to rest on the large overhanging branches of the Aden mango tree which extended several feet over her fence from the tree in the yard next door.

The entire tree was well-laden with ripening fruit and the branches which protruded over the fence and into Miss May's yard were bowing down low under the weight of the fruit they bore. She had picked as much of the ripe fruit as she could reach, but there was so much more beyond her reach. She would have to wait until her son came by to pick the rest, or get some of the youngsters who were always begging for fruit.

As Miss May looked at the tree she noticed something strange. Although there was no breeze, the tree was doing a kind of dance; the leaves were shaking, and one limb was practically touching the ground, rising and falling as if... Miss May went closer to the window and peered closely at the dancing tree limb.

"But you ever si mi trial!" Miss May marched briskly from the house, out onto the veranda, pushed open the grill and stepped out into her front yard. She strode purposefully across the lawn to the fence separating her yard from the next door premises and stood beneath, but slightly to one side, of the dancing branch, which was just above her head height. She glared up into the leaves and demanded to know, "And just what yu think yu doing, Sarr?"

The branch dipped and the leaves danced, and Miss May retreated a step, although she was not within reach of the branch. Then a bare foot appeared, followed by a leg in cut-off jeans pants, and then another foot and leg. Finally a torso in a torn merino, and then a head, came into sight as the person sat on the limb of the tree, one foot dangling and the other

14

wedged into the space between two limbs. The combined weight of the man and the fruit caused the branch to come down to Miss May's head height.

The elderly woman and the young man stared at each other; Miss May in stunned silence, the young man with an insolent grin on his face. Before Miss May could gather her wits sufficiently to speak, the man spoke.

"Maaning, Godmadda. Jus' picking dem few mango here. Nutten naa gwaan fi mi, and A figga A kyan sell two mango and mek two shilling, yu nuh seet?" The insolent grin remained in place.

"Well, of all the nerve!" Miss May was almost incoherent with outrage. "First of all, young man, I am not your Godmother, and secondly, how yu mean to be picking my mangoes to guh and sell? These mangoes don't belong to yu; they are in my yard…!"

"Is not your mango tree, Lady. It deh een-a fi-wi yaad; a fi-wi mango dem."

"Is not suh it guh." Miss May begged to dispute his statement. "The tree might be in your yard, but these branches that hang over into my yard belong to me, together with any fruit they bear. Your grandfather never give mi any problem in all the thirty years wi live beside each other; he knew these mangoes belong to me."

The young man yawned rudely without covering his mouth. "Papa dead and gone; him did too saaf, but is we run tings now, an' right now, mango a sell, and mi need di money. Suh I gwine finish pick dese mangoes and get out-a yu way."

Miss May was weak with impotent anger, but what was she to do? She could not physically prevent the man from picking her mangoes; she was sixty-eight years old and of small frame. What she needed was 'backative'; someone to stand up for her, and let this out-of-order young man know that his insolence would not be tolerated, and neither would the stealing of her mangoes. But she had no such backative to hand. She retreated indoors, defeated for the moment.

But Miss May was a woman of indomitable spirit. She would not accept defeat without a fight, but she would have to choose her battlefield and plan her tactics. She picked up the telephone and called her son, Calvin, who lived a few chains down the road. Calvin would deal with the trespasser; he was a strong, big-boned man with an intimidating appearance, and he was an attorney-at-law. Calvin would know what to do.

Within minutes, Calvin's SUV pulled up in front of the house. Miss May immediately took him over to the mango tree, which was still dancing and dipping from the activities of the young man.

Calvin said authoritatively, "Stop pick those mangoes and come down out of the tree!" A few tense moments elapsed, and then the first bare foot reappeared, followed by the rest of the body. This time, instead of sitting on the branch the man dropped to the ground in front of them.

"Waapen, Godfaada?" he enquired, before Calvin could speak. "A not doing anyting wrong, Sarr; juss picking mi mango dem. A fi-wi mango dem."

He spoke in a tone of reluctant respect, but hung his head down and refused to look directly at the person to whom he spoke. Miss May opened her mouth to speak, but Calvin raised a hand to silence her. He spoke to the bedraggled young man.

"These mangoes belong, under common law, to my mother by virtue of the fact that they are on her side of the fence. The fact that the tree is in your yard is entirely irrelevant, because in order to reach the limbs to pick these mangoes yu have to venture over the fence, which, in effect, means that you are trespassing on my mother's property.

"Furthermore, even if the mangoes did belong to you, there is nothing wrong with being a good neighbour and sharing the bounty. Look how much fruit yu have on your side of the fence. When yu grandfather was alive there was no dispute with him over the mangoes; it was share and share alike. We were good neighbours."

The young man was not impressed, as was evidenced by his bodily demeanour, but he was too much in awe of Calvin to be openly defiant. Nevertheless, he spoke his mind. "Look here, Sarr; if good neighbour is what yu want to be, why unnu don't share some an unnu money wid us. Nutting naa gwaan fi mi, an' mi have pickney fi sen guh school and bill fi pay. If unnu a-guh grudge mi di two mango dem, di lease unnu cyan do is help mi out wid some cash."

Both Calvin and Miss May were taken aback by the bold effrontery of the man. Calvin recovered quickly, as befitted his profession as a lawyer. "But yu bright and rude to! Is hard work provide my family with what wi have; wi never born with gold spoon in our mouth, nor get nuh hand-out. Yu young, strong, and able bodied. Why yu don't find some gainful employment that will provide a living for yu family? Why yu don't join the army or something? The pay good, and the discipline even better."

The man sucked his teeth and without another word, swung himself back up into the tree where he retrieved a bag half-filled with mangoes, and retreated along the limb until he got back on his side of the fence, where he vacated the tree. Calvin and his mother stared after the retreating man in confounded consternation. Miss May finally found her voice.

"Well, from I was born...! What a rude bwoy! Well, if the mangoes belong to him, then so do all the leaves that the tree shed on this side of the fence. In future when the gardener rakes up the leaves and 'drop-mangoes' I will see to it that they are returned over the fence to their rightful owner!"

Calvin reproved her. "Two wrongs don't make a right, Mama. Yu nuh have any need to descend to fi-dem level; I know yu bigger than that. A gwine pick some of the mangoes fah yu, and yu 'low him the rest. If it's that important to him, let him have them."

Calvin picked a dozen fit and turned mangoes and found one lovely ripe one nestling amongst the leaves which the poacher had missed seeing. He offered it to his mother, saying, "Yu can eat this one today; it ripe to perfection," but Miss May refused it. She had made up her mind that she would not eat any of the mangoes from that tree in future, but she would pick as many as she wished to give to the neighbourhood children who frequently came begging for mangoes, and the bwoy could go to the devil!

The next afternoon, Miss May was dozing on her day bed when she was jerked into full consciousness by a loud raucous buzzing sound which seemed to come from her front yard. She got up and went outside to investigate, and was just in time to see the Aden mango tree branch, which protruded over her fence, come down to land with a crack and a crash, onto her peppermint and fever grass. The buzzing sound ceased as the power saw was turned off, and a loud, pregnant silence filled the air.

Miss May was too shocked to move, let alone to say anything. She gazed in astounded silence at the large piece of mango limb with many secondary branches attached, and which was still loaded with young and almost fit mangoes. The limb had come to land with the main part resting on the fence, and the end branches and leaves in Miss May's herb garden.

The silence, which in reality lasted only a few seconds, seemed to stretch into eternity, but finally it was broken by voices from next door, which galvanised Miss May into motion. A loud angry voice was shouting. "God Almighty, Clovis! Weh yu chop off di mango limb fah?"

Miss May recognised the voice as belonging to the mother of the 'mango thief'. She moved toward the fence, galvanised by the voice and her burgeoning anger, but was arrested by the voice of the young man, Clovis, answering his mother.

"Juss cool, nuh Mama; wi ha' whole-heap-a mango lef'. Nuh worry yuself." His voice held no note of regret for his wanton act of destruction. His mother's querulous voice continued, and Miss May, who had been ready with angry words of her own, waited her turn, and listened to the dialogue from across the fence.

"But weh yu chop it dung fah? It wasn't troubling yu. Is bad-mind yu bad-mind. Yu nuh good, bwoy! Yu-a fi-mi pickney, but yu nuh good! Is a sin, wha' yu do!

"Yu nuh have nuh right fi deh 'arass Miss May; is ovah t'irty 'ears she an' Papa live side-an-side, and nevah a cross word. When A was a chile, shi was always good to mi, and now yu come here come-a trouble di woman. A shame a-you!"

Miss May felt slightly mollified at this vilification of the young man by his own mother, but still felt it incumbent upon herself to have her input. She covered the short remaining distance to the fence and called, "Miss Dorette?" to the young man's mother. The woman approached the fence and rushed into speech.

"Laad Gad, Miss May, A sarry fi what di bwoy do. A nevah have nuh idea seh him would-a do suppen like dat when A hear him deh grumble bout yu an di mango-dem. A shame suh till A cyan barely look pon yu!"

Miss May had known Dorette since she was a child. She did not blame her for what had happened today, although in truth, some little blame could be applied for the way the boy had been raised, without the proper amount of discipline. Nevertheless, she absolved Dorette. But the boy was a different matter. Miss May wanted justice, and truth be told, revenge. She was only human, after all.

She launched into speech. "A don't blame yu, Miss Dor, but A don't want yu to feel nuh way when A have yu bwoy up in court. He have no right to do what him do, even though the tree is in your yard. Those are my mango branches him cut down."

The young man spoke before his mother could respond; "A have every right fi cut dung di limb. A fi-wi mango tree, an a fi-wi mango dem."

However, later that day when Miss May instructed her son, Calvin, to start proceedings against the young man, she was disappointed by his response. Calvin said that in point of law, any neighbour having a tree which breaches another's property, has a duty to keep that tree trimmed and clear of his neighbour's property. In the case of fruit trees, which are of benefit, by mutual agreement, the neighbour may be excused from trimming the tree. However, if that neighbour wishes to cut off the overhanging branches, for whatever reason, spite included, he could do so if he wished, because it is his tree.

Miss May was outraged. "But yu said the overhanging branches belong to me, Calvin. I distinctly remember hearing yu seh-suh."

"I said the fruit belonged to you, Mama. Let it be. What's done is done, and although it's a sin what he did, still, let it be."

Miss May was loath to let it be, but she had no choice. But that boy could not be allowed to get away scot-free. "Well, him have to pay to have the limb removed, and have my garden cleaned up and my herb bed rehabilitated." Calvin replied that he would make sure that the bwoy came over and did the work himself.

Miss May did not want the boy anywhere on her property, and protested that he should be made to pay out of his pocket, where it would hurt him most, but Calvin, who was a Deacon in his church, and a good practising Christian, told her that "to err is human; to forgive is Divine." Miss May, who was also a good Christian, decided that, just for today, she would rather be human than Divine. Forgiving would be most difficult; almost impossible.

The young man was not chastened by his being made to clear the limb and tidy the garden, and went about it with a cheerful whistling, which fed Miss May's anger. But there was nothing she could do, so she sat on her veranda and watched him work, making sure that he did not help himself to any fruit from her garden. Miss May was a kindly woman, and willingly gave away scores of mangoes every year, when she could quite easily get them sold, but she was damned if she was going to let this boy have even one of her mangoes. She glared balefully at him as he worked.

The following Sunday at church, Miss May prayed for forgiveness for her anger and vindictiveness against the young man, and resolved that she would forgive him for the terrible thing he had done, sinful though it had been. Henceforth, whenever she saw the young man she would greet him cordially, and not hold a grudge. After all, she still had plenty of mangoes of her own; she could afford to forgive the poor sinful soul, poor thing.

And she would pray that God would cleanse him of his sinful and insolent ways.

A few weeks later Miss May was startled to hear her name being called from next door. If she didn't know better, she would swear it was the rude young man, but this voice sounded rather pleasant. "Hello, next door. Are yu there, Miss May? Could yu spare a minute of yu time?"

Miss May went out into the front garden and went up to the fence. The space where the mango branch had been was still obscenely empty, but there was nothing to be done about that. She had decided to let bygones be bygones.

Miss May had been right, it was the young man; only now, he looked quite different. He wore a clean starched white shirt tucked into black pants, and polished black shoes. His hair, which had previously been bushy and uncombed, was now cut low and had a clean, 'just washed' look.

Miss May was surprised to see the change in the young man, and it was not only in his dress. His very demeanour was the antonym of his previous attitude. He greeted her cordially as she approached the fence. "Good afternoon, Miss May. A hope a not disturbing yu from anyting too important, but a have something a want to seh to yu."

Miss May returned the greeting with like cordiality and waited for the young man to proceed. He met her gaze squarely, and said, "Miss May, A want to tell yu how sarry I am for cutting down the mango limb. It was a wicked and spiteful ting to do, but A want yu to know dat yu kyan get anyting yu waant from ovah here-suh, anytime at all, whether mango or orange or anyting at all."

Miss May gazed at the young man in amazement. Could this be the same bad-mannered and bad-minded bwoy who had been so insolent? If so, something miraculous had happened to change his demeanour. The young man gave her the answer to her unspoken question.

"Miss May, A don't know if is your prayers, or Mama own, but Jesas work a miracle eena mi life, and mi get saved. A want to invite yu to mi baptism next week. And any time yu want any Aden mangoes, just seh di word, for the bounty that God provide should be shared by all a wi. Fi-mi mango dem now belong to yu as well, Miss May.

"No more my mango, but fi-wi mango dem."

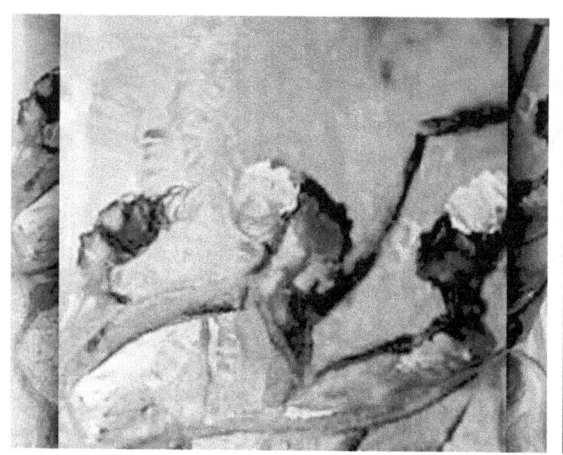

WHEREVER YOU MAY BE

BY RUDOLPH WALLACE

2000

Let phartz be phree, wherever you may be,

Phor that was the death of poor Mary Lee.

Epitaph in Lacovia Cemetery, St Elizabeth, Jamaica

You may have observed on your last trip to Lacovia cemetery that the famous Mary Lee gravestone, Lacovia's leading landmark, has fallen into disrepair and is now barely legible. Yet, the dusty path leading to the stone stands out like a beacon in the midst of the overgrown shrubbery, testifying clearly to its continuing reputation as an oasis for the idle and a Mecca for the mentally deficient. Little boys, rejoicing in the unmitigated vulgarity of the epitaph, spend hours after school frolicking in its precincts, and elderly matrons still come from all parts of the earth to peruse its asinine inscription and express socially acceptable levels of disgust.

To whom it may concern, the grave in question is mine. My fervent wish is that fifty years from now the ravages of time will have taken their full toll on the confounded stone and the fable it sought to immortalize will itself be expunged from the public consciousness. In the event that you have led a cloistered life to this point and have been spared the saga of "Poor Mary Lee" I will not lend currency to the tale by dwelling long on the distasteful epitaph. I wish only to observe that a facetious tombstone builder, seeking to establish himself as a rural wit, took the liberty of openly attributing my death to a misguided retention of gas, and in so doing sullied my reputation forever. My death certificate, if we are to be precise, reads *flatus interruptus*, capturing neatly an esoteric medical concept impenetrable to the layman and far beyond the comprehension of a common stone mason. For him to trespass on such delicate aspects of my life was a piece of unmitigated gall, and I cannot begin to understand how my relatives allowed him to defile my image and tarnish the family name merely to ingratiate himself with the baser elements of the Lacovian peasant class. It is not unreasonable to suppose that if appropriate action had been taken against this semi-literate poet in 1891 the people of Jamaica would not have had to suffer the equally senseless rhyming of his progeny in the dance hall more than 100 years later.

Be that as it may, the sad fact is that I, so admired while I lived, have come to be remembered in death only for the manner of my passing - a passing which has been crudely sensationalized by the bumpkinry and badly misconstrued by the nobility. You may perhaps ask at this point why, if I felt so strongly about the matter, I did not come forward before now to speak my piece. If you do so ask, you betray your ignorance of the metaphysical sphere. It is well known that we dead observe all things and can indeed make contact with the living, but our lack of corporeal structure prevents us from putting pen to paper or convening large gatherings. Accordingly, our means of communication have heretofore been limited to one-on-one Hamlet-type visitations, which only serve to expose the host to ridicule and detract from the content of the message. Now, thanks to the Internet, I can set the record straight despite my physical limitations and intend to do so without further preamble. If at the end of this treatise your thirst for knowledge has not been fully slaked, I urge you to visit my ethereal web site (www.phartz.com) for a fuller exposition of the details.

The story I am about to relate took place in the spring of 1890, several weeks before my twentieth birthday, when I was by all reports in the flower of my womanhood. So ravishing was my beauty and so elegant my bearing that it was being whispered in certain important quarters that I was destined to marry well above my station. That station, I must confess, had been considerably debased by the peculiar circumstances of my birth. My father was a Chinese merchant who had used his substantial wealth to secure the hand of a true-blue daughter of the British plantocracy. Alas, he was as delicate in body as he was astute in mind and succumbed to a tropical disease in 1874 when I was but four years old. In my earlier years I greatly resented my Oriental heritage, and servants were careful not to utter the word "mongrel" in my presence. All that changed one day when I was twelve or thirteen years of age and a perceptive manservant remarked that my still evolving beauty was derived entirely from my racial blending. Had that simple comment not fallen upon my ears I might not have come to harbour quite as keen a sense of loyalty to Lim Quong Lee, my formidable sire.

My mother, for her part, had the good fortune to outlive me and made her presence felt in every aspect of my upbringing. To ensure that I was thoroughly grounded in the principles of high society she retained the services of an English governess, one Miss Faversham, who taught me how a young lady of quality should flaunt her breeding in any and all situations. It was the same Miss Faversham who introduced me to the manifold nuances of wind-breaking and who, I suppose, must ultimately share responsibility for the manner of my demise.

In my day (as in yours) there were two types of gaseous emissions, the upper and the lower, and both, Miss Faversham taught, had to be controlled by proper timing. The upper emission, the belch, was the more socially acceptable and therefore the more dangerous of the twain. Many a young lady had been made to suffer public ostracism because of a poorly timed, badly managed or improperly disguised belch. As a young debutante, I learnt the skillful use of the folding fan in the execution of the belch. Among the uninitiated it was generally imagined that the fan, raised discreetly to the lips, was intended to conceal a whisper, or to mask a blush or giggle. That is what onlookers were supposed to think, and that is why the regular lifting of one's fan was guaranteed to improve one's coyness rating. Once, at a debutantes' cotillion, I was approached by a giggling Elspeth Smyth-Browne, eyes glowing as if about to impart a delicious bit of gossip. As she deftly raised her fan I cocked an eager ear, thereby exposing a full half of my face to what turned out to be a belch from hell, seasoned with wine and garlic. How I remained standing I will never know, but one matron who saw me stagger towards the door in search of fresh air later circulated a rumour that I had fallen victim to an unladylike excess of alcoholic spirits. The lower emission, which Miss Faversham insisted should at all times be referred to as the "tush", also required proper management if its socially damaging effects were to be mitigated. The secret here was to deflect all suspicion on to servants, a large body of whom could always be seen milling around in any household of quality. It was of vital importance that the lady of the house be constantly attended by a lady-in-waiting, carefully selected from among her most loyal maidservants. As far as I was ever able to gather, the lady-in-waiting in truth waited for one thing only: a sign that the mistress wished to relieve herself. This devoted attendant would then draw near and unflinchingly take responsibility for any foul odour wafting about. In a simple and elegant ritual Madam would direct a brief frown towards her trusty minion who, in the manner of an agile relay runner, would accept the baton of blame by adopting a suitably sheepish look. The fouler the odour the more disapproving would be the frown and the more sheepish the look.

While on this subject I must recount the strange case of Elfreda, a swarthy hireling of ample proportions who seemed ideally suited for the role of lady-in-waiting, but who was less than willing to take up the responsibility when the situation demanded. It was rumoured among the household staff that she took no pride in servitude and in fact harboured ambitions beyond her station in life. Be that as it may, her first mistake was to be her last. One day she caught a whiff of something _a third rate emission actually _and had the temerity to turn sharply towards me before I could turn on her. It was a purely domestic gathering but I nonetheless dismissed her on the spot, lest her insubordination infect the entire household. Mother thought me a trifle harsh but Miss Faversham wholeheartedly approved. The good Miss Faversham had been profoundly affected by what she had read of the French Revolution, and always kept a sharp eye out for incipient rebellion.

Without delving too much into the science of the tush I wish, with your indulgence, to address the dangers inherent in public emissions and to explain why technique was therefore so important. As every schoolboy knows, the loudest explosion is obtained by catching the pocket of air at its zenith and punching it forth with maximum gusto. For the daughters of gentry the containment of sound was of paramount importance, so we were taught to adopt the opposite course: to wait until the window of opportunity was on the verge of closing, until the gases, having found no release, were about to re-enter the body's innermost chambers. Then and only then were we to lightly squeeze, in a manner that gave no outward indication of the complex interplay of inward forces. Unfortunately, what you lose in decibels you gain in pungency, and it was impossible in a crowded room to conceal altogether the existence of the demon gas. What mattered was not whether someone had "tushed" but who — and I saw clearly, despite my youth, that the orderly functioning of Jamaican society would forever depend on the public response to that crucial question.

It stands to reason that it was the servants, those indispensable participants in the process, who best understood where real talent lay in this regard, and among the Lacovian servant classes there was none who would not have readily placed me in the first rank, fartwise. My most rhapsodic admirers stood ready to pit my skills against the finest ladies of the land, claiming that whenever I opted to go audible I could select a note in key with whatever the orchestra was playing at the time, and render my contribution with such immaculate precision that not even the keenest conductor could detect my input. One admirer likened me to a Mr. W. G. Grace, with whom apparently I shared the gifts of flawless timing and spontaneity, and though I did not know who this Mr. Grace was, I determined to redouble my efforts to one day surpass him.

Lest the reader become concerned that my simple treatise threatens to go beyond the pale or, God forbid, has already gone there, let me hasten to explain that an appreciation of the context is essential to a full understanding of the events leading to my demise on the evening of March 27, 1890. Suffice it to say that a well executed tush spoke as clearly to a young lady's breeding as a well-turned curtsy and required even more practice. When Miss Faversham had finished with me, I had developed such a level of expertise that I welcomed, nay, caressed every opportunity to demonstrate my prowess. Each belch became a melody of manners and each tush a virtuoso performance. At banquets and parties I was wont to select legumes, vegetables and meats purely on the basis of their ability to generate flatulence, and it was not unusual after a large meal for me to have at least three servants standing by to assume responsibility for my emissions, so copious was my output. I even developed a technique, later to be known as the 'Mary Lee Manoeuver,' which allowed me to channel the air athwart the bias so as to produce a sound that could not be accurately identified with any known bodily function. I was a genius, and I knew it.

Sometimes, after a particularly active day, I would lie awake in bed recalling in loving detail the day's emissions and the often hysterical reactions of the inhalers, who never imagined for one moment that odours so gross could conceivably emanate from one so delicate. Mother had coined a clever phrase: "a little knowledge is a dangerous thing," but what she had failed to mention was that too much knowledge, to the extent that it leads to hubris, is infinitely more dangerous. I had been taught to control and to manipulate. I knew when to hold back and when to let fly. But at the governor's soiree on that fateful day, I was confronted with a set of circumstances not anticipated by my tutor, and that, as it turned out, would be my downfall. Mother and I had been frequent visitors to Kings House in the days of Governor Clark so we were not overawed by the invitation to a welcome soiree for his successor, Sir Morton Higgins. We thought it significant that only four families from the parish of St. Elizabeth had made the list and the blue-blood Kerr-Jarretts had not. Sir Morton, who had two grown sons, had been careful to invite only those families with nubile young ladies, which was a clear sign that he was scouting for prospective daughters-in-law, and mother was thrilled that my Chinese blood had not disqualified me from consideration. Today a party guest, tomorrow a bride. She saw it as a natural progression and the inevitable culmination of her many years of hard work. Miss Faversham's expertise had not come cheaply but the finished product seemed more than worth the price. With a modicum of good fortune, she reasoned, our small family would be set for life.

In the days leading up to the big event, I pondered an interesting fact to which I had not given any previous thought. I had never met a man, young or old, married or single, who had not fallen completely under my sway, and although I knew nothing about the Higgins boys I was firmly resolved that regardless of the competition I would overpower them both with my charms, if time allowed.

The banquet hall was more crowded than we had ever seen it, with at least five hundred guests and an appropriate complement of servants. The governor had indeed managed to gather into one room the cream of Jamaican pulchritude and I wondered whether his sons would measure up to the occasion. There were, by my rough estimate, more than eighty eligible young ladies, most of whom I already knew, including some of the island's truly famous beauties. Amanda Eccleston was looking better than ever, but at twenty-five was a good three years too old to pose any serious threat. We had a good laugh at the Antonio girl from Portland whose backers continued to labour under the notion that her short stature might somehow be mistaken for youth, though to the rest of the world the hardness of her features clearly indicated that she was approaching thirty. Elspeth Smyth-Browne could on her day have been a force to be reckoned with, but the style of her hair and the design of her gown betrayed her mother's kwashi tastes and I ruled her out of contention from the start. Mother chatted on and on about the poor standard of the competition and however much I was predisposed to feign humility, I had to agree with everything she said. No one in the room could hold a candle to me, and the governor's sons would have to be mentally retarded not to grasp such an obvious fact.

I distinctly recall the emotions that gripped me as I stood waiting in the reception line. The next few minutes would be the most important of my life and I had to be sure to follow my instructions to the letter. I was permitted to size up the sons from a distance but was not supposed to look at them once they came within ten feet. I was to make prolonged eye contact with Lady Higgins, whose opinion was certain to carry greatest sway in the early rounds; I should smile at the governor, then turn my head away lest I be considered forward; and I should pay no particular attention to the sons but be sure that they caught my best profile. From a distance, I could see that the two sons were vastly different in age and appearance. Morton Junior, the elder son, was a grown man in his mid-thirties who straddled, with difficulty, the thin line between plain and ugly. For him to be arriving in Jamaica without so much as a fiancée, suggested on top of everything else that he was either a playboy or a clod. Regardless, I ruled him out from twenty feet. If I may be perfectly frank it is possible that my main reason for dismissing Junior was to create extra room in my plans for Alexander, his younger brother, who came as close to my ideal physical specimen as any young man I had ever beheld in the flesh. When the time came for us to be introduced, I extended my hand casually towards him as instructed, while continuing to smile with his father, then, in a moment of wild improvisation, squeezed his fingers so tightly that he blushed and hurried on his way. Luckily for me, mother detected none of this brazen and disgraceful behaviour and assumed that it was my beauty alone that caused the staff to hurriedly rearrange the seating and place us directly opposite Alexander at the dinner table.

During dinner, I spoke just enough to enhance the mystery of that initial encounter. Every comment of mine was carefully thought out and fairly bristled with intelligence, which is more than could be said for Alexander himself or the overdressed tart to his left. By the time we were halfway through the main course, I began to perceive a grave risk that vacuous chatter and childish giggling might win out over mature discourse. The girl, who was pretty in an artificial kind of way, had started to recount an incident involving a puppy and for some reason which I could not fathom Alexander was quite amused by it. Never one to cast my pearls before swine I decided to embark on an entirely different course of action, one calculated to dispose of my giggling rival, and to treat Alexander like an ordinary twenty-year old youth, albeit one with better breeding than the young men I had previously encountered. For more than five minutes I tried vainly to catch his eye, since I could harbour no realistic hope of orally distracting him from the tart's asinine, rambling story that was holding him in thrall. When finally he did glance in my direction, the dense youth seemed not to notice the sensuality in my eyes and averted his stare after a couple seconds. In desperation I sought experienced counsel.

"Mother..." I whispered, "This thing isn't going right."

I could tell from the look on her face that further dialogue was unnecessary.

"Don't worry Mary, we'll get another chance."

"When?" I asked. "A year from now, after he's married to that ...that trollop?"

"He's seen you my dear; he's not going to marry her!"

Mother was trying to maintain her own composure and may well have raised her voice a trifle too much. The puppy storyteller stopped yapping and looked towards us.

"Could you please pass me the salt, mother," I said, deftly changing the subject.

The request was quite ordinary in the circumstances, but mother's response was truly inspired. As she stretched over to reach the shaker, her hand struck a glass of Burgundy, spilling its contents directly onto the lap of the girl, who squealed like a stuck pig.

"Oh dear, that was clumsy of me," mother apologized, proffering her napkin in a gesture of genuine contrition.

The tart and her chaperone were already standing and servants were hurrying forward from every angle. This was an opportunity for me to demonstrate my graciousness and I milked it to the full.

"Why don't you go with them, mother," I suggested, "I'll be all right."

Flushed with embarrassment and with all eyes staring, the poor girl hurried away, closely followed by her chaperone... and mine. I now had the field all to myself and could feel the adrenaline returning.

"I'm so sorry, sir. I hope you didn't get wet too."

"No I didn't," he smiled, "and please call me Alexander"

"Alexander... You don't strike me like an Alexander"

"Well, I'll definitely strike you if you keep calling me 'sir.'" We both laughed. "You have a very pretty laugh. Has anybody ever told you that?"

"I didn't think you'd noticed," I remarked, not having the heart to tell him that his compliment paled in comparison to the praises normally showered on me for my astonishing beauty.

"You were so taken up with your friend…But who could blame you, she's so beautiful ... and she seemed to be such a good storyteller."

"I didn't realize that she was making such a great impression on you," he said, totally unmindful of my puny attempt at sarcasm.

"I'm talking about the impression she was making on you." I blurted out. "You couldn't take your eyes off her!"

I had gone too far. God only knows what had possessed me.

"I can see you're a different girl when your mother is not around"

"Oh? Different how?" I asked, hoping somehow to retrieve the situation.

"You know how," he insisted.

He was staring at me intently now, and I realized that I was blushing; not the contrived debutante's blush I had been taught to affect whenever I wished to appear demure, but a genuine blush brought on by his piercing unrelenting stare.

"I... I think it's a little warm in here, don't you?" I asked.

"I've been told that this is normal weather for the tropics," he countered.

I mumbled something and went back to my food. In less than two minutes, I had entirely lost control of the situation and had been reduced to the level of an ignorant peasant who could do no more than fidget and stare at her plate. At that moment, I wished the entire conversation had not happened, that the naïve young lady now sobbing in some remote ante-chamber had been allowed to finish her silly story and that I had never lain eyes on Alexander what's-his-name.

When we had finished dinner, I politely excused myself and resolved to go in search of mother, who would surely still be rejoicing in her exploits and would need to confront the unpleasant reality without further delay. For some unexplained reason, tears were welling up in my eyes and I knew that they would start rolling down my cheeks if I did not soon reach the exit, but the aisles were fast becoming crowded as dinner guests rose from their tables. As I made my way in between the elegantly dressed bodies, my racing mind sought to come to terms with what had gone wrong. I had prepared all my life for precisely this moment, but was there a chance that, like the Five Foolish Virgins, I was not ready for the Bridegroom? It was said that I lacked nothing in beauty and manners, but could there be, in that grey world inhabited by personality, character and temper, some fatal flaw which mother, perceptive as she was, had not detected? Surely it was she who should be made to answer for this unfolding tragedy?

A few yards to my left I spotted a half-open door through which a servant was exiting the hall, and decided to seek refuge there regardless of where it led. Alas, before I could advance further I felt a firm, almost violent grip on my arm and turned to confront a grim-faced

Alexander. This unexpected and quite inappropriate public spectacle brought an entirely new perspective to the proceedings. To the dozens of guests who must have wondered at my strange behaviour, Alexander seemed to be sending a clear message. Their opinions did not matter at that moment; perhaps for him they never did. I too, suddenly, stopped caring. In a matter of seconds we were weaving through the crowd, arm in arm, pausing occasionally only to look into each others eyes. The seriousness of Alexander's demeanour added an element of fury to what was already the most exciting moment of my existence. For all I knew, he was whisking me off to some distant hilltop where he would ravish me to within an inch of my life, Good! I had always been fond of "Wuthering Heights" and this was a Heathcliff/Cathy moment if ever there was one.

Once outside the great hall, Alexander relaxed his countenance and lengthened his stride. Within a matter of seconds, we traversed a long corridor and entered what seemed to be an unused bedchamber. Only after bolting the door behind us did he slowly let go of my arm.

"Alexander,' I panted "what was that all about?"

"It is I who should be asking you that question", he replied, staring deep into my eyes. "Why did you run off and leave me like that?"

"I don't know," I sobbed.

I was crying and laughing at the same time, and he had the good sense not to pursue the same line of investigation. He pulled me close to him and it was as if my entire body was encased in a warm furnace.

"Here, dry you eyes," he said, offering his handkerchief.

"What's the use?" I asked, "there are many more tears where those come from, and they're just waiting to spill out."

I could tell from the bewildered look on his face that he didn't know what to do, so I smiled and hugged him. The warmth that had engulfed my body before now seemed to permeate my pores and invade my entire being. Was this love? Probably not. I had never felt love before and this was a familiar feeling... An all-too-familiar feeling, come to think of it.

"Alexander," I whispered, "where are we?"

He thought for a moment before answering.

"To be precise we're in the west wing of the governor's mansion. But what is more important, we're somewhere they can't find us."

His face had been getting closer to mine, and I was sure he would try to kiss me in another few seconds. My debutante's training required that I hold him at bay for a while, but that was not my main consideration. The chill that was starting to grip my stomach dispelled whatever doubt I may have had regarding my inner sensations. I had dined liberally on legumes and was about to pay the price.

"Where can I go to powder my nose?" I asked, still very much in command of the situation.

"Your nose is perfect, my dear, don't worry about it," he replied mischievously.

"Really Alexander, I must.." He grabbed hold of my wrist as I attempted to turn away.

"Enough of these childish games Mary," he breathed heavily, "let me kiss you the way I've wanted to from the moment I laid eyes on you."

Ordinarily, I would not have been averse to the suggestion, but as mother used to say, 'first things first.'

"We will get to that later, if you behave." I said, placing a finger on his thrusting lips. "Right now, you will show me to the powder room."

I was handling the occasion brilliantly, all things considered, but unbeknownst to me my sensuous beauty had unleashed in the young man an animal passion which coyness and diplomacy could not easily overcome. Brushing my hand aside he drew my face towards his and pressed his lips on mine. The jerking motion of my outward frame seemed to precipitate the movement of the gases within, and I could tell from the churning build-up that we were not dealing here with any simple playground tush. I had to tear myself away and I had to do so immediately. With luck I could make it to the banquet hall where accusable servants would still be in attendance.

"Alexander, please"... I cried, "You're hurting me!"

His eyes were glazed like a man in a trance. I could not help thinking that the impending explosion would be the surest means of bringing him to his senses, and that it would serve him right. Of course it would also signal my departure from polite society, since no lady of quality, as far as I was aware, had ever been caught in a tush, and no gentleman of substance would ever consort with a lady who had been so caught.

The moment of truth was fast approaching and I could not break free from the grip of the hapless youth. All thought of making it to the banquet hall had now vanished from my mind. I would be lucky to make it to the doorway. No sooner had the thought crossed my mind that the doorway was no longer an option. Any sudden move and it would all be over. At most, I had a couple seconds at my disposal and I needed to summon every fibre of my being for what was shaping up to be a monumental contest between man and nature or, more precisely, woman and wind. I tightened my stomach and held my breath, determined to ensure that no portion of this monster should see the light of day. I stiffened as the pressure reached its apogee and then, after what seemed an eternity, it was over. The vile gases slowly receded and my body relaxed, trembling, in Alexander's arms.

"Oh you inscrutable Orientals," he remarked, "Why do you try so hard to conceal your true emotions?"

For him, evidently, my shuddering frame confirmed what he dearly wished to believe: that I had been totally overcome by his charms, my passion had peaked and I was now in the throes of some kind of afterglow. As history records, he did not preen himself for long. I was quickly overcome by dizziness, my eyes rolled over and my body fell limp.

"Mary... Mary..."

Alexander was gradually becoming aware of my contorted features and the cold clamminess of my skin.

"God, what have I done?"

To be fair to the young man we must conclude that it was out of panic rather than cowardice that he dropped my lifeless form like a bag of hot coals and hurriedly departed the bedchamber, pausing only to ensure that nothing of his was left behind.

The servants discovered my body within twenty minutes of my demise. It is said that they were led to the location by the noxious fumes that hung like a cloud over the entire west wing of the governor's mansion. There was no great mourning in Lacovia, from what I was able to observe. The cognoscenti surmised that, like some famous gladiator expiring after a bruising encounter in the arena, Mary Lee had fought the good fart and lost. She had been felled by the Big One, true, but her essence lives on.

The astute reader should have no difficulty placing my accomplishments into proper perspective. Unlike those athletes who throughout the ages achieved notoriety by excelling in arcane endeavours, with many spectators but few real practitioners, I was hailed as the premier exponent of an art practised by all of mankind. This is indeed a monumental accolade, and my humility, in the circumstances, is astonishing. The day will never come when we spirits will be in a position to do our own carving. Perhaps a compassionate reader will do me the favour of altering the offending inscription as follows: "The bold Mary Lee instinctively lived life to the full, but in the end could find no refuge from the consequences of her bravado." Now there's an epitaph!

DRY RIVER
BY VERONE JOHNSTON
2003

America, 1777

Some people are born to be mothers. I was known as the Mother from Tennessee, but over time it became Ma Tassie. In fact, my birth name was Nina, which in our tongue means 'young mother', so in a way I really was born a mother...

Those are the first words of the little book on my lap. *Memoirs of a Centenarian Slave Woman*. They tell me 'centenarian' means someone who is one hundred years old. But I'm not a hundred. At least, I don't think I am, not yet. Not ever, I hope. The burden of life is crushing me, slowly. Each breath, in, out, in, out, I hear and feel it raking its way through my thin body like a serrated knife dragged backwards through a soft membrane.

It's strange the way my life feels so heavy now that I'm free after a lifetime of slavery. Too old to enjoy it, they whisper. Too used to hard labour. I'm proud to admit I don't know how to be idle. The devil makes work for idle hands, they taught us. True enough, I never saw the masters do any work.

Hard work stops you from being able to think. I'm told it's a way to control the poor. For me it was a mercy, or how could I have borne the separation? But now that my body rests, I can't stop thinking about my children – the children of my body, the ones I lost. You see, children are our reason for living, just as our ancestors lived for us. And they continue to live in our memories. Will my blood children remember their mother? Perhaps not, but some part of me will be in their nature, their looks.

I feel strong this morning and have made them help me down the stairs into the sitting room. I'm sitting in a shaft of sunlight, where I can see dust floating like little fireflies. I rock myself gently, while Honey sits near me writing. She and her brother Daniel work for the Anti-slavery Society here in London. Twice a week the house is filled with people crying out for abolition, all of them white. They pretend not to notice that Daniel and Honey are coloured – after all, they're not that different, the way they look and talk and dress. And there I sit in the middle of them all, hissing and sizzling like a doused kitchen fire as I smoke my pipe, sucking in my thin black cheeks. I must look very strange to them, but perhaps they find me simply 'exotic'. They were always asking me questions, but soon gave up when I refused to talk. Could anything I said bring back my five lost children? It would only make them pity me – the poor old Negro woman.

It took all four of them – Daniel, Honey, Freddie and Elmer – almost a year to make me agree. They said my story could help others, but I just wanted to be left alone. I didn't trust writing. It's not the proper way to teach anything. But they said I was old-fashioned. That if I did it I would be remembered…

My tiredness, my fear, my sorrow – all in this little book! My fingertips brush the rough surface. It feels like any other. There's a picture of me on the front. It's my face, but I'm wearing something from the Bible and I'm in a garden with people behind me lying on cushions eating grapes and being served wine by little cherubs.

When they began to read to me from it, I was sure they'd brought someone else's story by mistake. Had I really said those words? Daniel told me they'd fought to keep my voice, but that writing has certain standards and etiquettes. I didn't know what he was talking about until Elmer explained: "It's the difference between biting into a chicken leg and having slices carved for you at the dinner table." That sort of makes sense, I think.

I turn the pages and roll my eyes from side to side as though I'm reading. Words must have some special magic that I can't understand.

It was hard to resurrect a sixty year old memory and live through it again. But I finally managed to pull together the events like a drawstring through a sack. And here it is, *Memoirs of a Centenarian Slave Woman* – me.

…A great number of us set out on the journey north from Hope Farm: men, women and children, with a few fowl, vegetables and dry foods, as well as the master's personal effects, like clothes and books and tobacco. I believed it was to be a short trade journey, such as he

had undertaken before, though this was the first time I had been made to accompany him. I think the others felt sorry for me, which is why they did not tell me the truth. After the buggies deposited us and our belongings at the river bank, they turned around and drove away. When they did not return, I grew anxious that we would not find our way back without them; but no one else seemed concerned. There was just sadness on the faces of the other slaves, and the usual resignation.

The master had gone to find some accommodation for himself so the rest of us sat down on the bare earth and waited to find out what we were to do next. I hugged my three children and tried to relieve their boredom with stories.

My son Assa soon found a way to indulge his favourite pastime by digging into the ground with his fingers, pulling out great handfuls of earth, and fashioning them into human and animal shapes. Meanwhile his brother Usayy, who was always hungry, kept darting into the bushes and coming back with various kinds of berries for my approval. To his disappointment, most were poisonous, but Assa found a use for them as eyes for his model people. Eventually they both wandered away with some other children and I continued to comfort my infant daughter, who had begun to fret under the sun's heat. From our place on the high ground we could look down onto the river which cut a narrow path through the sun-baked earth, moving slowly and lazily south towards the sea, intensely blue.

Even when the keel boats slipped up silently and moored, it did not occur to me that they were intended for us. When the others began loading the goods, I still did not believe it. Finally, a little after sunset when the heat had melted away, the loading was complete and everyone was commanded aboard. I began to cry because no one would tell me where we were going. I do not think the slaves knew, for they had all lived on the plantation most of their lives, like me. The master was already established in the central cabin, and the crew were waiting to cast off. With the heedlessness of youth, Assa and Usayy had already scrambled on board and I could hear their laughter mixed with that of the other children. I had no choice then but to follow them aboard, clutching my daughter tightly.

Late that night, the other slaves told me the dreadful news: he had sold the farm. Before they had a chance to block my way, I was out and up those steps onto the deck, faster than a scurrying lizard. "Nahri! Taruba!" I screamed into the night, and tried to climb overboard. I had both legs over the railings by the time anyone was able to restrain me and pull me onto the deck, where I collapsed, half fainting.

They carried me below and laid me on a mat, and called to Assa and Usayy, who had to be dragged forward, since they were shocked to see their mother in such misery and terror. But the people pushed their hands into mine and held us together, even as the two boys tried to pull away. They were trying to remind me I still had these children to think of; but it was no good.

Hope Farm was sold, and my eldest son Nahri, being big and strong for his age, was needed to continue the work for the new master. And as I had taught my daughter Taruba to cook, she was to take my place in the kitchen. I lay in the dark surrounded by my misery, and I called to Nahri and Taruba, hoping my voice would carry south with the flow of the river until it reached them at Hope Farm. If only I could tell them I would come back for them one day, so that they would be left with kind hope in place of their mother.

We were days on the Chattahoochee, with only a feeble wind to carry us. Quite often, the men had to lower the canoes, tie them to the boat by broad ropes, and row vigorously for hours to keep us on course. I stood at the stern looking back and listening to the oars plunging and creaking, wishing they would all snap and the canoes sink, so that the boat could take its natural course back south.

Inevitably the tide changed, pushing us into Atlanta, from where we continued cross country to the coast. And there, the reward of those strong men who had tirelessly rowed us to safety and carried our provisions, was to be sold on the riverbank to the highest bidders, who descended like jostling hyenas. When we moved on, it was with only half our number.

The ship that was to take us further on this reluctant journey was much larger than any I had ever seen. Rumour had reached us of great vessels trapped at the river mouth like frightened cattle penned in for slaughter; with only their dwindling supplies to sustain them in the face of a British invasion.

This time, as we were herded up the gangplank by foul tempered sailors shouting and shoving us, even the children dragged their feet and hung onto their elders. Nothing could have prepared me for the filth and squalor which we were expected to inhabit. And the other poor slaves we saw were lashed together, some with weeping sores from the chaffing of the shackles; women were shamefully exposed, and children left to wail in hunger and fear.

As usual, the master retired to his cabin and took no notice of us. The Carolina crew were a set of ruffians who took pleasure in tormenting the other slaves for their amusement.

To avoid their vicious attentions, our little group from Hope Farm stayed below, enduring great heat, rank odours and overcrowding. Since the master would not eat food prepared by anyone else, I was able to escape to the kitchen for the better part of the day. The air was stifling, but it was a change from the cramped cabin where children cried throughout the night and men and women groaned and retched. I carried my little girl on my back, while Assa and Usayy were stowed under the table where I worked. Usayy loved food, so he would gather up and eat the fallen scraps like a little bird. Assa liked to make people laugh, so he spent his time moulding the surplus dough into funny faces and putting them in unexpected places for the other slaves to find. He even made a striking likeness of the captain, but I prevented him from going anywhere near that man. So we stuck it on the door and the kitchen hands spat and threw rubbish at it.

Eventually, news reached us that Georgia was being abandoned to the Crown and slaves were escaping by the thousands to join the Loyalist cause. That explained why the men on our ship were chained and we were confined below.

In those conditions sickness was inevitable. Even though I washed and fed them and kept them with me in the kitchen, the fever found its way to my two boys. There was nowhere to nurse them except the hot airless room, where I stayed up all night fanning them until my hands seized up and I could barely knead the dough in the morning, and my eyes were as red as though I had been pounding salt.

Three days later Assa died. I remember waking suddenly. There was no noise, and I could feel Usayy's feet digging into my back. I felt his heart, still beating, but the breath had gone from Assa's body. I knew it had just happened, at the moment I awoke. His small body was still warm and beaded with sweat.

He would have been flung overboard like so much rubbish, except that I was able to conceal his death long enough for the kitchen boy to find an empty flour sack and have him properly covered. Even in their casual brutality they would not deliberately unwrap him – it would have been too much bother. So, in a rough old sack with the string drawn tightly over his head, my son's remains were dropped overboard to sink silently to the bottom of the never-ending river.

When the ship moored at the next town, it was a silent, depressed group that assembled on deck, with eyes screwed up against the bright sunlight. The master himself looked cross and dishevelled, as he marched in front of us, counting. When he reached the end of the line, he came back and stopped in front of me. "Where's the other one?" he demanded. I could not answer. "Answer me, woman! Where is he?" My neighbours looked at me in fright, willing me to say something, anything other than this silence which would be taken for insolence. But it was as though some demon was squeezing my throat and I could not speak. When he struck me, someone behind quickly snatched the baby from my back before I fell down. "Will someone tell me where that boy is?" he shrieked, red with fury.

"He died."

I do not know who said that. It seemed to come from the whole group. I could feel their sympathy, even though no one dared help me.

"I don't believe it. Where have you hidden him?" He dragged me up by my arms and shook me roughly. "Is he in the kitchen?" I shook my head. "The cabin?"

To every place I shook my head, until finally I broke down and burst into tears. My crying grew into a loud lament that took hold of me until I was completely overcome and could not stop.

On the plantation someone died every day, but we were not allowed to mourn them in the proper fashion. I used to wonder what would become of their souls – if they would haunt us for not performing the rites. They ought to haunt the masters who prevented us, but ghosts are not always logical.

That day on the river I bawled loudly enough to satisfy the departed souls of everyone who had ever died in the whole world.

When my distress abated and I was once more conscious of reality, the master had gone. They said he realised I must have been telling the truth, since no one could fabricate such extreme emotion.

Two days later I lost Usayy too. Not to the fever – he recovered from that. But the master had begun to find the children a hindrance, so he started selling as many as he could in each town we passed through. Usayy was sold somewhere along the Savannah. And I could do nothing but keep on baking, stirring and chopping. My life had no other purpose.

At Port Savannah I was sure we had reached our journey's end, since there was only sea ahead and no sign of the dreaded naval blockade. The port was, for the time being, safe. Very few of us remained, but whatever he proposed, the master would surely need us to look after him. However, I was wrong again. The master intended to leave these shores for good. Meanwhile, we enjoyed a few weeks rest waiting for a ship to arrive and then for favourable weather. During that time, I explored the port with Niha on my back. She was just beginning to take her first stumbling steps on the slippery green stones, and starting to look around her with interest, pointing at the Indians who squatted along the walls. She was attracted by their colourful beads, while I was drawn to the little clay pipes smoked by women as well as men. When I found one discarded in the sand, I picked it up and dusted it off, pushing it absently into my pocket. I did not start to use it until much later, when the life had been sucked out of me and my hollow carcass needed the sensation of fire to remind me I was still alive.

Although I learnt the names of the places we had passed through, I had no real knowledge of where we were or how far we had come. I just knew that everything was flowing in the wrong direction, and that I had to go back and gather up the links of the broken chain. People told me it was a miracle my children and I had been able to stay together so long. That made me start thinking about some of my companions who had neither children nor parents. What could they leave behind, and how would their souls find rest?

The days of inactivity coupled with the contemplation of the calm sea comforted me and hope dared to blossom in my breast. We were going to a new place, Niha and I together. I would have her to pass on my knowledge, so the link between past and future would not be broken and there would be somebody to give me the last rites when my time came. These thoughts reassured me as we sat side by side on the ramparts watching the people ambling on the quayside.

"Oh look!" pointed the white lady with flowers in her hair and lace at her breast.

"Get her for me, Arthur."

She stooped down to scoop Niha in her perfumed arms while the man named Arthur went to find the master. A short while later he re-appeared and met her anxious look with a little nod.

My baby did not cry when they took her away. She rested her little hands trustingly on the woman's bare shoulders. No one looked at me. But I cried, great streams that ran to the ground to join with the river going south; the river we had left behind. South, where they took my last baby.

I have never cried since.

Jamaica, 1757–1820

By the time we reached the island they called Jamaica, war had given rise to a new country, America. The master and my former companions were scattered to unknown shores, and there was nothing left of me but this withered old woman, working all the hours God sends to stop the pain from welling up.

In the windy hills where we settled dust was blown everywhere, in great red whorls that splattered against the whitewashed walls as though a great monster had coughed. The soles of the slaves' feet flashed orange when they walked, and even their palms were similarly stained. I often wondered how the people who were white all over managed to stay that way.

I spent the longest years of my life on the St. Ann sugar plantation, pulling the guts out of chickens and kneading dough until my fingernails chipped and split down the middle and the hard skin around them flaked. My knuckles turned black and hard like burnt meat and the oven's searing heat singed my arms in a dozen places. My dry lips cracked so that a yawn would have me tasting blood at the corners of my mouth. And my shrivelled eyes saw only despair.

Then a child named Elmer came. The new master liked to buy children, as he believed it bred loyalty. This little boy chose me, in some ways like a master picking out a new slave. He scanned the strange faces before him, then broke away from the line of boys, put his thin little hand in mine and buried his face in my skirts. I took him with me to the kitchen, where he played under the table eating the raisins that dropped from the buns, just as Usayy had done. I would look after him for his mother, just as somewhere someone was looking after my son Usayy.

Honey and Daniel were the master's offspring. I do not know if the mistress realised this, but in any case, she took a shine to Honey and had her brought up in the house. They love us when we are children, like kittens or puppies. Daniel was a loner, but he worked all about the plantation, looking after everyone's needs in his quiet but effective manner.

The mistress died young and the master decided it was time to travel to a place called England. We set out together – Daniel, Honey, Elmer and I with the master, right across the ocean to the land of their fathers. Fear was my constant companion, glaring at me like a snorting bull and jangling its fearsome chain for the duration of the journey. I must have crossed the Atlantic in the other direction, from Africa to America, but I do not remember.

Even when I hear the tales told at the meetings, the stories and articles they read out all about the terrible Middle Passage, still my stubborn brain refuses to remember. I suppose that is a mercy.

But no fresh horrors awaited me in England. Honey and Daniel became mine, and looked after me as Nahri and Taruba would have done, had we not been parted. After the master died, leaving us stranded in this cold, foreign land, white men preyed on Honey, and Daniel could not protect her. That was when our kind friend Freddie stepped in and gave us all a place to stay. His people turned against him when he befriended us, and even his family disowned him. So I became his mother too. He was a simple man who liked to paint seascapes, but to amuse us he drew caricatures of everybody, and he and Daniel and Elmer all threw darts at the ones we did not like, which had us all rolling about with laughter. He supplied the humour in an age where there was little to laugh about; just like my son Assa.

I had loved my children with all of my being, and when they were taken from me I shrivelled up and grew old overnight. But luckily no one notices an old woman, and under cover of that age and decrepitude I began to love again. I was like a hen with an empty nest to which others were drawn like lost chicks yearning to be mothered. On the outside I was as stern and cold as ever. I hoped that if no one realised how much I loved the new children I had taken into my heart and adopted as my own, then we would not be parted again.

Nahri, Taruba, Assa, Usayy – their spirits had returned to me in Daniel, Honey, Freddie and Elmer. But there was always one soul missing: Niha's. And then Dolly was born...

from Memoirs of a Centenarian Slave Woman. London, 1828.

The doorbell rings and in comes Freddie, my tall, fair-haired English son, who kisses my dry sunken cheek and presents me with flowers as though I were a girl again. He peers over Honey's shoulder, picking up and dropping papers until her careful order is ruined. She's patient with him until he grows bored and starts hurling paper planes about. This is too much and she shoves him off the armrest. After pacing about the room looking for something to do, he rings the bell. Freddie never could settle down and be still. He was raised a gentleman, you see. Born to be idle – but loveable all the same.

A maid answers the bell and he sends her to fetch Dolly, grinning at Honey, who gives up, throws down her pen and folds her arms. The maid returns with a precious sleeping bundle. The child's growing legs dangle against the woman's skirts, her cheek rests on her shoulder, and her glossy black curls hang down like ivy. I make a sound in my throat, it comes out like a growl, but the maid turns and gently, with Freddie hovering behind, places the sleeping child on my lap.

She's baby Gwendolyn, Dolly for short. I feel so much love for this beautiful child I'd cry, if there were water left in this old body. The soft warmth of her skin and the smell of rosemary in her hair invade my failing senses. I feel alive again. Honey watches us smiling, head to one side, as I rock her daughter back and forth, murmuring a tune deep in my chest.

There is so much I want to say to Dolly, to make her feel and understand. Memories pour into my poor old head until it swells and aches. If I could only lay my thoughts out in her mind, because I no longer have strength to put them into words. The air in my chest grows shallower with each breath.

In my motherland, we didn't need to write. Knowledge was carried in the memory of the people. I try to teach that to Dolly, but I will be gone before she is much older, and she will forget. This great nation of writers can't even remember the date most of the time.

Maybe I have been squeezing her too hard, because she wakes up and scrambles off my lap towards her mother. After a few moments, she's ready to play with Freddie, who has her on his shoulders, horsing about the room, making her giggle and scream. Honey tries to quiet them, fearing the noise will be too much for me. But loud noises remind me I'm alive. I have to keep my senses sharp, or I'll lose the use of them forever. So saying, I have a sudden urge to smoke my pipe again.

Honey's reluctant to bring it, but I demand to know why a woman as old as me can't have her pipe when she wants it. I have to stop to breathe. Breathing and talking isn't easy. I hide my face behind my hand, so she will not see my labour. After a long time, she returns with the dusty pipe. She must have turned my old trunk upside down to find it.

My fingers pack in the tobacco as neatly as though I'd done it yesterday. Neither too much, nor too little, none spilled on my dress. I light the pipe and breathe deeply until the tobacco glows. It takes me back to those late nights on the steps of the old plantation house, puffing away until my nostrils are filled with the smell of dry pampas grass. Burning up the moist leaves always made my throat raw, but I never sipped water to soothe it. Finally, when the fumes had made me mellow, I'd rest my head back against the wooden door and roll my eyes up to the night sky, where the fireflies winked beneath the stars.

The night was filled with the noise of crickets and roaches scraping their legs and beating their hollow wings. Lazily I swatted the mosquitoes away and scratched at my chapped legs, leaving dry white lines on my black skin.

My hair never got used to the dry heat of Jamaica or the cool English climate. It had recoiled like the eye of a snail when touched, and no amount of oil could coax it out into its African glory. My people used to part and twist their hair tightly and train it over wire frames. Each style told a story: she's ready for marriage, she's the mother of many sons, she's a rich lady. My ancestors would gasp in dismay at my shrunken crop. But it tells its own story.

I couldn't love anyone more than my four grown up children, and the little one. Except perhaps the five I lost. But I realise now it's not about blood ties. Honey, Daniel, Freddie, Elmer…I'm their mother, and they'll always do things the way old Ma Tassie taught them. They'll teach their children's children, and so on 'til the end of time. The chain isn't broken – merely twisted – and life will continue long after my feeble body has given up its spirit.

Dolly is standing by the settee, listening to some nonsense of Freddie's. What makes her turn her head and smile at me, briefly, with the knowing eyes of an old soul? In that moment I know my life hasn't been in vain, and that she'll grow to understand. A dam bursts and a river gushes out, washing away the pain in my head and giving new life to the earth that's been dead for so long. My heart dissolves in gratitude, and I close my eyes. The smoke fills my body and something inside me lets go. I lay my head against the chair back, with the sunbeam on my face. It's a warm summer's day I'm told, but I can barely feel it. My senses are dead to this weak English sun, like the fingers of a cane cutter are dead to the stroke of a feather. I don't even know my face is wet until drops gather on my chin and splash onto the book in my lap, making the ink run.

My children were taken from me. God gave me five new ones in their place. I lie back and watch the fireflies dance in the failing light. Somewhere in the distance, thunder rolls.

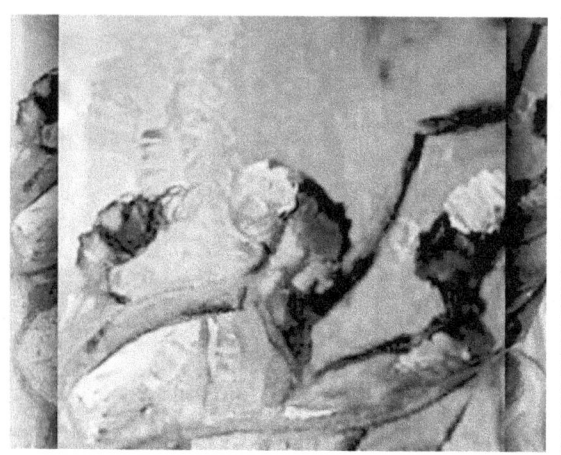

MISS AFRICAN GEM

BY CLAUDETTE BECKFORD-BRADY

2005

Miss Jemima McIntyre was extremely upset. Furious, in fact. How dare that dreadlocks Rasta bwoy come call her African? She with her high colour, straight hair and European features! She, whose great-grandfather had been a Scottish laird, and grandfather a planter class Jamaican who owned vast acreage.

It wasn't her fault that her white mother had chosen to marry a mulatto man, against the wishes of her family. And when he had run off with another woman, leaving her mother with two young children to raise, with no help from her family who had cut her off, Jemima knew it was the black half of her father that made him act that way.

But even though she got one quarter of black genes from her worthless father, the other three quarters were absolutely pure, unadulterated white. Huh! African indeed! The bwoy was an idiot.

Miss Jem's mother had instilled in her that, even though they had been reduced to the lowly status of having to 'keep shop' in order to survive, she must never forget that she was of aristocratic stock and must conduct herself at all times with that in mind. She had lived by these precepts all her life and at 73 years of age was too old to change her way of thinking.

And now this Rasta bwoy with his knotted up, matted rope of hair on top of his head come telling her that if she only have one teaspoon of black blood in her, she is African! But after all!

Miss Jemima kissed her teeth in outrage, straightened her aristocratic back and glared at the Rasta man from behind her shop counter and her bifocals. "Young man," she boomed in her English educated voice, "it would serve you well were you to go and trim your hair and beard, bathe your body and change your clothes, instead of coming into my shop and telling me that I am African. I know my own family history better than you do, and I can assure you, I am of the Scottish aristocracy."

In fact the young man's clothes did not need changing, as Miss Jem noticed belatedly. He was neatly dressed in clean denim jeans and a spotlessly white tee-shirt with a picture of Haile Selassie emblazoned on the front. His long dreadlocks were neatly tied behind his head and his beard was hardly more than a five o'clock shadow. But Miss Jem did not notice this initially. She only saw a dreadlocked Rasta man who had been insolent enough to suggest that she was not only black, but African to boot.

The young Rastafarian man looked her in the eye and refused to back down. "Are you trying to deny your bloodlines, Miss Jem? My grandmother tells me that your father was a mulatto, half black and half white; that makes you at least one quarter black."

Miss Jem looked at the young man in part anger, part perplexity. She was slightly intimidated; this young man looked like a Rastafarian but spoke like an educated person, and he had a way of looking directly into her eyes which was most disconcerting.

She was used to people like him treating her with the respect that befitted her station, and not thinking they were equals with her. But this young man not only seemed to believe he was her equal, he actually gave the impression that he thought he was superior!

Pushing her feelings of intimidation aside, she glared at him and said, "Now look here, I am well aware of my bloodlines as you call it, and as for your grandmother, she was my mother's servant, and too fast and feisty by far. She has no business discussing my family history with you. Now take your purchase and your change and remove yourself from my shop!"

She slammed a bulla cake on a piece of brown paper, a bottle of cream soda and some coins onto the shop counter and turned her back. The young Rastafarian vacated the shop, calling out as he left, "One Love, Miss African Jem."

Miss Jem sat down on the stool she kept behind the counter. She was more upset than the situation warranted. Why did that boy's grandmother have to dip her mouth in people's business? No one looking at Miss Jem or her sister Bridie could tell that they had a taint of black blood in them. The people in the District looked up to them and treated them with the respect that befitted their station. But now this old servant woman of her mother's had to go and divulge the dirty secret.

And why? Hadn't Miss Jem's mother treated her well as a servant, giving her food and cast off clothing to take home to her family? These Negroes could be so ungrateful! No matter what you did for them, or how you tried to help them, they never appreciated you.

Miss Jem closed up shop for the day and retired to her apartment behind the shop.

Miss Jem dressed carefully in a dignified grey linen suit, donned a small black hat which she secured to her head with a deadly looking hat pin, and finished off with black leather shoes and handbag. She checked herself in the looking glass and was satisfied with what she saw; a dignified, stately lady as befitted her aristocratic pedigree.

She said goodbye to her sister Bridie who was minding the shop today, and stepped outside to the waiting taxi which was parked outside the shop. At her approach the driver started the engine and waited for her to get in. Miss Jem, however, seemed to have no intention of entering the vehicle.

She folded her arms and glared severely at the driver, who stared back at her impassively. When it became apparent that Miss Jem was not getting into the car, the driver sighed and said, "Lady, yu waan di taxi or yu doan waan di taxi? Time is money y'nuh."

Miss Jem drew herself up to her full height and pierced the driver with her glare. "Young man, do you not know that you should always open doors for ladies, even car doors!"

The young man grinned. He was new in the District and this was the first time he had been hired to drive the old lady, but he had heard about her high and mighty ways from some of the other drivers. "Oh, sarry, Miss Jem; A nevah rememba," and he leaned across the front passenger seat and pushed the door open.

Miss Jem sighed in exasperation, pushed the door shut, opened the rear door and angrily got into the vehicle, shutting the door with a resounding slam.

As the car drove off, rather faster than she would have liked, she ruminated angrily to herself. "These insolent young pups have no respect for their elders and betters. That bwoy knows he should have gotten out of the vehicle and opened the door."

She knew that he knew that he should have gotten out and opened the door. She knew that he had purposely set out to annoy her. It was her lot – first the Rasta bwoy the other day, and now him. They had been sent to try her. Aloud she said, "Please to drive within the speed limit, young man."

"But a not driving fast, Miss Jem."

"Nevertheless it is too fast. Please reduce your speed."

The car slowed to a crawl, while the driver grumbled below his breath that she "should-a hire one donkey kyart." Miss Jem fumed silently in the back of the car until she could take it no longer.

"Young man, kindly attempt to find the happy medium between this death crawl and your former break-neck speed! I have an appointment to keep and punctuality must be observed at all costs."

The poor beleaguered driver sighed resignedly and increased the speed a little.

They arrived in the town and Miss Jem paid the driver and alighted from the vehicle in front of the bank. She dismissed him and told him she would make other arrangements for the return journey. Under normal circumstances she would have let him wait until her business was concluded, and drive her home. But she was damned if she would ever use him again.

As the car moved off and Miss Jem turned to enter the bank, some-one suddenly and unexpectedly grabbed her handbag from her grasp, pushing her to the ground in the process, and sped off with her bag and the weeks' takings from the shop, which she had been about to bank.

Miss Jem was dazed but not hurt. A small crowd had gathered and some-one was helping her to her feet. She was escorted inside the bank where she was given a seat and a glass of water while some-one fanned her with a piece of cardboard.

She was beginning to come back to herself now. She sat up straight in the chair and said, "Thank you kindly. I shall be quite all right now."

"Take it easy Miss McIntyre, there's no rush. Take yu time." The voice belonged to the nice young brown skinned teller who was always so pleasant and polite. She gave him a weak smile and said, "Thank you, young man. If I may just sit here quietly while you process my transaction I would be most grateful."

She looked around her to locate her bag and the young bank teller said quietly, "I'm afraid the person who pushed you down stole your bag, Miss McIntyre."

"Ooh no!" Miss Jem let out a wail before catching herself. Then she regained her composure, glance furtively around to see who had caught her in her unguarded moment, and said to the young man, "Then I shall have to change my plans. I was going to make a deposit of the proceeds from my business, but now I shall have to make a withdrawal instead. My bank book is gone with my bag, are you able to facilitate me, nonetheless?"

"Of course, Miss McIntyre, everyone here knows you. There will be no problem. How much would you like to withdraw?"

Miss Jem was about to give the young man the figure when a commotion drew their attention. They looked toward the door to see two dirty, sweaty, bedraggled men, one of them a Rastafarian, entering the bank with a small entourage of people following behind. Some-one pushed something at Miss Jem and she realized with joy and relief that it was her bag, a little the worse for wear, but essentially intact.

She rummaged quickly inside and satisfied herself that all was as it should be. Her wallet and the money in the small canvass drawstring bag were still there, although she had no opportunity to count it. Some-one was saying to her, "See'm ear, Miss Jem, si di dutty t'ief ear."

Miss Jem looked up, straight into the eyes of the Rasta man who had berated her about her bloodlines. "You!" she ejaculated. I should have known!"

She stared at him scornfully. He obviously had been restrained by force. He had a bloody nose and his clothes were torn and dirty as if he had been rolling around on the ground. His accomplice looked to be in even worse shape than he.

Miss Jem addressed herself to the young bank teller. "I'm not at all surprised that this Rasta is the thief. Just the other day he was extremely rude to me in my shop. He and his accomplice must have been watching me and realized that I bank the profits every week. People are usually robbed on their way out of the bank, not on the way in. He must have been watching me."

Miss Jem glared icily at the two dirty looking men and demanded to know if anyone had called the police. The nice young bank teller was saying something to her. What was that?

"Miss Mac, you don't understand. Is not the Ras who rob yu. Him run down the robber and drag him come back here, and get back yu bag fi yu. And he had to fight to get it back too."

"What's that yu seh?" Miss Jem was confused. "Is not this dirty dreadlocks boy who stole my bag? Then who?"

At this point the police arrived on the scene and handcuffed the culprit before taking him away. The sergeant took a statement from Miss Jem and before leaving, addressed himself to the heroic Rasta who had chased down the thief and caught him. "Good work, Ras. A gwine need a statement from yu and yu gwine have to guh-a court fi give evidence. Come down-a station when yu ready."

"Nuh problem, Sarge," the Ras replied. Then he turned to Miss Jem and asked, in the educated voice which had so intimidated her, "Are you alright, Miss Jem? He didn't hurt you?"

Miss Jem did not know where to look. This young man, whom she had been berating scornfully was not the thief, moreover, he had taken it upon himself to chase the thief, getting hurt in the process, but bringing back both thief and booty. And she had publicly castigated him. And now here he was solicitously enquiring after her well-being.

She knew what she had to do. She must apologize publicly and give the boy a reward. She stood up and looking the young Rasta man directly in the eyes, she said, "Young man, I have misjudged you. I owe you not only an apology, but my sincere thanks and eternal gratitude. And thank you for your concern; no, I am not hurt."

The young Rasta smiled, and his eyes lighted up his whole face. Miss Jem thought to herself that he was not a bad looking young man after all. If he would only trim and comb his hair he would be quite handsome for a dark-skinned man. She found herself smiling back at him.

"Well, my young hero, if you will present yourself at my shop at your earliest convenience I will see to it that you are adequately rewarded for your efforts on my behalf."

The Rasta man replied with dignity, "Thank you Miss Jem, but the only reward I need is to know that you are unhurt. Perhaps you will allow me to see you home safely?"

"SERVE!"

Miss Jem went into the shop to serve the customer. Her lined old face broke into a smile as she recognized the young man standing on the other side of the counter. "Well hello, Ras, it's good to see you. How is your grandmother?"

"Howdy, Miss African Gemstone. Granny is fine, thanks, and she sends you her best regards. How yu du?"

They exchanged further pleasantries and the young man left, after paying for his purchases. Miss Jem had never been able to persuade him to accept a reward for retrieving her bag from the would-be robber, and this had further endeared the Ras to her.

They had become firm friends and from time to time they would hold discourse, sometimes fiery discourse, on various topics and Miss Jem was constantly surprised at the young Ras's intelligence and the extent of his knowledge; he was obviously well read.

Their friendship gave Miss Jem a new lease on life; she had found someone who was worthy of her intellectual attention. And she had come to accept his habit of calling her "Miss African Gem" as a compliment of sorts; he obviously held Africans in high regard. In addition, she rather liked the spin he put on the word by adding "stone"; it made her feel precious.

Their friendship had also softened somewhat her tough, austere persona. Every one in the community noticed a softer, kinder Miss Jem, and the children occasionally found sweets mixed in with their mothers' change after their purchases. And often, now, she would allow regular and well known customers to 'truss' which she had never been known to do formerly.

A few bad-minded people with smutty minds was sure there was something more intimate than mere friendship going on, but neither Miss Jem nor the young Rasta paid any attention to it. They knew what their friendship was all about, and they were above idle gossip.

And as Miss Jem said often to her sister, Bridie, "That young man is a credit to his family, and if at first he appeared rude and insolent, he has certainly redeemed himself. I would be proud to call him my son."

Miss Jem's funeral was well attended. Bridie had died the year before, and having no other kin, Miss Jem, anticipating her own demise– had left with her attorneys instructions for her burial and the disposal of her estate. She had named the young Ras as sole beneficiary.

She also left him a letter in care of her attorneys, which thanked him for the pleasure he had given her during the last years of her life, and she signed it:

Miss African Gemstone.

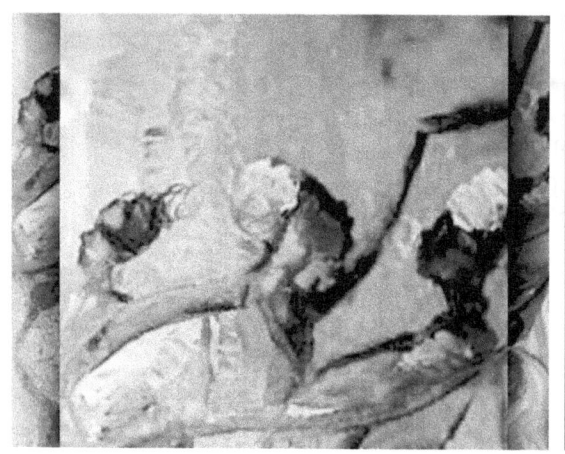

OF LOVE AND LIES

BY A-DZIKO SIMBA

1999

Errol found Ma Ma Tenky rocking on the verandah, winding cotton around her fingers the way she did when she was meking story. He spat out the last of the sugar cane, dragged the cloth across his mouth and then circled it around his face to mop up the wetness. For three weeks the sky had not produced a drop of rain, the ground was hard and brown and, though it was after four, the day remained unbearably hot. And now the sugar was bringing up the sweat in him; it seeped from his whole body. And the climb had not helped. It was not like before. Twenty-eight years and seventy-five pounds ago it had been fast, urgent, delicious, for she would have been there, sitting on the verandah with her feet up on the railing, pretending not to be waiting. Cynthia. Cynthia with her iced-lemonade out front, and inside, her warm softness.

He caught hold of the rail and wheezed heavily. It would take everything he had to deal with the old woman. She was uglier than the last time. Her bad eye was all but closed now and from it oozed a thick yellow milk. Her mouth lolled limp on one side – "A stroke?" he'd asked, repeating Lukie's news, "Humph, well, lying mout mus suffah."

"So wha yuh bring fa mi beside dat dead ol funeral face o' yours?"

He bit his bottom lip and silently pulled himself up the stairs. As he mounted the last step he pulled a crumpled bill from his pants pocket and flung it onto the table beside her. Knowing not to wait for thanks, he moved quickly to the end of the verandah, jammed himself against the column and fastened his arms across his chest. It was hotter there but it was as far from her as the space allowed. From this position the lines on her face appeared darker, like charcoal scrawled on a dead leaf. It wasn't so much her looks that made her ugly, bad mind, that's what it was, bad mind.

She smoothed out the note and held it up to her right eye. "Five 'undred," she mumbled and her few working muscles pulled her face into a dis-satisfied scowl. "So," she said, folding the money in half and sliding it under the table cloth, 'yuh decide fi set yuh y'eye pon yuh ol mudder 'for she dead eh?"

"Chuh, jus talk wha yuh haffe talk an let me goh 'bout mi business, yuh ear?" Ma Ma Tenky's rattling cough loosened up some phlegm, which she spat into a rusty biscuit tin at her feet. Errol grimaced and turned his back to her, See dat, he thought, she woulda nevah carry on soh if Lukie ere.

"Is hate you hate mi, don't it?" she accused, leaning towards him, "Anyway, noh worry yuhself, mi soon dead."

"Dead or alive, mi noh care. Wha yuh call mi fa?"

"Aiee sah!" he heard her sigh and realised he had wounded her. That's just how it was between them. It would have been better if Lukie could have come. Lukie had a way with her – he had a way with everyone.

From inside the house the sound of a metal dish striking the floor rang out amid the hysterical screeching of startled chickens.

"Damn fowl, I gwine kill every last one of dem – yuh watch."

Errol shook his head. Nothing here changed. Generations of chickens had grown fat on the pickings in her kitchen, in spite of her threats. Even when she threw out Mr Philips and they hit hard times, not even then could she kill them. He and Lukie had to do it. They would chase them until the birds went crazy, then Errol would fall on one and hold it fast while Lukie, with one pass of the machete, would slice off its head and they would cheer at the headless body staggering around the yard. The chase was fun but Errol had no stomach for the slaughter – that was Lukie's job. One time Errol had hold of a fat hen in the wedge of space between the house and the latrine. There was not enough room to properly swing the machete and he had wanted to bring the chicken out to the middle of the yard. Lukie had blocked the way, pushed him back to the fence then raised the cutlass above his head.

"Wha happen? Yuh noh trus me?"

Before he could answer, Lukie had brought down the blade so swiftly that Errol still had hold of the head, with its red eye staring in horror and its beak twitching as though it had something to say. That's how it was between him and Lukie; even when Lukie told him the truth about Ma Ma, they were still brothers – tight, just like brothers. Only once was he glad they weren't blood. 'When Ma Ma Tenky's sister, Gertrude, sent her eldest to stay with them, he avoided the girl for weeks. His brother had first choice. Then Lukie had caught him, pressed flat against the hole in the galvanise, watching her bathe.

"Relax man," he'd said, patting Errol on the back, "She a mi cousin – do wa yuh wan do. Feel free man."

And if it hadn't been for Ma Ma, all now he and Cynthia...

"Mm mmm Lord, yuh alone knoh is not a ting mi do dis chil to mek him hate me soh."

This, he reminded himself, was why he had stayed away. First she would stick him up with guilt. Then she would dance around with him, weaving her stories in and out of him, turning him fool. But this time he was ready for her.

Pearl had never put up with her nonsense. Straight after the wedding she had told him,

"Listen, me married to yuh, not yuh an yuh mudder. Noh involve me inna she stupidness. How yuh let she twist up yuh head soh? Jus mek up yuh mind to knoh wha yuh knoh an 'tand firm pan it," she had shouted, one hand on her hip, the other brandished inches from his face.

"All she could do is chat. Jus chat. An all yuh haffe do is listen – noh even listen, jus act like you a listen and let all de chatting pass yuh by. Yuh jus haffe knoh wha yuh knoh – simple."

And even though when she left she took every last piece of everything from him, he was grateful for her wisdom. So when Lukie had come home last Friday all rushy-rushy throwing this and that into his grip, 'bout some urgent business down South, and telling him, in between packing and eating, that Ma Ma had sent for him, Errol had gone straight to the back room and thrown himself down on the cot. Immediately Pearl had come to his mind because, with the Miami job almost certain and the old woman not being in the best of health, he knew he had to go to her. And if that was the case, he decided, he'd better lie there and think about all the things he knew. Just how Pearl wooda do.

He was not in the habit of thinking. He was more a hands man, like Mr Philips – tek piece a wood mek anyting. Thinking – that was Lukie's department. But, in the end, to his surprise, it had been easy. First he thought about Ma Ma Tenky and how much he disliked her, so much so that it felt just like hate. And after that he remembered when he passed over to the upper school and the children from Redunda had followed him home for a week chanting, "Bwoy yuh gat no mudda, bwoy yuh gat no farda, a donkey mussa bawn yuh, a donkey mussa bawn yuh."

The words had burnt so deep that each day he had arrived home trembling. On the Friday, when they began to stone him, his rage had burst out and he had flung his little self on them with fists flying. That afternoon he had come home with his clothes in shreds and his eyes bulging with fury begging to know the truth but she had insisted that, she was mother and Mr Philips his father.

He had tried to believe it until one day he'd stood next to Lukie in the glass and finally realised that they not one bit resembled each other. And he had just cried and Lukie had broken down and told him that no, Ma Ma Tenky was not his mother but she had made him swear on the Holy Book not to tell. And a feeling had swelled up inside of him and he had run to the backyard and, before Lukie had got close enough to tear the cutlass from his hand, he had hacked four of the chickens to pieces.

"Anybady lie to me again ah gwine kill dem Lukie, kill dem dead."

And Lukie had thrown the cutlass out of his reach and said softly, "Bwoy, come – let we clean up the yard before Daddy Philip reach home... come noh." And later they had slashed each other's thumbs and pressed them together like they'd seen in a cowboy movie at Uncle Win's and from then they were brothers. Blood brothers.

Then he thought about Lukie and the fat hen. And the last thought, the biggest of all, made all the rest look small-small for it concerned Cynthia and it had ruined his life. Of course he and Pearl would never have made it for she came behind Cynthia and Cynthia was all that he loved. And Ma Ma knew that, yet still she had stood in the kitchen watching the cornmeal and worrying the cotton and talking her story so good that even though he could not understand how on earth the child Cynthia carried could not be his, he had no choice but to agree to give her up. And if it hadn't been for Lukie all now he wouldn't have known that yes, of course the boy was his. But by then it was too late. Cynthia and her son had already gone – sent to America, Canada perhaps, Lukie had said. And that same night he had tied up his things in brown paper and gone, for if it were left to himself alone he would have killed the old woman stone dead, but there was Lukie to think of.

So in the end it came down to three knowings and when he considered it, he had known them for almost his whole life. One – most times he hated her. Two – she would die lying and three – he would chop off his right hand and give Lukie.

He glanced at her out of the corner of his eye. Her chair sat motionless now but she continued to pull at the cotton. He sensed from her a sort of satisfaction. It was like she didn't know he'd only come for his own sake – so that when she finally went his conscience would be clear. Irritated, he stared into the middle distance willing her to finish. It was nearly five. With any luck Iron Man would soon pass on his way down from his ground; he could beg a ride and be away from her.

"June gwine mek me eighty-six, but mi not gwine see nex year..."

Errol shrugged.

"Carry on however yuh want Mr Errol, but the Lord tell me if me want to res good in me grave me haffe mek peace wid yuh, wedder yuh willin or not.

"From de time yuh fin out dat mi is nat yuh blood muddda, me knoh yuh start turn yuh mind 'gainst mi and nuttin mi do right wid yuh. And yuh and de Lukie him wrap up so til yuh nah listen me. But yuh si, me did have it pan me mind fi de longes to tell yuh dese tings but, chuh, why waste me bret?

"Anyhow, me a get ready to meet my Savior an me noh want nuttin pan me ches."

Ma Ma Tenky picked up the tin and spat into it once more.

"Noh care me noh bawn yuh, me start raise yuh before yuh even si sun rise. Mi wash yuh, care yuh, put clothes pan yuh back and food inna yuh belly. So as far as me concern, me a yuh mudda, yes. And if is sour yuh sour yuh insides so till yuh noh knoh me a yuh mudda, well, you jus tell me, ah who yuh tink me be?

"Anyhow, everybady have a right to dey owna story," she said then turned her face to the road and inhaled deeply. "One preacha man, Williamson, from Redunda, had a daughter name Ursula. Ursula pretty-pretty is a shame and Williamson – 'e noh stupid after all – 'e kip de child lock up inna de ouse from mawning til night. Only place she goh, school and church, school and church. Nex ting boops! Ursula gan. Some seh she run wey wid man, some sey she get mad fe go out an cuss Williamson stink and 'e beat er in such vexation im kill har and got har bury in de back yard.

"Anyhow, six, seven months pass, nobady see Ursula, everybady forget bout she. Den one night – de moon jus goin off – mi hear one scratch-scratch at de window – noh Ursula? She look like smaddy yuh ooden even piss pan. Clothes dutty, hair noh comb... and smell? Lard Jesus! Mi fix har up wid some dumplin and bully beef and soh and she noh gi mi good night or howdy. All she do, she jussa eat an a watch mi, eat an a watch mi. When she done eat, she jump up and run out de back. When me falla er, mi see one little bundle on de step and when mi look, well, a one little black baby.

"After mi don clean yuh up mi tek time examine yuh unda de kerosene lamp – mek sure yuh all right. When mi pass de lamp over yuh face, mi nearly drap. Yuh black like yuh mumma yes, but every damn thing else, yuh nose, yuh y'eye, yuh mout, even yuh y'eyebrow dem for guess 'ho – noh Mr Philip.

His mother paused, coughed some more, this time pounding her chest and massaging the flesh over her left bosom.

"Seem like whatever I give im ere not enough, 'e haf to go look more elsewhere. Haffe," she quarreled, "Dutty daag."

When Errol caught himself he realised he must have been listening for some time. He kicked at a post angry at his lack of vigilance. It sounded true, but then all her stories sounded so.

"Anyhow, dat a ol talk," continued Ma Ma Tenky, "Oh, ol talk an all dem people deh dead an gan long time an mi knoh you noh really care 'bout none o dem, fa none o dem is de reason fo yuh hate, Mi knoh dat. Mi knoh all yuh love still wrap up inna de Sin-tiah."

"Grandma, I figure I'll take a walk over to Hubert. You want me to lock up?" Grandma? It was the voice of a young man – twenty-five, thirty? American or Canadian perhaps.

The sweat started up again and rings of metal muscles fastened around Errol's neck. He stumbled away from the rail.

Ma Ma Tenky stopped the winding and raised her hand, "Wait Errol, just wait." She settled the cotton onto her lap and answered, "Clifton, come 'ere son, sombady out ere I wan yuh meet."

And here he was at the door, shielding his eyes from the sun's last rays.

Errol stared, taking him all in. His smooth brown skin and stubby fingers and his nose, almost straight, with a slight hook at the end. And his thin red lips, the top one with a sharp V in the middle. Everything, every damn thing, right down to the eyebrows. Every damn thing for guess 'ho? Noh Lukie?

The sound of a pick-up negotiating the steep curve beyond the house caught Errol's attention and he pushed passed the stranger's extended hand.

"Errol...Errol, Where yuh goin?"

Errol climbed onto the back of the truck and, without looking back shouted, "Down South, Mummy, ah goin down south."

NO PHYSIOLOGICAL REASON

BY RUDOLPH WALLACE

2003

"If you grab after mi blurtnought titty one more time, you bathe youself tonight."

The new girl's voice is soft, but carries a menacing edge that stops the old man cold. He cannot risk alienating her. Not now, not with the best part of the bath still to come. Shakily, he lowers his hand, until it is completely submerged in the soapy water, then angles his head towards his right shoulder, tucking his chin into his collarbone, as if to embellish his handicap with an element of grotesquerie. This pose has never failed to mine whatever vein of sympathy exists in the bosom of an onlooker, and he fully expects that soon he will feel forgiveness in her fingers, or detect, at the very least, a note of pardon in her breathing. Contrition should be made of sterner stuff, true, but sheepishness doesn't call for more than this.

As she prepares to lather his torso, the brusque squeak of soap on rag betrays her washerwoman background. What has the institution come to, he wonders, hiring as a practical nurse a girl so unbelievably impractical that she would attempt to chastise a man of his pedigree, and in his condition at that? Can anyone this coarse or this insignificant begin to understand what he went through to get here? Never in a lifetime of minimum wage bliss. Still, this is no time for reminiscing. The girl's soft hands and plump arms bear witness to her undoubted potential. He is half-inclined to explain that his reaching out in the general direction of her breast is not a sexual overture at all, but a feeble attempt on the part of a visually impaired man to bond with his caregiver. He knows, however, that if he does convince her of his innocence such conviction will be short-lived. Story will come to bump two minutes from now when her hands attend his scrotum.

****

Jasper Harriott is nowhere listed as one of Kingston's founding fathers – he was born two hundred years too late for that. But if a man's historical significance is measured by the size of the mark he leaves behind, rather than by its shape or colour, no one can deny Jasper a place in the history books. For longer than we care to remember, most of the glory has been reserved for a few old English missionaries who established our now half-empty churches, and for a handful of slave-owning colonial masters who created our now marginally-relevant institutions. Yet it does not take a sociology genius or a foreign-trained urban planner to identify the most conspicuous features of 21st century Kingston – a poverty of spirit that corrupts everything in its path and a physical blight that reaches beyond sleaze. These features did not evolve by chance. Where do we go to find the stories of the men who systematically undermined the achievements of the founding fathers and, by so doing, shaped the city into what it really is today? Where, by all that is fair and just, is the plaque to Jasper Harriott, who nourished the people's baser instincts and manfully chipped away at their moral foundation, sowing the seeds of the sex and gambling industries that spawned our far-flung underground economy? If you seriously need to ask such questions, it is probable that you have been cloistered for too long. Jasper himself would be the first to tell you that marble statues do not go with his territory, but that is okay; the city itself is monument enough.

You may want to question Kingston's claim to one million inhabitants – it depends on where you draw the boundaries, surely –but you should never underestimate the many ways it can take your money. Every type of criminal and confidence trickster is represented here – from the one-legged squeegee boy at the traffic light who can grab your wallet and disappear while you are still rummaging around for coins, to the squinting albino who demands that you pay him for being born a dundus in your stead. Be especially wary of the mother, hitching a ride to wherever you are going and brandishing her meal ticket, the babe in arms, now approaching seven, who would much prefer to stand on his own but must remain aloft to elicit your sympathy.

At the heart of the city lies Cross Roads, a bustling intersection by day and a den of iniquity when the sun goes down. It is the perfect setting for Harriott, the oldest of six or seven gambling houses within a 100-metre radius of the clock tower. All other vehicles for the extraction of your cash pale in comparison to Harriott, which – as if things were not bad enough – doubles as a cut-rate whorehouse. Take note that we are referring here not to The Harriott, as in The Hyatt, or The Marriott. Nor is it Harriott's with the dignified apostrophe.

Any such affectation could lead the unwary to expect of a better class of establishment. This is Harriott – plain, simple and seedy beyond belief. Its nondescript entrance on Half Way Tree Road – two columns moistened at their bases by regular applications of fresh urine, framing broken metal gates that never close –gives access to a yard that can, under pressure, accommodate a dozen cars. The building, set off to the western side of the property, is a dilapidated Georgian two-storey that continuously regurgitates, but never fully empties itself of, the dregs of Kingston society.

Harriott's motley clientele would hardly stand out in a Jamaican crowd any more than its rusty roof of corrugated zinc would attract attention in one of the army's regular helicopter inspections. Archie, the sky juice vendor with a facial wart bigger than Aaron Neville's; C.T. Swaby, the homosexual tailor; Fingers Reece, no more than twenty-five, but with the potential to be one of the all-time best (already banned from all card and dice games in the area, he is now coming under scrutiny for dominoes as well); Precious, who seems biologically incapable of distancing herself from the odour of the roast fish that is her stock in trade; dozens more. They come and leave in an unending stream, twenty-four hours a day, the good, the bad, the ugly, the hopeful, the desperate, and the depraved. They may differ widely in their exposure to formal schooling, but you may rest assured they have one important characteristic in common. They are all seasoned lowlifes – women who will suck the breast off a lizard if the price is right, and men who will lay bets on the outcome. For more than half a century, characters such as these have headed for Harriott the way maggots head for the heart of the sore and they have not been disappointed.

Harriott, as you have already discerned, takes its name from the building's registered owner, who is now blind, bed-ridden and bidding hard to become the ranking stud in his nursing home. It is said that when Jasper Harriott was young his cleverness and ambition were matched only by his dusky good looks. Scion of the richest black family in Jamaica in those days – his mother was a Kelly – he missed out on the hue that his father, a mulatto spree-boy from St Elizabeth, had been widely expected to bring to the union. There had been muted jubilation when he emerged from the womb looking like he had been dipped in bauxite but, to his family's abiding disappointment, he was unable to hold on to the Harriott redness. By the time he attained puberty, his lips were an ounce too full and his skin perhaps a sunburn too dark to earn him a 'brown man' classification. These negatives notwithstanding, he nonetheless boasted a head of hair that was fine and straight like a new house-broom and a physique that was sufficiently agreeable to guarantee him his fair share of female companions.

After such a promising beginning, it has to be said that Jasper paid dearly for his father's spendthrift ways. One only has to look at the paltriness of his inheritance. When in the late 1930s Daddy took a knife to the groin in a Havana alley, the only thing the seventeen-year-old Jasper was able to salvage from his estate was the property in Cross Roads, which then housed a still-viable buggy-repair business. While this might have been an adequate legacy for most people, it was less than satisfactory for Jasper, who had no stomach for hard work. He was easily seduced by the glamour of war and joined his friends in volunteering for the Jamaica Regiment in 1939.

The first batch of recruits, two hundred and seventy-two strong, was scheduled to depart for Britain on 11th December. They were, in the main, hardy youths who had kicked the living hell out of their schoolmates and figured to do the same to the Germans. They were already being hailed as heroes, this ragtag bunch, though all they had mastered to this point was a hastily concocted diet of basic drills. They did not yet qualify for uniforms, but the more presumptuous of their number had attempted to set themselves apart with some kind of pseudo-militaristic look. Some had dusted off their old schoolboy khaki shirts, and a few had added epaulets for the occasion. (They had all, sensibly, eschewed their school pants, which in those days stopped at the knee and would have made people take them for prisoners.) Jasper Harriott, whose mother was richer and more doting than the others', wore a full suit of authentic seaman khaki, the green variety, that perfectly duplicated the British army issue in both cut and colour.

HMS Boadicea had docked at Victoria Pier three days earlier, and the crowds, starved in those pre-television days for visual entertainment, had started to assemble from then. Come the morning of the 11th, the air was rent with pomp and circumstance. The military band outdid itself, saving the old chestnut, "I Was Born of the Red White and Blue," for the end. Governor Richards, bedecked in white ostrich plumes, conducted the inspection himself. (He had not yet embarked on his campaign to imprison dissenters and still retained a vestige of popular appeal.)

The march past over, it was time for the recruits to board. The foghorn sounded, the old men – mainly WW1 veterans – applauded heartily and the ladies shrieked. Jasper, already standing over six feet, his spanking new tailor-made uniform resplendent in the bright mid-morning sun, assumed that he, and no one else, was the toast of the female onlookers. Alas, a bizarre incident occurred on the firing of the 21-gun salute. It was Jasper's first exposure to the sound of sustained gunfire and the shock was more than he could stand. He was overcome by a terror so intense that he promptly soiled himself and had to be hustled discreetly from the parade square. Despite the best damage control efforts of the regiment the thing slowly leaked out leaving an ugly stain on the young man's reputation. As one wag later remarked, Jasper Harriott did see WW2 action, albeit of the bowels only. His mother defended him stoutly, claiming that her son had merely swooned from the heat, and citing as evidence the fact that spectators in the general vicinity were seen fanning vigorously as the adjutant led him away. Still, she wondered in her heart whether she had erred by allowing him that extra helping of hominy corn at breakfast.

Over the next few months Jasper discovered how brutally unforgiving Jamaicans can be in cases of spontaneous public defecation. Children called him names like 'Doodooman' and 'Filthus', even while keeping a safe distance, and among his acquaintances the curled top lip pointing upwards to the nostrils became the greeting of choice. Elsworth Smart, whose daughter Jeanie had always worshipped the ground Jasper played on, summed up the feelings of a disappointed nation. In a memorable speech on 'cowardniss' delivered while Jeanie looked on Mona Lisa-style from the sidelines, Mr Smart (presumably on the authority of the King of England) banned him for life from the upscale community of Richmond Park.

Whether he liked it or not, the parade square incident was his defining moment. There was no point in trying to piece together a reputation so completely in tatters. A return to the buggy business, aside from placing him at the mercy of the snooty carriage trade which now, to a man, despised him, would also bring him into regular contact with horse droppings, and provide additional ammunition for would-be comedians and pranksters. In desperation, he sold off all the raw materials and equipment belonging to Harriott's Hansom Works and opened a gambling house, in effect abandoning the buggies for the horses. Because of his mother's Kelly connections, he was able to secure the patronage of the great Lord Frigsby and other card players of equal stature, whose names (being less colourful than Frigsby's) have not survived the passage of time.

The profits early on were enormous, and would assuredly have guaranteed him a lifetime of contentment, but that was not enough for the new Jasper Harriott. He longed to show the world how far he had come from the parade square, how immune he now was to any form of embarrassment, how devoid of shame or pride. He ventured into the business of prostitution, ostensibly to thumb his nose at the men who had ridiculed him. He stayed, because nothing he had ever done before excited his passions quite as much. He was comfortable in the company of his ladies, social outcasts themselves, who (in those pre-M.L. King days) judged a man not by the colour of his sin but by the content of his wallet. He it was who received the credit for recruiting the notorious Caucasian prostitute, Pearl 'Pearl Harbour' McCarthy, the darling of the United States Navy, though it has to be said in the interest of fairness that Pearl needed neither sponsorship nor persuasion to take her rightful place in the profession. Indeed, by the time she came to Harriott she already had a handful of loyal clients, whom she generously brought under the firm's umbrella. And even in later years, when her body could no longer command a decent fee, she was content to offer it for whatever it could fetch on the streets of Kingston. For her, as for all of history's great courtesans, money was not the goal; but the excuse. Pearl Harbour was to copulation what Columbus was to the New World – not its discoverer in the truest sense, but an avid spokesperson who provided an opening for the multitude.

To be sure, Pearl was not Harriott's only gem. Many wayward downtown girls, who had previously been involved in aimless and unprotected intercourse, found in Jasper their direction and shield. An unspecified number of St Andrew maidens, their bodies grown plump from lack of use, discovered under his tutelage a way to make idle organs provide their own upkeep. And rural enclaves, not to be outdone, yielded up several world-class beauties to the rapidly growing stable. Among the country girls, none was more exciting than the lascivious 'Sesame' Scarlett, so called because of her childhood predilection to open up to all comers, young and old. After two months under the maestro's guiding hand she had become so particular in her choice of clients that only gentlemen of title and wealth could qualify for an appointment. Had Sesame not abandoned the profession prematurely – whisked away, some say, by a sea captain when she was just nineteen – there was no limit to what she might have achieved. We could tell of many more. Of stalwarts like 'Miss Bog Walk,' so called because of the many men who are said to have perished in her treacherous gorge. But why go on? There can be no disputing the fact that Jasper Harriott overcame the odds and went on to become a whoremeister of the first water. Men who had scorned him now beat a path to his door, in search of the satisfaction they could not find at home. Dowagers who did not deign to spit on him wept as he drafted their daughters to his service.

Perhaps he was too good. It was well known even then that, in Jamaica, usury and trafficking in female flesh lead inevitably to blindness. Local scientists, having not witnessed this phenomenon in other countries and unable to posit a causative link, dismissed as coincidence a correlation so strong that even toddlers sat up and took notice.

Jasper Harriott, as time went by, grew increasingly contemptuous of those who sought to caution him. In his heart he harboured no fear for the vicissitudes of life. There was nothing fate could throw at him, he was apt to boast, that could compare with what he had already endured. Laughing in the face of danger, he rejected the evidence of history and rashly cast his lot with the Doubting Thomases of science. Alas, there is a price to be paid for arrogance and, not surprisingly, it is the arrogant who have to pay it.

"Daddy, why you don't put on you glasses? Look how close you have to be holding the paper to your face." The ten-year-old poked her father in the ribs as she spoke.

Jasper flinched. It was moments like these that reminded him why he had never embraced domestic life with the requisite enthusiasm. He loved Tina as much as he had ever loved anyone, but wished half the time he could find a humane way to put her to sleep.

"I tell you already I don't like that glasses. Them cut the lens too thick."

"The lens haffi thick because you eye bad. Mamma say is vanity why you won't put it on, and she say one day car going bounce you down."

"Tell her mustn't hold her breath."

It was 1982 and Jasper, sixty, was paying the price for stumbling into fatherhood late in life. By his account, Tina's mother, an employee one-third his age, had deliberately become pregnant to set herself above the other girls and perhaps trap him into marriage. The lucky lady's professed desire for a baby was not matched by her postnatal deportment and she was often heard to complain that the child was cramping her style. Jasper, on the other hand, soon warmed to the role of proud father, and grew increasingly reluctant to expose his daughter to her mother's wanton lifestyle. The result was that young Tina, when not in school, could always be found at Harriott, seemingly in her father's care but, more accurately, in the company of doting gamblers and off-duty prostitutes. Slightly built, with bulging eyes, she reveled in the attention, being by turns petulant, innocent, authoritarian, playful and precocious. She learned early – and from the best – how to deceive and manipulate, and honed her skills in daily verbal by-play with her gullible and indulgent father.

The gambling side of the business boomed in the eighties and early nineties as harsh economic times forced many to seek, through games of chance, the fortune they despaired of finding through hard work and sacrifice. Harriott the institution flourished, even as Harriott the man went into decline. Jasper's rapidly deteriorating eyesight became a matter of concern for his friends, as doctors could find no physiological reason for it. While the business was able to thrive under the stewardship of Jasper's long-time friend and manager, Lenky, there was no corresponding bulwark on the personal side. Tina was attending college in the United States, and no one else was prepared to minister to his needs. After much discussion, Jasper reluctantly agreed to be placed in a nursing home, the most luxurious in the country. For the first year, Lenky visited regularly to update him on the progress of the business, but after a while those visits no longer seemed relevant. The old man's advice was not needed, his ideas were outdated and he was there to stay.

****

"Mr Harriott, guess who come to look for you?"

The old man sits up with a start. He is a creature of strict habits, and they know better than to disturb him. He is enjoying his glass of burgundy, the one drink allowed him for the day, and is basking in the sickly-sweet aroma of dove soap that clings to him like a Chinese condom. He has already listened to the six-o-clock news, so he knows that the visiting hour has passed.

"Nurse, you know that I don't accept no visitor after I have mi bath."

"This is one visitor you going be glad for," the nurse assures him.

"Daddy!" the familiar voice cuts off all further debate.

"Tina?"

Before he can go on, Tina comes forward and smothers him in a tight embrace. The nurse props him up on three pillows to make him more comfortable, adjusts the thermostat and closes the door on her way out.

"I never know you remember say you have a father."

"That's what you say the last time I come here… just the other day. What? You memory getting bad?"

"What you call 'just the other day' is four months ago."

"That long? What a way time fly!"

The old man detects, from the tremor in her voice and the long pause after, that he has struck a nerve.

"Have a seat Tina."

"I'm okay Daddy, really."

He extends his hand towards her but she doesn't take it. That's the way it has been for some time now. She knows how much he likes to hold her hand while they speak, yet, aside from the perfunctory embrace at the beginning and end of each visit, she avoids all contact.

"The only time you come here is end o' month, every three or four months, when the cheque due."

Tina forces a chuckle. "Wha' kinda foolishness that? You well and know say that when it come on to them things Lenky is the one who—"

"Don't lie to me girl! Lenky don't come here in years."

"Okay. So I bring the cheque. What's the big deal?"

"The big deal is that you keeping something from me. Why? Is you running the business now?"

Her silence answers the question.

"How long?"

"The business belong to you Daddy. And I'm you only child. Why shouldn't I run it?"

"That's not the life I want fi you chile. Is a nasty business; not any kinda business fi a woman... 'specially not you."

"Why not me?"

"I send you go college. You don't need that."

"It was good enough fi you Daddy, and it good enough fi me."

"I train Lenky fi that business, and him very good. I tell him mus' gi you any amount o money you want. There is no need fi you go dutty up youself with dem dey wutliss people."

"You figet say I grow up with them same people dey Daddy? I know every gambling game ever make. And I can run the house better than Lenky. Inna my first month I take in three times what Lenky used to draw."

"So what him doing now?... Answer me girl! What you do with Lenky?"

"Him was getting rich at your expense Daddy."

"You don't think I know that? But what difference it make? I don't need no whole heap o' money inna this place."

"Well it make a big difference to me. Is a very profitable business, and I not going make no employee take 'way mi birthright."

She is the living, breathing duplicate of her worthless mother. The old man is afraid to ask the question again, but he does. "So... what happen to Lenky?"

"I send him home. Him lucky I never lock up him backside."

Jasper Harriott doubles over in the bed as if trying to hear his knees – a good sympathy-grabbing pose usually, but one that is wasted on Tina.

"I sorry him never come and warn me what you was up to... But I suppose you mussie stop him from coming here too."

"I had to tell the nurse them not to let him in, and not to put through him calls. Since you assume is him was paying you bill, I never see the need to make you no wiser."

"Oh... I see... So is you control... *the whole o'* Harriott?...

"Yes Daddy."

"...The girls too?"

"Everything."

"How long now?"

"From around six months after I come home. Ninety-three."

"Ten years? I don't believe it."

"And business never been better."

The pride in her voice is more than the old man can stand.

"I never wanted this kind o' life fi you Tina," he whimpers.

"Nuh worry Daddy, I can take care o' myself."

Another clumsy embrace and she is gone.

Back in the hall Tina chokes back the tears. She has said too much, and is glad to get out before the recriminations start. She does not want to hear again how much he loves her, how reckless he has been with his health, and how badly he fears for hers. It is better this way. Better for him to live out his last years in the bliss of ignorance, while she pays the nurses extra to cater to his whims.

"Everything all right Miss Harriott?" a nurse asks.

"The room feel a little cold to me," Tina responds, "but if that is how him like it…"

"Yes. Him love it when it well cold."

Tina fishes around in her handbag and takes out an envelope.

"This should take care of everything for the next six months."

The nurse mumbles her thanks, and stands back while Tina unfolds her long white cane. Then, moving slowly but confidently, she advances to the front porch where her chauffeur sits waiting. He rises, takes her by the elbow and together they descend the steps to the cobblestone walkway.

THE GUARDIANS
BY NADINE TOMLINSON
2000

See that you do not despise one of these little ones; for I tell you that in heaven their angels always behold the face of my Father who is in heaven. (Matthew 18:10, RSV) Don't forget to be kind to strangers, for some who have done this have entertained angels without realizing it! (Hebrews 13:2, The Living Bible) The two angels came to Sodom in the evening; and Lot was sitting in the gate of Sodom. When Lot saw them, he rose to meet them...and said, "... Turn aside, I pray you....and spend the night... so they turned aside to him and entered his house, when morning dawned, the angels urged Lot, saying, "Arise, take your wife and your two daughters who are here, lest you be consumed in the punishment of the city" But he lingered so the men seized him and his wife and his two daughters by the hand... and they brought him forth and set him outside the city. (Genesis 19:1-3, 15-16, RSV) Elijah was afraid and ran for his life...and went a day's journey into the desert. He came to a broom tree... Then he lay down under the tree and fell asleep. All at once an angel touched him and said, "Get up and eat." He looked around, and there by his head was a cake of bread baked over hot coals, and a jar of water. He ate and drank and then lay down again. The angel of the Lord came back a second time and touched him and said, "Get up and eat, for the journey is too much for you. So he got up and ate and drank. Strengthened by that food, he travelled forty days and forty nights until he reached Horeb, the mountain of God. (1 Kings 19:3-8, NIV)

Saving Grace

The hairs were erect on the back of my neck. That happened only when something terrible was about to happen or if I was no longer in control of a situation. I sensed, rather than saw that Peter was not beside me and as my eyes blearily found the alarm clock on the night table, I realised that I should have been up already. Slowly, I sat up in the bed and smoothed a palm over my nape as I surveyed the bedroom. Its immaculateness was undisturbed. I tried to reassure myself that I was being absurd, but my stomach knotted as beads of sweat broke out on my skin in spite of the chilled room.

I tried to calm myself, but my heart rate only soared. I thought of calling Lloyd Bawkins about the Morgan-Atkins contract. Maybe something had gone wrong. Halfway through punching his number, I remembered that he was in Portland with his family for the weekend. I bit my lower lip hard as I mentally scrolled through my memory for another name. A second thought interrupted and I felt perspiration making my palms slick as I began punching my mother's number.

A high-pitched scream from the corridor outside the bedroom made me drop the handset, and I scuffled off the bed, after disengaging my feet from the tangled sheets. My heart pounded rhythmically along with my feet, which swiftly ate up the distance to the source of the sound. Quiet sobs led me to my six-year old daughter's room where I saw my husband comforting her. He was kneeling on the carpet as he held her, and he looked up as I rushed inside. He had been shaving, and foam still bearded his jaw and the sides of his face.

"It's all right," he smiled reassuringly. "Bad dream." He turned his attention to our daughter. "See, baby, but it wasn't all that bad, 'cause someone rescued you, remember?"

She sniffled and nodded. He tickled her sides and she giggled, then began playing in the foam on his face. I smiled as I watched them, then suddenly realised that the hairs were still standing on the back of my neck.

My best friend from high school, CeCe Mignott, and her husband Patrick hosted an annual barbecue every August at their home in Mandeville. Peter and I had gone every year for the past twelve years, ever since we had gotten married. Later that morning, I stood in front of the mirror on my dresser as I applied my make-up with a precise hand. Through the mirror I watched Peter as he came into the room from the adjoining bathroom and went to the walk-in closet.

"I've already picked out something for you," I said. "It's on the bed."

"I was thinking of wearing this." He held out an outfit that had been worn more times than I cared to remember and which I detested.

"I should have thrown that out the first chance I got," I muttered, as I surveyed my face.

I turned away from the mirror and began to get dressed.

"You have so many things to choose from. Why do you insist on wearing that –that ...?"

"Because I like it. I feel comfortable in it." He sat on the bed as he put on his socks.

"This has nothing to do with comfort," I said. "It's about good taste. You've never worn this outfit I bought you."

I gazed at myself critically in the full-length mirror by the closet before turning to face him. "What, don't you like it?"

"I never said that."

"Okay, so wear it then instead of that. I'm sick of it and I'm sure everybody else is."

He dropped his hands between his legs as he hunched forward slightly.

"Boy don't you ever stop? Does everything have to be done your way?"

He spoke evenly, which meant that he was trying to control his annoyance.

I sighed exasperatedly and went once more to the dresser where I began to fiddle with my already perfectly coiffed hair.

"Why don't you just come out with it and say that you don't want me to embarrass you in front of all our friends? That you're still embarrassed?"

I didn't answer and the silence thickened around us as he looked at me for a long time through the mirror. I could feel the hairs rising on the back of my neck again. When he finally spoke, his voice was incredibly soft.

"Have I been doing that all this time, Syril? What – it's been over a year now. Are you still mad at me?" He didn't wait for my response. "What are you gonna do about it? Troubleshoot me like you do your problems at work?"

He stopped and began to put on his clothes. His movements were jerky and his hands shook a little as he buttoned his shirt. I watched wordlessly as he finished dressing and started to leave the room. At the doorway, he came to a slow stop and remained motionless for several moments. He did not turn around when he said, "If it's a refund that you want, I'm sure you'll find a way to get it."

I stood rooted to the same spot after he left, pain filling my heart. The sounds of his rumbling laughter mingling with the high-pitched squeals of our daughter wafted down the corridor into my room. I closed my eyes and rubbed the back of my neck as I wondered if he had meant our marriage or the outfit that lay forlornly on the bed.

I listened to Grace's soprano voice as she sang along with the Kids Praise tape that filled the vehicle. She's heard that tape about a million times, I thought, as I gazed unseeingly at the passing scenery.

"C'mon Daddy," she urged. "Sing this part."

Peter laughed and joined in. He had a good tenor. He had been on the church choir as a youth, but that was a lifetime and another world ago. Grace interrupted my reverie.

"You next Mummy. Sing this part, sing this part."

I groaned. "Uh-uh. I don't think so, honey."

"Why?" sounding puzzled.

"Mummy's not feeling up to it, darling. Maybe next time, okay?"

There was a long and thoughtful silence before her little voice piped up once more from the back seat. "Are you sick, Mummy?"

Sick. Maybe I was. Sick and tired of having to prove myself all the time, of trying to be in control, of trying to be perfect. 'Almost isn't good enough,' my father's words surfaced from a distant memory. 'failure isn't an option. Why, your brothers...' And my mother's, 'It's not that your father doesn't love you, honey. It's just that after having three boys, he thought that you...anyway, that's why he didn't bother to change your name. I just changed the first letter. I saw it in a novel once, so it's not that strange. And honey, you're just as good as any boy.'

Yes honey, I said softly. "Mummy's sick."

Out of the corner of my eye, I saw Peter glance at me. After a while he asked, "do you need anything?"

I shook my head no. It was just like Peter not to keep a grudge, to forgive and forget and move on. He could never stay angry for very long. It was one of the things I had always admired and loved about him. It was one of the qualities that had kept us together for so long.

"Daddy, when are we gonna reach Auntie CeCe and Uncle Patrick?"

"Soon, baby."

As I listened to their easy rapport, I was glad for the close relationship they both shared. Grace had what I had never experienced and I lived vicariously through her. Yet, a part of me wished that I was the first person she called for when she didn't feel well or if she fell down and scraped her knee or if she had a nightmare. I knew that she loved me and was aware that I loved her, but I also realised from quite early on that she and Peter were kindred spirits.

'You're my soul mate,' Peter had said to me a long time ago. 'We belong together.' We had been good together for as far back as I could remember. I tried to recall when the tide had turned.

Peter, paced the floor agitatedly. 'Syril, you asked me to wait and I've waited five years. When will your schedule ever be right to have this baby? Do you even want a child?'

"Peter, you can't just give up all you've accomplished all these years to be what – an artist? What are people going to say? What about the reputation and credibility you've built up over the years?"

"All I need is for you to stand by me. I don't expect you to understand everything I do. I need to do this. Just trust me."

"You're acting like a fool, Peter. What's gotten into you? This is suicide. Think of what you're doing to your career, to yourself, to us."

"It doesn't have to do anything if you'd just give it a chance. Give me a chance, Syril."

"Syril?"

Peter's voice was real. I turned and saw the concern on his face. "Are you all right?"

"Mm-hmm." I smiled to reassure him. He had stopped on the long driveway that would take us to the familiar spread of land and the ranch-style house. I realised that the tape had started over again and I could hear Grace humming softly behind me. Peter started the vehicle and drove off again. I rubbed the back of my neck in spite of myself.

The barbecue was another success and I told CeCe so. Everyone was in high spirits. The hot, August afternoon lured some of the guests into the Mignott's swimming pool, while others lounged on wicker chairs beneath spreading lignum vitae trees. Children hurled their seemingly boneless bodies around in gaily coloured bounce-abouts, while some rode on docile ponies and horses under the skillful handling of a trainer.

The tension that had been building up inside me all day melted under the warming effect of both the fun-filled laughter and sun that soaked me all the way to my toes. I relaxed on a lounge chair by the pool, glass in hand, shades shielding my eyes. I wished that I had brought a swimsuit. For the first time, I didn't care about messing up my perfectly combed hair or ruining my perfectly applied make-up or eating too much for fear of spoiling the perfectly maintained figure I had achieved through a rigid training programme over the years. I smiled mischievously at my rebellious thoughts.

"What sweet yu so?" I peered over my shades to see CeCe towering over me, hands akimbo. "It mus' be something good fi mek you a smile so." She eased her large, voluptuous body into the vacant seat beside me. "Share it nuh."

"Aww it's nothing really." I shrugged noncommittally. "I guess I just feel good, that's all."

"Hmm. 'Bout time."

I turned my head to look open-mouthed at her. Her body heaved with laughter at my expression.

"Nuh badda gi mi dat look. Yu kno seh is true."

A heavy splash sounded dangerously near us and she whipped away from me and on to her feet with surprising agility and speed that belied her size.

"Owen and Andrew, if oonu so much as wet up me and these people, oonu going to find out what next never look like. And don't 'but Mummy' me. We look like we need another bath?"

She turned to find me overcome with futilely suppressed laughter.

"Syril," she sat down once more. "Don't laugh. Them boys going mek me old before time. See," she grabbed a handful of long, thick, natural twists, "I find 'bout five gray hair since week. I swear I going ship dem off to Marjorie, but yu know how she finicky a'ready."

I chuckled again as I imagined CeCe's younger sister having her two nephews for the rest of the summer holidays, then remembered CeCe's earlier statement.

"By the way, what did you mean about what you said earlier?" I sipped my drink and wished again that I wore a swimsuit.

CeCe took my drink from me and drank long from it. "Bwoy, that did good," she stated when she had finished, then laughed heartily at me before calling to Owen and asking him to bring her two glasses of orange squash.

We watched his lithe figure racing off into the distance. There was a small pause before she said, "Syril, yu know seh yu always act like yu have something up your …"

"Don't bother to finish it," I cut her off. "Do you always have to be so graphic?" I was a little wary of her serious tone.

"Look at how yu even talk. Yu know seh in all the years I know yu, me never hear yu talk patois yet."

I sat up and stared at her. "Now there's something wrong with the way I talk?" I sputtered incredulously.

The twists bobbed as she shook her head. "You're missing the point," she said, using her professional voice.

She drew her chair closer to mine, drained the last of my drink and set the empty glass down beneath her seat. She continued, "You've never been able to really relax and let go. Even during high school, remember? You always had to be the first in the class. Granted, you were bright, but it was always like you were trying to prove a point. And even with Peter," she ignored my warning look, "even with Peter turning down that senior management position to fulfill his dream. You try to tell him what to do and how to do it. You act like his mother instead of his wife. Honey, you're not God."

I could feel my muscles contracting again. I was glad when Owen returned with the chilled drinks. CeCe took them from him, the thanks barely from her lips before he dived into the pool again. I held the glass she handed to me and thought about what she had said. The truth in it was thrusting me towards a crossroads.

"Hey, yu know seh me an' yu a bonafide," she was once more the old CeCe, "Mi jus' want yu fi stop act like a tight - I mean, jus' relax and be yuself for once."

I nodded, unable to release my tongue that seemed to cleave to the roof of my mouth. Hastily, I gulped my drink and almost choked. Tears sprang to my eyes as I struggled to regain my breath. Cece gently patted and rubbed my back and a strangled sob escaped my lips. I was horrified. I never cried.

"Bout time fi dat too." I glanced at her through blurred vision to see that she was grinning good-naturedly.

I looked around me and for the first time, saw all that I was not in the people around me. I had become my father. CeCe had seen it all along. My mother had closed her eyes to it because she wanted harmony and to preserve her fantasy of the perfect family. Peter had tried to heal it with his love and understanding.

Peter. He was walking briskly towards me. I couldn't see the expression on his face, but his stride was enough to make the hairs stand up once more on the nape of my neck. There was something strange about him, but I couldn't say what it was. CeCe's hand was still on my back and so she glanced at me when I stiffened.

"Syril?"

I didn't answer. There was a sudden shriek from the pool and I jumped violently. Two girls were trying to out-dunk the other and it was then that I realised what was wrong. Grace was not with Peter. She never went anywhere without him. She was his shadow.

I leapt out of the chair, almost dropping my glass. He reached me then and I saw the tight, controlled look on his face that meant he was all knotted inside. I pulled the shades from my face, afraid to ask the question that burned in my brain.

"She went with Janice to use the bathroom," he said quietly. "Janice said she didn't know where she turned after that. She thought she was behind her..."

A movement in the distance behind him attracted my attention and my gaze wandered in that direction. Everyone seemed to be focused on a central point. Even those in the pool had stilled their frolicking and were staring in the same direction. Peter saw that I wasn't paying attention to him and turned to see what I was looking at, just as CeCe gasped, "Oh my God!"

The hairs were practically screaming from my neck now. Pushing past Peter, I raced towards what attracted the crowd, unheeding of Peter and CeCe's shouts for me to stop. With each pounding step of my feet, I berated myself for becoming so complacent. The warning signs had been there all along, like flashing red lights, and I had ignored them. Now I would have to pay the price.

Nothing, however, could have prepared me for the sight of Grace, her tiny figure surrounded by the Mignott's Doberman and five Rottweiler dogs. She stood several helpless metres away, between the house and anyone's reach. I dropped the glass in my hand and tried not to scream like a madwoman. Yet a force stronger than my suffocating fear held me rooted to where I stood. I was apart from the rest of the guests, but I noticed Janice, the Mignott's helper and Patrick in front, a look of despair on his drawn features. I knew, as well as he did, that trained as the animals were, the slightest movement on the part of anyone would set them off.

I prayed silently, my first prayer in years, "Oh God don't let her, please move, help her the dogs." What came out didn't make much sense, but I was past caring about grammar and syntax. All I cared about, in those unendurable moments, was saving Grace. And I realised then, ironically, that it would take another kind of grace, the one I had once heard about a long, long time ago and had ignored, to save her, to save my marriage and to save me.

As we all stood there, as if in some strange tableau, it struck me quite forcibly that this was what all my premonitions were escalating to. This was the ultimate test. This was where I had to be in order to finally admit my utter helplessness and give up the fight to be in control. As I dropped my hands, which I found I had been wringing, to my sides, I felt the last twinges of the struggle with my inner self twitch and die as I surrendered.

It must have been at that same moment that I noticed that the dogs had not attacked Grace. Through all those hellish moments, she had stood surrounded by the snarling beasts, foam at their mouths. Her eyes were not focused on them, but instead were locked in my direction. One hand was by her side and a finger from the other rested comfortably in her mouth. I couldn't tell if she was terrorized into a stupor or if she was thinking of bolting. I could only imagine her trauma.

The Doberman, who was the leader of the pack, paced before her with lowered head and coiled muscles that danced beneath his sleek coat. Once he attacked, the others would move in for the kill. He seemed to deliberate, making short darts towards her, then pulling up short as if restrained by his collar. The Rottweilers growled, but waited with patient discipline for his tacit command. The Doberman again made another impotent rush forward, then halted, as if he had changed his mind. He made a few more of these attempts, all the while unaware of Patrick, who had left the crowd and skirted the perimeter so that he approached Grace from behind, facing her captors.

"Zeus" he called firmly to the Doberman leader, "heel."

Zeus cocked his ears and looked up in the direction of his master's voice. He growled at Grace through a closed mouth, but obeyed. The others remained motionless, appearing confused at the turn of events, then one by one slowly sank to their haunches. Grace was still looking in my direction. Suddenly she smiled. I smiled at her, my heart bursting with an emotion greater than joy and relief. Lifting my hands to my mouth, I became aware that my face was wet with tears.

Patrick scooped her up into his arms and held her tightly for several minutes before he came over to where I was. Janice immediately hurried over to the dogs and began leading them away to their kennel around the side of the house. The guests, it seemed, broke through their frozen spell and surged towards him. I was oblivious to all else as he placed Grace in my arms. I sank to my knees, uncaring of the grass that would stain my trousers, clasped her to me in a fierce embrace and showered her hair and face with frantic kisses. I had never been this emotional with her before and I felt deliciously free in expressing myself.

She squirmed against me and my heart sank sickeningly as I thought that she wanted the familiar comfort of Peter's arms instead. Reluctantly, I released her enough to look into her eyes. She didn't pull away, but instead, took a dramatic, deep breath and said innocently, "Mummy, I can breathe now."

Everyone around us laughed. Someone touched me on my shoulder and I turned in mid-laugh to see that it was Peter. CeCe was beside him, beaming with wet eyes. Peter and I looked at each other in silent communication as the crowd pressed around us, touching Grace and all talking simultaneously. I felt detached from them as we gazed at each other in tacit agreement. What had happened that afternoon had somehow altered our lives in a way we could scarcely begin to imagine or express. I knew, for one, that I would never be the same again, and as I looked at the man who had always accepted me as I was, I knew that I could be the person I saw in his eyes. All that had gone before didn't matter anymore. It was what lay ahead that was important.

Patrick was encouraging everyone to give us some space and time for ourselves. CeCe excused herself and began to work her charismatic charm and magic and before long, the guests scattered, some returning to their previous activities, while others lounged and rehashed the incident.

As Grace and I huddled closely together, I noticed when Janice approached Patrick and spoke with him. Her gestures were obvious that she was baffled as to the sequence of events. After a while, Patrick patted her on the shoulder and she returned to the house. Patrick then beckoned to Peter, who left us and went over to him. They exchanged words before Peter returned to us and hugged us both.

"They still don't know how the dogs got out," he explained, whispering discreetly in my ear. "Pat's gonna check it out, but everything's still a mystery."

"Tell Pat to forget it," I said calmly. "Grace is okay and that's all that matters."

He gazed thoughtfully at me for a while before asking quietly, "And us?"

"We've got a lot to talk about," I said seriously, but I smiled and saw the relief in his eyes.

Grace was apparently tired of being ignored, so she sandwiched herself between us and flung an arm each around our necks.

"Are you sure you're okay, princess?" Peter asked, as he looked her over keenly.

She nodded vigorously, so that her two plaits swung. "Mm-hmm, Daddy."

"I'm so proud of you," he continued and kissed her temple. "I'm glad you remembered not to run."

"Course I remembered. And the nice man told me not to."

Puzzled, I pulled her arm from my neck. "What man?"

She began fingering the hem of her dress. "The man that was beside you."

I stiffened. "Grace, there was no one beside me. You were looking straight at me, remember? I was by myself."

"He was beside you," she insisted stubbornly. "Then he came to me. He knew my name and he told me that I shouldn't run. He said that he was my friend and that everything was going to be all right."

I started to protest, but Peter stopped me. "What else did he say, honey?"

"He put his hand on Z-Z-,"she struggled to pronounce the word.

"Zeus?" Peter prompted.

"Mm-hmm. He put his hand on Zeus's head and said something to him," she hesitated, "but I couldn't hear what he said. Then he put his hand on his neck and stopped him from jumping on me. And he spoke to the other dogs too."

I listened incredulously to her story, then slowly remembered my fumbled prayer, the moment I surrendered and the immediate calm that had washed over me. I stumbled out of my reverie long enough to hear Peter ask Grace if she had been afraid.

She looked thoughtful for a moment then replied, "Yes, Daddy. I was very scared, but I'm fine now." She stopped, something slowly dawning in her eyes, then beamed excitedly at us. "Now I remember where I saw him before!"

Peter and I exchanged confused looks. "W—where, honey?" my voice quavered.

"Daddy should know." She looked expectantly at him. "I told you about him."

Peter gazed blankly at her, then at me. He shrugged his shoulders in defeat.

Grace sighed dramatically, her hands akimbo. "Daddy, my dream, remember? He's the man that saved me."

Guardie

Is two week now since de incident wid de dawg dem but mi cyan 'top tink 'bout it. De likkle girl, Gracie, she get ovah it in no time. If it was evah mi, yu si, oh woulda piss up miself. Grace an' mi a good good fren, dough. One sweet likkle girl. Bright, yu si. 'Ar fahda love 'ar dung to de grung she walk pon. An' de modda, no badda talk 'bout she. 'Ar heart tring woulda bus' if anyting did evah 'appen to dat chile. Mi 'ear seh dem 'tart go back a church. Well at least dem did a send Gracie all along, but mi know seh di only time di modda she 'tep inna church is wen somebody ded or if weddin' a gwaan. Di 'usband use to go church one long, long time, but 'im did 'top. Anyhow, up till now nobody can seh 'ow de dawg dem get fi cum outa di kennel, an' mi no know 'ow Gracie did jus' vanish so wen mi did tek 'ar from de batroom. 'Ar parents dem did good dough fi jus' tek it so nice. Anyways, dem an' Miss CeCe and Missa Mignott a good good fren fram whappi kill phillup.

Wah fascinate me more dan anyting dough, is wha Gracie did seh 'bout de man dat did talk to har. 'Ow she did describe 'im, me know seh nobody like dat was dere, an' dough mi young – me is twenty-five – mi know all a Missa Mignott fren dem. Is invitation dem sen' out every year, so mi know seh a no any an' anybody can jus' cum. An' dem no stush, 'cause trus' mi, wen Miss CeCe ready fi chow har patwa or tell Owen an' Andrew dem seh she wi still bus' dem backside as big as dem be, yu woulda nevah believe sake a 'ow she look. Mi modda did always tell mi no fi judge book by de covoh. One ting 'bout Miss CeCe weh mi like, is dat she doan forget weh she cum from an' she roots, yu kno?

Anyways, de ting res' pon mi mine wah Gracie did sey, 'cause mi did 'memba one incident dat did 'appen to me wen mi was at primary school, long, long time before mi did haffi 'top. Ah was in grade five at de time an' it was one lunchtime. Well, me nevah did 'ave any lunch fi eat dat deh day. Ah tink me an' some a mi fren dem did go raid de mango tree an mi good, good fren Latonya did 'ave some tam'rin'.

Well, it was lunchtime, as ah did seh, an' a group a wi girls dem, me, Latonya, Selena Graham, Annmarie McIntosh an' one next girl, whofa name me caan memba. Wait; ah tink is Novelette she did name. Well, all a wi did a play dandy shandy. Me an' Latonya did always team up 'cause wi did bad, yu si. 'Ardly anybady coulda get wi out.

Anyways, wi did a play dandy shandy, stucky an' one 'hole 'eapa odda game dem till we did bus' some sweat. Mi 'memba 'ow mi uniform did soak an' mi did a tink seh 'ow mi woulda haffi go 'ome afta school an' wash it, 'cause it was de only one mi did 'ave. Di bell did ring fi wi go back a class an' mi did tell Latonya seh mi woulda go wash mi face. Di playfiel' did crowd dat deh time, so mi did decide fi go one 'nodda route, roun' de side a di school.

Now, di secondary school did deh nex' to my school an' di bwoy dem use to cum ovah to our side an' gwone wid dem tings, like smoke weed. Dem wasn' suppose to cum ovah by wi, but no mata 'ow my principal an' dere principal did talk, nutten nevah cum outta it. So, anyways, mi did run roun' di side a di school fi get weh from di crowd an' buck up pon a group a di bwoy dem from ovah di secondary school. Ah tink it was 'bout five or six a dem an' dem did ben' ovah someting. Mi 'memba seh mi did 'top an' a wonda seh if mi shoulda run tru dem 'cause dem did a block mi way. As mi did ready fi jus' bus' tru dem, mi 'ear somebody behine me sey,

'Janice, what yu doin'roun' 'ere so?'

Wen mi tun roun', mi si one tall man inna one khaki lookin' uniform jus' a 'tan up a look pon mi. Mi neva did si 'im before, but 'im did look like a watch man, so mi did tink seh it was di new guardie, 'cause we shoulda get one new one since di ole one did get sick an' haffi lef.

Well missis, wi did jus' a tan up a look pon wi one anodder. Den mi did start wonda 'ow 'im did get fi know mi name since wi neva did know wi one anodder fram Adams. But mi neva did ask, 'cause mi did like 'ow 'im look. An' im neva did bawl afta mi like di odder one use to. 'Im did too miserable. No wonda 'im did drop a grung.

Anyways, mi did look pon de man an' sey, "Mi a tek one shortcut, guardie."

'Im did smile one nice smile an' sey, "What yu madda tell yu 'bout shortcut?"

Mi did jus' come quick wid, "Seh it draw blood."

'Im jus sey, "Come round' dis side an' go to yuh class." An' den him jus mek like mi shoulda pass 'im.

All dat time di bwoy dem neva pay wi any mine. Mi did look pon dem, den pon 'im an' a consida wah fi do. Finally mi dis decide fi listen 'im, 'cause mi did like 'im. 'Im did seem so nice an' mi did glad seh 'im was wi new guardie. Mi dis shout out, "Awright, guardie" an' run past 'im. But wen mi did reach di middle a di playfiel' an' tun roun', mi neva si 'im. Mi neva did tek it fi nutten, so mi did jus' a run go a class wen mi buck up pon Latonya. She did a go a class too, so wi did 'tart fi talk an' mi did 'bout fi tell 'ar 'bout di new guardie, wen mi notice seh dat blood did deh pon 'ar uniform. Wen mi show it to 'ar, she neva do nutten more dan 'tart fi scream an' holla, only fi fine out seh no part a 'ar no cut. Wen wi look good, wi did see seh dat blood did deh pon di grung, an' dat it did go all di way down di corrida.

Wi folla it till wi buck up pon one piece a crowd a di pipe weh we use to drink water. Wi see Novelette, di girl dat did a play dandy shandy wid wi. 'Ar 'ead did bus', 'an' she did a try fi wash off di blood, but di 'hole a 'ar uniform did blood up. We hear seh she neva do nutten more dan go roun' di side a di school an' run tru some bwoy fram ovah di secondary school who did a swing one ole someting look like pickaxe an' it did bus' 'ar 'ead.

Mi seh, wen mi 'ear dat mi nearly piss up miself. Den mi 'memba di guardie an' mi did realise seh dat it coulda be mi 'stead a Novelette, an' dough mi did feel bad fi 'ar, me did glad seh it wasn' mi.

Di Principal tek 'ar to di 'ospital, an' she did get one 'hole 'eap a stitches an' some piece a injection mi did 'ear. Wen mi tell Latonya 'bout di new guardie, she did look pon mi like mi did a smoke weed an' sey dat di new guardie no cum yet, 'cause 'im shoulda 'tart work Monday comin', an' dat until den, dem did a kip de gate lock a certain time. Mi sey, wen mi 'ear dat, mi did nearly piss up miself again.

From The Sky

A week after the incident with the dogs, the novelty of the miraculous rescue started to wear off. CeCe had teased me and said, "You're a doubting Thomas."

"Well, until I meet one that drops from the sky, I guess I'll keep saying that what happened was a fluke," I had replied.

It wasn't that I didn't love my goddaughter and hadn't been grateful for the danger that had been averted, but I was never very religious to begin with.

One Wednesday, almost three weeks after the episode, I decided to go to Kingston to transact some business concerning the farm. The weather was good, although this summer was the hottest one ever, so I decided to make the best of it. The boys were at camp, so I asked CeCe if she would come with me since she had taken some time off from work. Usually, she would have gone up to New York to see Marjorie or to some other part of the U.S., but she had decided to stay in Jamaica this time around.

"No, Patrick," she groaned, as she watched me putting supplies into the back of the pick-up. "It too hot fi go pon de road."

"Honey, the sun hasn't even come up yet."

She shuddered and pulled her dressing gown tighter around her. "All dat to. Mi a go back a bed. It goin' to get hot later. An' yu know how Kingston hot a'ready, much more now."

"Yu just too lazy."

She stuck her tongue out at me, then asked, "Is you one goin'?"

I finished packing the last of the items. "No, I'd asked Nigel to come with me."

Nigel was my right hand man. He managed the farm when I wasn't around.

"Oh awright then. Be careful now." She hugged me tightly and kissed me. "An' doan badda stay late. Yu gonna stop at Peter an' Syril?"

"Only if I get the chance." I gave her a quick kiss. "Be good now."

"Baby, ain't I always?" She laughed and squealed as I swatted her on the behind.

As I got into the pick-up, I saw Nigel running towards me. CeCe waved at us as I drove off. By habit, I looked in the rear view mirror and saw her watching the pick-up until we disappeared from sight.

The meeting with my client had gone well and the transactions had been completed, although it had taken a little longer than I had planned. It meant that I wouldn't be able to visit Peter and Syril. Since I was near to the hills of rural St. Andrew though, where a friend of mine had a place where he grew orchids, I decided to check him to see if I could get a plant for CeCe. She was wild about them, and I knew that she would be more than pleased if I returned with even a small one. Kingston had been an oven, but now as I headed with Nigel up the rugged terrain, the sky darkened and nimbus clouds bunched above us. The air now cooled us as we went further and further up, surrounded by lush vegetation and forestry, and bumped over rutted roads. I glanced at the clock on the dashboard and saw 3:30.

An hour later when I left Jerry, a potted Phalaenopsis in hand, the sky tore and rain sheeted down. The wipers worked bravely against the water that lashed the windscreen. I guided the pick-up slowly down the incline, hugging the corners as I negotiated them and blowing my horn to warn any oncoming vehicle of my approach.

The drive seemed interminable. Nigel was quiet, but I knew that he was alert and was keeping a sharp eye out in case anything happened. And something did. As I rounded a corner, the pick-up unexpectedly bucked and wheezed to a stop. I sat, still gripping the steering wheel and wondered what went wrong. Then I quickly turned on the hazard lights.

Nigel looked at me and asked, "Boss, yu waan wi go check the engine?"

I stared at the downpour outside and sighed. If we didn't do something, we'd be stuck in the middle of nowhere. I imagined CeCe at home worrying, then said, "Might as well. We can't let night catch us here."

I flew the bonnet and we alighted from the vehicle. We were both drenched in a matter of seconds. A brief but thorough check revealed nothing that could have caused the problem.

"Awright boss," Nigel suggested, "try it again."

I did as he instructed, but nothing happened. I jumped outside once more and shook my head at him.

"Come back inside," I said. "We can't do anything in this rain. Let me try and see if I can call for help."

He looked dubious at this, but remained silent. We entered the vehicle and sat dripping, while I tried a few numbers. They proved unsuccessful, however, because of our location. Finally, I tried Jerry, who told me that he would send someone to tow us back up to him.

"Okay, Nigel," I said, after I had replaced the cell phone on the charger. "Look out for a white van. Jerry's sending somebody."

I glanced at the clock again and saw 5:02. In a little while dusk would settle. We should have been back already. I leaned my head against the headrest, feeling cold, yet relieved, and watched the rain.

I must have dozed off because I came to with a start when I felt Nigel shaking my arm. It felt as if I had been sleeping for hours, but I saw that it was now almost 5:15.

"What happen?" I asked, feeling slightly groggy.

Nigel indicated behind us at something outside. The rain had ceased and a white panel van was making its way slowly towards us.

"When did the rain stop?" I questioned.

"Bout five minutes ago, boss."

I rubbed my head and looked at the van, which had now stopped. The driver put on his hazard lights and alighted from the vehicle. A young man, about in his mid-twenties approached my side of the pick-up.

"Evenin'," he greeted us.

"Evenin'," we responded.

"Engine trouble?" he asked, going around to the front of the pick-up.

I flew the bonnet and alighted. "Yeah, I guess," I said, as I joined him.

He opened the hood and secured it. "I don't know what happened though. It was tuned up just last week."

He gave everything a cursory look. "Awright, let me see what ah can do."

Nigel joined me and we watched as the young man went to the back of the van. He returned a few moments later with a can.

"Okay," he said, "I'm goin' to use this and then ask you to start up."

I nodded and headed back inside. It was only after I had been seated that I heard Nigel telling me to start up. I tried and the engine roared to life. Amazed, I left the engine running and alighted. The young man closed the hood as I joined Nigel and him.

"Boy, I don't know what's in that can, but it has saved the day. Thanks a lot." I made to shake his hand.

He smiled. "That's awright. Glad to help out anytime." He started walking back to the van.

"Guess I won't need you to tow me up to Jerry," I laughed. "I'll call him but tell him thanks anyway."

The young man waved at us before he drove off, heading down the hill. It would have been difficult to manoeuvre in that spot, so I knew he would have to go a bit further down before he could turn and head back up past us. As we entered the pick-up, I realised that Nigel was quieter than usual.

"Nigel, you all right?" I hesitated to drive off.

He looked confused. "Boss, dat guy..." His voice trailed.

"Yes, what about him?"

He shook his head as if trying to clear it.

"Nigel, what's the matter?"

"Di can, boss. Nutten was comin' outa it wen 'im was sprayin'."

"How you mean nothing was coming out? You weren't seeing right."

I started to drive off, then heard a horn blowing frantically behind us. I glanced in the rear view mirror. Nigel was insistent.

"No, boss. All de spray 'im a spray, mi neva si anyting cum out." Puzzled, I turned off the engine and alighted, then stopped dead and stared.

A young man was running towards me. I drew back warily.

"Mr. Mignott," he said breathlessly on reaching me. "Sorry ah tek so long to reach yu, but mi did 'ave a flat tyre. But ah si yu get it fi start."

"B-b-but h-how, w-who, d-did anyone else pass you w-when you were c-coming?" I stammered, as my mind tried to work.

He looked surprised. "No, sar. Two week now dem block off di road after yu go up likkle bit pass Missa Jerry place, so nobody can come from up dere so, or seh dat dem a go up furder. Is a good ting seh is only 'is place up dis side." He laughed. "If anybody did pass me, sar, 'im woulda haffi drop from di sky."

I started violently at his choice of words. Nigel came up behind me. We didn't look at the young man who continued talking at a rapid rate. We could only stare in stunned silence at the white panel van parked at the side of the road, its blinkers flashing.

Quintessential Mama

"I hate the summers here," she thought, although she had lived in New York for the past ten years and should have been used to the weather by then. She glanced out the bedroom window of her apartment as she rolled up her stockings over her thighs and past her hips. She dreaded going outside into the suffocating heat. She stepped into her skirt, and zipped it up, then smoothed her palms over the front of her thighs, hips, and then, derriere to erase imagined wrinkles. It was a habit with her. All this she did while looking out the window, as the air conditioner hummed and delayed her inevitable entry into the forbidding heat.

She would take a cab to work because the traffic was insufferable, and her car was in the garage for a few days anyway. She never took the subway and the single reason stood out starkly from any other that she may have had. But she wouldn't think about it now, especially since the phone call she had received from CeCe. It didn't matter that that particular conversation had been three weeks ago. She had a photogenic memory. The subtle nuances in CeCe's voice were indelible in her brain. But she wouldn't think about it now.

As she stood outside at the top of the steps of the brownstone she lived in, waiting for the cab she had called, her silk blouse starting to cling to her skin, she absentmindedly watched the passersby. It was another habit with her. She liked to observe people and imagine what they were like or what they did for a living. Her vivid imagination would conjure up exciting scenarios involving espionage, some thrilling adventure or a scorching romance. CeCe ascribed it to too many hours spent in the insurance firm where she worked. But then CeCe had always been adventurous as a child. She was wild, extroverted and daring. She lived life with a passion, as if sucking the very marrow from it. Marjorie could almost see her now, voluptuous and copper-coloured. Then she thought of how, in contrast, she appeared bloodless, as if life itself, on a whole, had blanched her complexion into a sort of anaemia.

When her cab arrived, she was glad for its air-conditioned comfort. And although the route the driver took was familiar to her, the shops and buildings, even the trees, she gazed at them all, as if seeing everything for the first time. Her mind sifted, collected and filed memories away for future retrieval.

At a traffic light, pedestrians crossed before her while the WALK sign glowed a bright green. The crowd was dense, but her eye still picked out the floral printed dress and straw hat tied with a brightly coloured bow. She bolted upright in her seat and pressed her nose against the window next to her in an effort to see more clearly, but all she caught were glimpses of the multi-coloured flowers and bobbing straw hat. The lights changed and the cab surged forward with the rest of the traffic. She turned around in her seat and stared in vain out the rear window; her target lost from sight, swallowed up in the hustle and bustle that was New York City. She remembered again why she never took the subway. She remembered another time, another floral dress and another straw hat.

She was always glad when the part-time job she had was over so that she could go to her class. It meant another three hours, but at least she was much closer to getting into the comfort of her bed. She wouldn't complain, because this was what she wanted. For the first time in her life she was going to be independent and stand on her own two feet. Plus, she had a better chance of completing her studies here in the States.

After her class was over, she would take the subway, and then walk the few blocks that would lead her home. Home. The word struck an ironic note, for the New York City studio she rented was a far cry from her family home in Jamaica. But she wouldn't cry now, because she was closer to getting her degree.

Usually, she would be so exhausted she would fall asleep on the train and wake up in time to come off at her stop. She would walk briskly, her head hunched down into her shoulders, her knapsack slung over a shoulder, eyes scanning the perimeter all around. She knew enough to know that she didn't want to end up a statistic.

One night, after a test, she took the subway, as was her routine. The air was nippy, for it was almost fall. The car she entered was vacant, so she settled into a seat at the rear, propped her knapsack into a pillow behind her head and drifted off into sleep. Just before she lost consciousness, she imagined the high score she would get. She had studied so hard for it, even on her lunch breaks. She just knew she had done well. It would all pay off in...

She awoke with a start. The train wasn't moving. She knew something was wrong. She felt groggy as she rose unsteadily to her feet and picked up her knapsack that had slid to the floor. The stop looked unfamiliar as she peered out the huge windows into the station with its many pockets of darkness. Her mouth became dry as it dawned on her that she had passed her stop and was now at the terminus. Fear clutched her throat in an icy grasp as her mind numbly analyzed her situation. She was hopelessly, helplessly lost and penniless. She had used up all her tokens. She was new in New York. There was no way she could find her way home.

It was useless to remain on the train, even worse in the station, its darkened areas looming menacingly around her. Hunching down into her shoulders and clutching her bag to her, her heels clicked noisily against the pavement as she headed towards the stairs that yawned upwards and led out of the station. She wished her shoes wouldn't make so much noise and thought of tiptoeing, but when she tried it, it only slowed her down. Her breathing sounded loud in her ears. The shadows seemed pregnant with unimaginable horrors.

A few metres away from the bottom step, she spied a lone figure crouching by the wall, half-hidden by the shadows. She slowed her pace a little and tried to remember to breathe. At first, she thought it was a drunk or one of those street people, but then she noticed he was watching her surreptitiously, and that his posture was like that of a coiled panther she had seen once on Discovery. If she screamed, no one would hear. She was already a walking statistic. Her mind clicked. The steps loomed closer, as did the darkness and shadows. Her breath whistled in her ears.

The stranger watched her feet. She remembered how her mother had taught her and CeCe how to pray. She recalled the pastor in the pulpit and her own feeble attempts, a long time before she had given them up. But she had never forgotten.

'Oh God, "she prayed silently, 'help me and my feet.' She never broke stride as she measured the distance between where she was and the beginning of the stairs. She didn't look at the predatory figure almost parallel to her. She was never good at sprinting like CeCe, but her prep school dance instructor would have been proud as she took a flying leap and dashed up the stairs two at a time and out of the station. She would have continued running if she hadn't almost collided into a large figure.

Before her stood the epitome of the quintessential mama, from the straw hat with flowers and brightly coloured bow, to her spreading bosom that spilled over like huge watermelons, down to her floral dress and patent handbag that hung from her forearm. The woman looked kindly at her and asked, "Chile, are you lost?"

Marjorie gaped at the woman as she struggled to regain her breath. She forgot all about the stranger in the station and wondered if probably she had jumped from the frying pan into the fire. New York City was filled with all sorts of weirdos and wackos, but the sight before her had to top them all. This one was straight out of some "To Kill a Mockingbird" story. It was strange, however, that she felt safe with her, in spite of her initial shock. She reminded her of Nana back home, except that Nana was much, much smaller.

Marjorie smiled weakly and said, "Yes, I'm lost. I passed my stop and I don't know the way home."

The woman nodded and said, "Come baby, follow me."

Marjorie followed behind the woman, looking at her wide hips and spreading bottom that rode up and down like rolling mountains with her every laboured movement. Finally, they came to another flight of stairs and the woman slowly ascended, stopping frequently as she panted for breath. Marjorie longed to speak, but she didn't know what to say. What would they talk about? And how was she going to ask her for money to get back home? She had never begged for anything in her life before.

At the top of the stairs, the woman stopped and turned to face Marjorie. "You take this train here when it stops an' it will take you back home, honey."

Marjorie gulped as she tried to frame the words. She could hear the train roaring into the station. She watched its noisy approach, then looked at the woman again, only to see her holding something out in her hand

"Take this, chile," she said "You're gonna need it if you wanna get on that train."

Marjorie's throat was choked with emotion as she took the tokens from the woman, tears filling her eyes.

The woman smiled "Go on, honey," she said softly. "It's getting late."

Marjorie hurried to the turnstile and slipped the tokens in, then spun around to tell the woman thanks. A brown paper bag and a few scattered dry leaves were the only inanimate witnesses in the empty corridor.

Marjorie paid the cab driver and then walked towards the towering building that housed the insurance company where she worked as a manager. She thought of what CeCe had told her about how her goddaughter had been rescued, and then she thought of her own epiphany all those years ago. For one moment in time, her gray world had been coloured by the stuff her fantasies were made of. Recalling what she had been told, and catching a glimpse of a picture from her past, had awakened something in her during the drive. She felt something akin to renewed faith stir within her and a desire to drink from life, maybe not the way CeCe did, but in the way planned just for her. One day soon, she would tell CeCe about that night. And she'd go back to church again too and reclaim the faith she had when she was a little girl.

The security at the front desk in the lobby greeted her by name and she smiled brightly at him and headed for the bank of elevators. As the doors slid closed and she punched 18, a thought skittered across her mind, causing her to smile once more. She would first start by taking the subway again.

No Name

The day after they returned from camp, two weeks before school was slated to start, and a month after the incident at the barbecue, Owen and Andrew were told that they would visit their Aunt Sylvia in Kingston for a few days. She was their father's older sister. She wasn't anything like the aunts their friends at school had. In fact, she wasn't like anyone they knew. Probably a bit like their mother, because they both got on together like a house on fire.

Aunt Sylvia was old, they thought, because she was in the same age bracket as their parents and Auntie Syril and Uncle Peter. But she didn't look old, if they were to judge by the wolf whistles and catcalls she got whenever they were with her. Once, while she was gardening outside her house, wearing short tights and a tank top, a man riding on a bicycle crashed into a neighbour's parked car and broke his nose when he landed face down on the windscreen and lost two of his front teeth when he hit the ground. Aunt Sylvia did that to men. They crashed their cars while driving, or fell down the escalator, or got caught in the escalator, or their wives or girlfriends walked out on them in stores and restaurants.

She and their two cousins, products of a failed marriage, lived in a block of townhouses, about a five-minute drive from Half Way Tree, there being no traffic. The pastel walls were filled with purchases from the many art shows she frequented, along with her own work as a freelance photographer. She especially loved black and white photos, and from a conversation with their cousins, those were the hues to be used as the theme for the interior decoration of her house once summer had ended.

"Pastels are in now," Maya-Angelou had told Owen sarcastically over the phone.

"She still not goin' to get any furniture?" he had mocked good-naturedly.

She had snorted, "If she keeps this up, Marcus and I are gonna come live with you guys. I wish she'd just be normal for once in her life. Oh, and Mr. Freeman from next door? He fell off his ladder while painting and broke both legs. Wanna guess how come?"

They couldn't wait to get to Aunt Sylvia's.

Owen and Maya-Angelou were both twelve. Andrew was eleven, while Marcus was the baby of the group, at ten years of age. Still, the cousins always had fun together, even with Maya's moments when she thought she was a sophisticated adult. Miss Thang, Owen would teasingly call her, as he twanged. "You child," she would retort, forgetting that she was still one herself.

When Owen and Andrew saw her, however, after their father dropped them off that Tuesday morning, she looked anything but a child. Gone were the Pollyanna-style plaits to be replaced by a flowing mane that fell way past her shoulders. She also seemed to have grown since the last time they saw her. Her knees didn't look so knobby and she actually had hips that were accentuated by the jeans shorts that hugged her snugly. Shell-pink toes peeped out from her sandals. They were the same colour as her tank top. Her tank top!

Owen's eyes bugged as he stared at her chest. She caught the direction of his gaze and glared.

"Don't you dare say anything, Owen Mignott or I'll knock you out," she hissed through clenched teeth.

He stifled a laugh as he and Andrew passed her into the house, but he knew she was as good as her word.

"So, Miss Thang – a now mi ago call yu dat." They were all in Marcus' room, lounging on his bed.

Her eyes were daggers. "Bite me."

He ignored her and held a fist to her lips as if it was a mike. "So, tell me Miss Baley, how does it feel to be a wooomaaan?" He stretched out the last word dramatically.

She boxed his hand away.

He tugged at the sleeve of her top. "What's this underneath?" He feigned surprise.

"Could it be –? No, wait – is this a bra you're wearing, Miss Baley?"

"Owen," she said warningly, as Andrew and Marcus chuckled.

"Why, Miss Baley." Owen covered his mouth in mock surprise. "I do believe you've gotten – hey!" he yelled, as she suddenly lunged at him and pinned him beneath her weight.

He made strange, gurgling sounds in his throat as she proceeded to strangle him.

"Lunch's ready whenever you are guys." Aunt Sylvia appeared in the doorway and without batting an eyelid, continued, "But I see you're kinda busy at the moment, so I'll just put it in the oven. Oh, and Maya, try not to get any blood on the sheets, will you sweetheart? It'd be such a dickens to get out in the laundry."

"So, is it true?" Marcus asked Owen and Andrew later, while they all sat on beanbags in the living room and ate their lunches.

"Bout what?" Andrew asked in a muffled voice, his mouth full of fried chicken and rice and peas.

"Oh gross. Andrew!" Maya exclaimed.

"What happened at the barbecue?" Marcus looked curious. "You think it's true, y'know, that she saw one of those –?"

"Oh give me a break." Maya pursed her lips and looked arrogantly at them. "She's what–five years old?"

"Six," Owen corrected.

"Six, schmix, what's the difference?" She set her plate down on the carpet. "She's a little girl. They make things up, y'know, at that age."

"Yeah, Freud," Owen mocked.

Marcus looked confused. "What's a froid?"

Maya ignored him. "What I'm trying to say here is, that all of that, y'know, angels and stuff like that, they aren't real."

"So how yuh explain what happen den?" Owen challenged.

"Well, y'know," her hands gestured as she searched for a plausible excuse, "uh – it was –uh – just one of those – uh – lucky breaks. There you have it." She folded her arms and gave him a smug smile.

"I doan know," Andrew said slowly. "She say dat she saw him before in a dream."

Maya threw up her hands. "People, I rest my case."

Marcus looked at their almost empty plates. "By the way, who's gonna wash up?"

"Mother," Maya called up the short flight of stairs that led to the bedrooms. "We're going outside for some air."

Behind her, Owen mouthed, "Mother?" at Marcus, who rolled his eyes and shrugged his shoulders.

Aunt Sylvia appeared at the top of the stairs. "What, there isn't enough inside?" she asked dryly. She wore her reading glasses and a pencil behind an ear and held one of those scratch pads that she used as a journalist.

Maya sighed dramatically and pursed her lips. Aunt Sylvia pushed a wave of her hair behind the other ear and scrutinised them over her glasses.

"Try not to overdose, will you? And remember what I said about any strangers that bother you. You can always say later that it was self-defense."

"God, please let me normal when I'm forty," Maya muttered beneath her breath so only the others could hear.

They discovered that there wasn't much to do once they had spent a few minutes outdoors. Finally, they sat on the steps outside and decided to play an old favourite of theirs; counting the number of white cars that passed by on the main road that faced the entrance to the townhouses. When they got tired of that, they changed the colour and model then switched the object of the game to the people that walked by.

A noisy batch of teenagers strolled by, probably on their way to the plazas, they thought aloud, followed closely by an old, white-bearded man with a white cane and wearing huge shades. Marcus said he was probably as old as Rip Van Winkle was when he woke up after his long sleep, to which Maya scoffed and responded that there was no such person, it was just a fable, like Santa Claus and the Easter bunny and angels. Two attractive young women, fashionably attired, strutted by and Owen and Andrew whistled shrilly then ducked, laughing. Soon they grew tired of that activity.

"So what are we gonna do now?" Maya yawned, looking slightly bored. She propped her chin up with the heel of a hand.

"Let's play basketball," Andrew suggested.

"Yeah, let's," Marcus agreed excitedly. "Owen, you an' I can team up."

Maya looked disdainfully at her brother and cousin. "Hel-lo-o," she said, with characteristic melodrama. "I don't think so."

"Hey, who died and made you God?" Marcus asked testily.

"Oh, roll over and play dead, turd," she retorted.

The argument was about to erupt into a full-blown fight, when there was an unexpected commotion at the entrance to the townhouses. A scruffy, bedraggled dog was being viciously abused by a group of teenaged boys. Cowering, his head swivelled rapidly, seeking an escape route. His tormentors surrounded him, stones in their hands, some with a foot raised to deliver a well-aimed kick, all with blood in their eyes.

Owen stood up and descended the steps. The others slowly followed him into the open. They could see anger burning in his eyes. Andrew knew that, as much as he and his brother were always getting into scrapes, cruelty to animals was unthinkable and intolerable. Growing up on a farm had taught them that much.

"Hey!" Owen shouted.

The boys paused and glanced in his direction, momentarily distracted. The poor creature took advantage of the brief respite, dashed between the legs of one of the boys and headed straight for Owen. He cowered next to him, his entire body shivering.

Realising their prisoner had escaped; the boys strode on to the grounds toward Owen and the others. A motley crew of five youths, between the ages of thirteen and fifteen years, they presented a formidable front. One of their numbers stepped forward, obviously the leader. He was the biggest of the lot, unsmiling and scar-faced.

"W'appen," he said menacingly, "oonu si wi a trouble oonu?"

"Di dawg nah badda oonu," Owen returned. "Why oonu no lef 'im an' gwaan 'bout oonu business? Oonu deh pon private property."

At this, the other boys let loose a string of obscenities and began to goad their leader to "defen' it" and "deal wi dem case."

"Ow-en," Maya said warningly, as the posse moved in on them threateningly, and he heard the fear in her voice. He took a quick glance beside him and saw the worried look on the faces of Andrew and Marcus. He looked down and saw the quivering dog at his feet watching the boys warily. He wasn't afraid to fight and he knew Andrew could hold his own, but these boys were much bigger and more dangerous. Marcus was no match for them and Maya – well, that went without saying. Already, the leader was reaching into his back pocket for something, an ugly sneer on his face.

All at once, a car turned in to the entrance. As it neared them, Maya waved frantically. The leader halted, his hand in his pocket, then slowly withdrew it. The others began to shuffle as the car pulled up alongside them.

"Mi mark yu face," he threatened, pointing a finger at Owen. He looked at Maya and a nasty look creased his features. "Brownin', mi ready fi yu nex' time, yu' 'ear?"

"What are you boys doing here?" the middle-aged driver asked sternly as he turned off the engine and alighted. "C'mon, leave this children alone and go on now."

He positioned himself between both parties then touched his hand to his waist. From behind, Owen and the others could see the handle of a gun tucked into his waistband. The other boys saw it too and began to slowly retreat. As the leader walked backwards, he pointed at Owen, then the others and finally at the dog.

When they were gone from sight, their rescuer turned to them and asked what had happened. They related the incident to him and he shook his head as he looked at the pathetic creature, which seemed to be waiting on them to determine its fate.

"That mangy mutt?" he asked incredulously. "All that was over him?" He scratched his head. "My God, all you had to do was just run 'im. Look at him! Yu cyan harbour him here, anyway, so you'll just have to get rid o' 'im."

He went back into his car. Before driving off, he said, "Yu betta all stay inside too, in case those boys come back. I'll make a report, but if yu si them again, you call the police, understand?"

They nodded and said their thanks, then watched as he drove off and headed towards the visitors' parking area. Then they looked at the dog that sat on its thin hunches looking up at them almost expectantly.

"What are we gonna do with him?" Marcus asked. "It is a him, isn't it?" He checked.

"Yep, it's a him all right."

"We?" Maya was furious. "He almost got us killed. Just run him like the man said. Go on," she shouted at the animal. "Shoo!'

"But look at him," Marcus persisted. "He likes us and he won't go away. We can't just leave him. Suppose those boys catch him again?"

"Like I'm its keeper." Maya folded her arms and glared at the dog, which stared at her, panting.

"I dunno, Maya," Owen said, looking from one to the other. "I think he's got a thing fo' yu."

"You can't keep him here," Aunt Sylvia said, when she found Owen and Andrew drying the dog off with old towels in the washroom, after they had hosed him down outside and given him three baths.

"But Aunt Sylvia," they began, in unison.

She held up a hand like a police officer. "I understand the situation," she said, "but do you want me to lose my lease, which, I might add, expressly forbids pets?"

"But what are we gonna do with him, Mom?" Marcus asked.

She sighed. "Give him something to eat. That's the most we can do now, then you'll have to send him away. Sorry guys."

"That's what I've been trying to tell them from the beginning," Maya interjected, "but nobody listens to a word I say."

Aunt Sylvia turned to her and smoothed a hand over her daughter's hair. "Now I wonder why that is?"

The next day, they found the dog outside on the steps waiting for them.

"I don't believe it," Maya said, a look of disbelief on her face. "Look how far we took him yesterday. How could he have found his way back here?"

"I knew we shouldn't have sent him away," Marcus exulted. "He like us." "Him look like 'im hungry," Andrew observed. "We betta give 'im someting to eat." "Y'mean we better get him out before they throw Mom and us out of here," Maya retorted. "You heard what she said."

"What are gonna call him?" Marcus stroked his head and the dog licked his hand. Maya went ballistic. "Don't touch him, you bonehead," she shrieked. "He probably has rabies or something."

"Look like she's di one wid it instead," Owen whispered to Andrew, who chuckled.

"Let's call him Benji," Marcus offered. "Y'know, that dog from those movies? He reminds me of him."

Maya snorted disdainfully. "Benji, indeed."

"Nah," Andrew said, surveying him critically. "Da name deh nah go fit 'im." He stopped and looked thoughtful for a moment. "Why we no call 'im 'No Name', den?"

"Yeah," Marcus agreed excitedly.

"Not bad," Owen said slowly. "It corny, but it can do fi now."

"For now?" Maya looked at him with narrowed eyes. "Look, you guys will be going home in a few days, so if you think you're gonna leave him here you –"

"Who sey anyting 'bout leavin' 'im here?" Owen asked her coolly.

"Well," she said, looking sheepish. "Where's he gonna stay? Plus, Uncle Patrick will never let you keep him."

"Wi tek care o' worse." Owen folded his arms and looked at her quizzically. "Anyway, why yu giving 'im such a hard time? 'Jus' because 'im is not a pedigree, doan mean seh wi mus' treat 'im like 'im is nutten. 'Im 'ave rights too, jus' like any odder animal." He suddenly laughed. "Maya, ah tink yu really like 'im, but yu a try hide it, y'know."

Before Maya could give a biting remark, the door opened and Aunt Sylvia appeared.

"Okay guys, I'll be ready in the next fifteen –." She stopped on seeing No Name. "didn't you guys take Lassie here someplace yesterday?" She held her head in both hands. "What did you do, give him a homing device?"

"Mom," Marcus said excitedly. "He found us again. That means something, doesn't it?"

"Yeah, it means something all right. It means we get to live on the streets like Benji here."

"I told you he looked like Benji," Marcus told Maya triumphantly. He then turned to his mother and informed her," His name is No Name, Mom."

"How...apt," she said slowly, looking at the dog who returned her steady gaze.
Owen faced Aunt Sylvia and said, "Ah was thinking of tekking him back home wid us. Could wi hide 'im here till den? Ah promise wi won't mek anybody find out. We can, uh – uh keep 'im in the washroom."

She sighed and closed her eyes. "I just know I'm gonna regret this," she muttered to herself. She dropped her head back, then straightened it and inhaled deeply. After a brief pause, she opened her eyes and said, "Okay," then held up both hands as the boys gave high fives and touched their fists with each other's.

"But under no circumstance is he to be seen on these grounds, capisch?" She turned to re-enter the house.

Maya threw her hands up in the air and said sarcastically, "Why don't we just open up a bed and breakfast for strays while we're at it?"

Aunt Sylvia patted her on the back. "Good thinking, Maya. And since you're being so generous, our little friend here can stay in your room tonight. I think you two will hit it off, as it seems he brings out the beast – I mean the best in you."

An exasperated sound escaped from Maya as she glared at them all then stomped past her mother into the house. Aunt Sylvia gazed at her disappearing figure then turned to the others, who were hooting with laughter.

"I might be mistaken," she drawled, "but I think she's a tad upset at the moment." She glanced down at the animal waiting patiently beside them. "What d'you think, No Name?"

The dog only looked back at her and wagged his tail.

Over the next three days, No Name was their constant companion. When they went out, they bundled him up so that even the nosiest of persons would have been unable to determine his existence. The care he received had strengthened him somewhat, and even his appearance had improved a little. Although he spent much time with the boys, he seemed especially fond of Maya, who, although she would rather be hung by her toenails than admit it, had grown to tolerate the "little critter", as she referred to him with grudging affection. He spent the nights in her room, curled up in his little box, followed her around, or lay with his head on his forepaws, watching her as she painted her toenails or spoke with her girlfriends on the phone during the days.

On the fourth day, after spending most of it with some friends who lived nearby, they decided to walk the short distance back home. On the way, Maya decided at the last minute to stop at Devon House for ice cream. As they licked their dripping cones, No Name looked as if he hoped one of them would accidentally drop one. They strolled along leisurely, apparently in no rush to get home.

Soon, they finished their ice creams, except Marcus, who had just eaten half of his and given the rest to No Name. As they left the grounds, laughing at some joke Andrew had remembered, they heard a shout behind them. On turning around, they were all alarmed to see the same group of boys with whom they had had the confrontation running towards them.

"Oh my God." Maya gasped in horror and froze.

"C'mon, let's go," Owen urged, pulling her by the hand after him as he and the others fled, No Name at their heels.

The distance to their only place of safety stretched almost interminably before them. There were no other pedestrians nearby and the few they could glimpse were too far away to be of any assistance. No one seemed to be aware of their plight, not even the occasional vehicle that whizzed by them.

A few metres away from the entrance to the townhouses, Maya suddenly cried out sharply then stumbled and fell, her hand slipping out of Owen's grasp. Braking to a stop, he glimpsed his brother and cousin rounding the corner of the entrance before he swivelled to run back to her. No Name sniffed her, barking excitedly as if encouraging her to get up. Her jeans had protected her legs, but she had skinned an elbow and there were a few cuts and bruises on her forearms. She rose unsteadily and staggered towards Owen, No Name bringing up the rear. Again, he took her hand, sparing only a swift glance to see that their would-be attackers were fast eating up the distance that separated them. At any time, Owen almost expected to feel someone grab him by the shoulder or feel a blow to the head. The sudden rush of adrenaline had caused his head to start pounding, and his heart raced with the effort of trying to help Maya keep up with him.

Ahead, a pick-up slowed down at the curb, its hazard lights on. He saw four ferocious looking dogs tied up in the back and saw the driver, a security guard, alight, along with the passenger, another guard. The driver began looking at the rear tyre on the right and his gestures implied that he had a flat. He and the second man began to untie the dogs. As the second man led the dogs on to the sidewalk, No Name suddenly darted past Owen and Maya and into the path of the dogs then scampered under the pick-up.

Maya screamed. The dogs were driven into a frenzy, with the man holding their leashes struggling to subdue them. Immediately, Owen realised that he couldn't very well pass the crazed animals, so with a quick thought, he leaped into the back of the pick-up and hauled Maya up behind him. The driver heard the thud of their bodies as they hit the floor and immediately pivoted. Instantaneously, the group of boys, unable to stop their mad pursuit, careened into the driver, his partner and the dogs.

What occurred next happened so fast, Owen and Maya could scarcely take it in. The boys began screamed in terror and pain as the dogs turned on them. The driver shouting hoarse commands at the animals and tried to free himself from the weight of their bodies. The other man bravely tried to hold on to the leashes with all his might, as he thrashed about on the ground.

One by one the boys managed to escape, bruised and bleeding, their clothes torn and dishevelled. They were a sorry bunch as they limped away. Owen sighed with relief, then realised that their troubles were far from over. No Name was still beneath the pick-up, causing the dogs to become even more rabid. The driver rose to his feet and brushed himself off. When he saw the two in the pick-up, his features darkened.

"Oonu si what oonu cause?" he barked at them. "Come out from dere, now."

"Sir," Owen began. "Ah can explain."

The guard shook his head vehemently and pointed to a spot beside him. "Now," he repeated.

Reluctantly and slowly, they disembarked. By this time, the other man was on his feet and had the dogs somewhat under control. Both men glared at the two.

"Oonu a eediat or what?" the driver bellowed. "What oonu name an' where oonu live? Ah want to si oonu parents right away."

Maya began to cry. No Name apparently heard her, for he came out from under the pick-up and sat next to her. The dogs, on seeing him, began their uproar again.

"Lawd, one a yu tek up dat dog quick before anyting 'appen again," the driver yelled, as he went to assist his colleague. They tied up the dogs a few metres away.

Owen picked up No Name. "Sir," he tried again, on their return, "ah can explain."

"If ah was ever an officer a lock oonu up," the driver interrupted harshly.

Maya cried even harder and No Name began to whine. Both men began to look distinctly uncomfortable.

"Awright, awright," the driver tried to soothe her. "No badda bawl. Yu nah get lock up. But oonu cyan go on so on de road. Oonu realise what oonu almos' cause? Oonu could get us in serious trouble."

While Maya sniffled, Owen explained to them all that had taken place, starting from the very beginning, four days ago.

"Mm." the driver nodded his head understandably. "A so it go?" His features softened. "Oonu no worry oonu head," he assured them. "Ah mark dem bwoy face, so mi an' mi fren 'ere," he indicated his colleague who nodded at them, "will look into di matter for oonu. Wi still need to talk to oonu parents though."

Maya had stopped sniffling and taken No Name from Owen. She held him to her and began checking him for any injuries. The guard looked at the dog, then at her.

"Is your dog dat?" he asked, incredulity on his face.

For a moment, Owen could see the old Maya as her eyes flashed a challenging look at the guard. But she only tossed her hair and said, "Yes," in a clear, calm voice.

He and the other man exchanged surprised, amused glances. "If yu seh so," was his only remark, but his eyes told a different story.

The day before Owen and Andrew were due to leave, No Name disappeared without a trace. Maya moped around the house, to everyone's surprise. Marcus wondered aloud if he had come to any harm, but since the boys' recent capture, they ruled that one out. Andrew figured that he had run away. Aunt Sylvia had an entirely different perspective.

"He hated the cooking and he couldn't take it anymore," she said dryly, then on seeing Maya's depressed look, went over to where she lay on a huge, brocaded pillow on the carpet. She lounged beside her and stroked her hair. "But who knows? Maybe he found a better place to go to and somebody's taking good care of him."

"Maybe he was an angel," Marcus looked pointedly at his sister.

Aunt Sylvia's shoulders shook with suppressed laughter. "N-no, I don't think so. From the little I know, and believe me, it is, angels only take human form."

Maya raised her head to look at her. "I thought you didn't believe in that stuff."

Aunt Sylvia shrugged. "Well, let's say that your Aunt CeCe and I have been having some pretty interesting conversations on that stuff. Plus, look at how he helped to change your life. That bed 'n breakfast suggestion still open?"

Maya smiled, but became pensive. "Do you really think someone's taking care of him, Mom?" she asked.

Aunt Sylvia was silent momentarily, then said gently, "Yeah, honey." A beat, then, "Either that or your cooking finally did him in."

They both stared at each other for several moments then fell against each other laughing uncontrollably.

The little, scruffy-looking dog ran down the crowded street, avoiding the legs of the pedestrians that hurried by at a brisk pace. He trotted past various buildings, the many offices, stores and fast-food restaurants that dotted the square, past the empty fountain in the park and waited with the people at the pedestrian crossing, so that he could cross the street with them when the traffic light changed. He went by the congested taxi stands and the mini-plaza tucked into a corner, past the bank which sat beside it and into an open lot where a smattering of cars were parked. Under a spreading tree, a man conducted his business from a portable lunch cart, while under another, a coconut vendor also sold long stems of sugar cane.

He trotted up to the tree where the vendor was serving a customer, and went to on old, white-bearded man with a white cane, wearing huge shades, who sat on a dilapidated, metal chair next to the coconut cart. The dog licked the hand of the old Rip-Van-Winkle-looking man, which rested on his thin, bony knee. The old man smiled.

"So the children passed the test, hmmm?" he spoke softly. "Especially the girl, eh? Good work, boy." He sighed and turned sightless eyes, veiled by the dark glasses, to the sky. "Well now, looks like we'll be moving on from here. There's a young fellow in Spanish Town who's gonna need some help pretty soon." He chuckled, revealing gums with scattered teeth. "You make a mighty good partner, boy, a mighty good partner."

The dog licked the old man's hand again then sank to his thin haunches and rested his head on his forepaws.

Truly, Madly, Deeply

Seven weeks after the incident her granddaughter, Grace, had experienced with the dogs, on a cheery September morning, Eileen Wainwright sat on her front patio drinking a cup of lemon tea, her favourite, and decided to end her life.

It was not a recent, nor a rash decision. She reasoned that it had first settled in her mind the instant they had placed Leonard's elaborate coffin in the ground and covered it up, along with all that she was and owned, with the red dirt.

She had never worked in her entire life; well, not the stereotypical occupations that were recognised and accepted. She had been a housewife, homemaker or house manager were the politically correct euphemisms preferred within certain circles. She had excelled at her tasks of caring for her family, along with co-hosting the many functions that had sprung from her husband's business and political connections. But now she was alone, save for her cat, Aurora, and Susan, the housekeeper her eldest son, Charles had employed for her despite her protests. Leonard had passed on five years earlier, and her four children were all grown, with families of their own. There were the regular visits, Sunday dinners and family reunions, but when the pitter-patter of tiny feet and the sounds of children's laughter and frolic had faded into nothingness, she was left with only memories, like yellowed photographs.

The big house, renovated in recent years, was filled with them. She didn't need to look in albums or at photo frames on the mantel shelf and center table or on any other piece of furniture. Her mind was alive with them. But they no longer sustained her as in the earlier days when each of her children had left home, first to study overseas and then to start their own lives. And they had lost their edge much, much later, in those empty days following Leonard's death. She bitterly regretted the path her life had taken. She had sacrificed her dreams and instead, lived entirely for her family. She did not regret anything she had done or given for her children; for she saw and received the fruits her efforts had yielded in shaping their lives. Yet, she had always wondered what her life would have been like if she hadn't closed her eyes and said goodbye to the girl she once was.

Any recapture now was beyond her reach at this chapter of her life. Its possibility had been forever sentenced and condemned the moment she had accepted Leonard's marriage proposal and later said "I do." Its reality and her spirit had been forever entombed the instance her body had been sacrificed.

She felt something soft brush against her leg and as she set her cup and saucer down on the glass-top table, she saw that it was Aurora. She picked her up, placed her in her lap and began to rub her head. Her heart ached when she thought of the pain her action would cause to her children and their families. Yet, not even that and the tenderest ties could remove the desolation that filled her on waking each morning.

She didn't want her empty existence anymore. She didn't want to face what she had always said she would never become. She had said that she would remain free-spirited and independent, but she had sold her soul and Leonard had broken her spirit.

She could hear Susan going about her duties inside the house. Her two days off began the following day. Eileen thought of the letters she had written to each member of her family and her closest friends, tucked away in her writing desk, and of all the plans she had put in place. She had waited five years. One more day wouldn't matter.

The next morning, bright and early, as Eileen locked all the doors and closed all the windows before turning on the gas and leaving the oven door open, she heard a terrific crash outside. She would have ignored it if it hadn't sounded as if it had come from her front yard. Annoyed at the interruption, yet curious as to what could have caused it, she left the kitchen and went out on to her front patio. Her eyes widened in amazement, shock and disbelief at the sight of a large pick-up truck that had smashed through her fence and now lay on its side on her front lawn.

A young man, who had been running down the incline facing the cul-de-sac where her house was situated, came through the gap created by the truck and jogged over to where she stood, her mouth agape. He ran up the short flight of patio steps.

"Mrs. Wainwright," he sounded winded. "Ma'am, I'm sorry about this. The person who was washing the truck accidentally released the handbrake when he was cleaning the inside. We tried to catch it," he turned to gesture futilely at the overturned vehicle, "but as you can see..." His voice trailed.

Eileen remained dumbstruck as she stared helplessly at the damage caused and at her crushed azaleas, crocuses and sunflowers. A small crowd had gathered in front of the gate. Some viewed the spectacle, their hands over their mouths, while others pointed and implied by their gestures their speculations as to how the incident had occurred.

The young man suddenly began sniffing. "Is that gas I smell?" he asked, his brows knitted.

Eileen snapped back to reality. "Uh - uh - uh," she stammered, "y-yes. I-I-I was in the kitchen...cooking." She reached behind her to close the front door.

The young man looked concerned. "You'd better check it out, ma'am," he advised. We wouldn't want another accident. In the meantime, I'll see to it that Mr. Campbell gets in touch with you." He turned and began to run down the steps.

She called after him. "W-who's Mr. Campbell?" He turned to face her from the bottom step. "His grandson owns the pick-up. And ma'am, I'd turn that gas off now if I were you."

Eileen watched as he ran across her lawn, a vague thought eluding her. He went through the gaping hole in the fence before heading in the direction from which he had come. She looked at the growing crowd in front of her gate then slowly turned and reentered her house. As she turned off the gas and opened all the doors and windows, a towel over her nose, she tried to grab hold of the thought that still stubbornly evaded her.

The sound of her doorbell ten minutes later revealed a tall, graying gentleman on her patio.

"Good morning," he greeted her pleasantly in a rumbling, bass voice as he held out his hand to shake hers. "My name is Murray Campbell and I believe that's my grandson's pick-up on your front lawn."

His grasp was firm and strong. Her hand seemed swallowed up in his. She became aware that he hadn't released her hand and quickly withdrew it.

"Eileen Wainwright." She hoped she didn't sound as awkward as she felt. "I see your - uh, I really don't know who he was, but a young man was here earlier and said that he'd - uh, make sure that you contacted me." She inclined her head at the upended vehicle on the lawn. "about the pick-up."

Mr Campbell looked puzzled. "Young man?" he repeated. "Uh, my grandson isn't here at the –"

"Uh, he said that your grandson owned the pick-up, but he never really..." She searched vainly for an explanation.

He raised both brows. "Well, I don't know who you were talking to because the gardener and I were the only persons at the house."

Eileen stared blankly at him then suddenly remembered something else the stranger had told her. "He uh - said that the person who was washing the pick-up accidentally released the handbrake."

Mr Campbell nodded. "Yes, that would be Wayne, the gardener, but he was alone."

In a last effort, she described the young man and what he had been wearing. Mr. Campbell shook his head.

"No ma'am," he said ruefully. "I don't know anyone who fits that description. Maybe he's from around here."

She shook her head. "No. I've lived here for the past forty-odd years and I've never seen him here before." A thought flashed in her head, like a thousand-watt bulb, as the answer to the riddle in her mind finally crystallised. The stranger had known her name!

She suddenly noticed the odd look on Mr. Campbell's face. "Is that gas?" he asked, sniffing.

"Uh - e-excuse me a minute, will you please?" she said hastily, and then hurried from the patio as fast as her legs could carry her to her gate, where small pockets of people were still gathered. Before she could reach it, however, a woman around her age, wearing a hat and gardening gloves, had pulled the latch and entered and was now approaching her.

"Eileen, my God!" she exclaimed, on reaching her.

Eileen raised a hand in greeting to some of the onlookers then turned to her friend and neighbour. "Helen," she said, sounding rushed. "I need you to tell me something. Did you see what happened?"

Helen's eyes widened. "Did I? That pick-up came out of nowhere..."

Eileen cut her off and grabbed her gloved hands. "Did you see the man I was talking to?"

Her friend's eyes narrowed. "Man?" she asked, puzzled, then looked towards the patio.

"Do you mean him?"

"No, no. The young man who came here shortly after the accident happened."

Helen looked at her, a sympathetic expression on her face. "You're still in shock. I know I would be if it were my front lawn that had a truck sitting on it. Look at your azaleas. It's a good thing no vehicle was coming and no one was passing by. Why ..."

Eileen felt herself growing agitated. She gripped her friend's hands tighter, making her wince. "Helen, just tell me if you saw a young man talking to me this morning on my patio. Please."

Helen slowly released her hands from Eileen's death grip and took off her gloves. She massaged her wrists as she spoke. "There was no one with you on the patio and the only man I saw you talking to, is the same one who's looking at us now." She stopped rubbing and looked at her friend in concern. "Are you all right, honey? C'mon let me make you a cup of tea, how about that? We could also offer the nice man a cup too. By the way, Eileen, you didn't tell me you were having gentlemen callers now."

An hour later, the pick-up was removed and the fence temporarily patched until Mr Campbell had made the necessary arrangements for its restoration. Helen had returned to her gardening and the crowd had dispersed to their respective homes. Eileen stood on the patio with Mr Campbell. She thought of how the day had turned out and wondered at the strangeness of it all. She thought of postponing her plans, but found she had lost the taste for it in the drama of the morning's events. She remembered that she would have to collect Aurora from Helen and also destroy the letters she had written. Her mind constantly revolved around the enigmatic young man.

"Well I'd better be going," Mr Campbell's voice intruded into her reverie. "I'll have someone come over tomorrow to finish the repairs to your fence." He chuckled. "I don't know about the flowers though, but I'll see what I can do."

She smiled. "That's all right really. Uh, thanks for looking about things so quickly." She held out her hand to shake his. "Goodbye, Mr Campbell."

He took it and raised it to his lips. "Murray, please."

Eileen felt strangely warm as his mouth brushed against the back of her hand. She suddenly found it difficult to swallow. He gently lowered her hand but still held it in his.

"Goodbye...Murray." She couldn't quite meet his eyes.

He slowly released her hand. "Until tomorrow then."

Even after he had gone up the incline and disappeared from sight, she still remained in the same position on the patio, the back of her hand still tingling from the touch of his lips.

That night, Eileen lay in her bed and dreamed. She saw a young, slender girl with dark, wavy hair and an impudent smile as she danced, spinning round and round so that her thin dress sailed above her knees and exposed bare, shapely legs. Eileen tried to see her face more clearly, but it was slightly blurred, as things are in dreams. The image faded into another scene where she saw a young woman, an older version of the girl. She wore her dark hair up and her clothing, although stylish, was sedate. Eileen noticed the unsmiling expression on her face.

Then there were shadows and she felt very afraid, but they cleared and she saw the girl again from the first scene. She was smiling and beckoning to someone from the shadows, but Eileen couldn't see who the person was. The young girl looked sad for a moment, but then she began to laugh and clap her hands as the figure walked towards her. She ran forward and took hold of the individual's hands and together they began to dance. Then they both stopped and the figure turned and began to walk forward, as if coming towards Eileen. The young girl began to dance again, her short, wavy bob bouncing and her dress twirling as she pirouetted out of the shadows. Her face was uplifted and Eileen suddenly recognised her. The dark figure stepped out of the shadows...

Eileen awoke, gasping for breath, her hands over her mouth to keep from crying out. The girl and the figure she had seen had been her.

Murray returned the following morning with two young men. He introduced them as Neil, his grandson, and Paul, Neil's friend.

"You got your grandson and his friend to fix my fence?" she asked incredulously, trying hard not to stare too long at him. She struggled to quell the fluttering sensations that suddenly arose in her stomach.

He grinned, and she thought that he had a wonderful smile, then drew herself up short. What's the matter with me? She thought. You're a grandmother, for heaven's sake.

"...and so he didn't mind," Murray was saying.

"Oh," she said, and then stopped, at a loss for words. He gazed steadily at her and she fidgeted nervously then touched her short, dark hair streaked with gray.

There was a sudden loud blast of reggae music and she jumped violently, her hand pressed to her chest. Murray laughed.

"I'm sorry, it's only Neil. I keep telling him he's going to be deaf before he reaches twenty, but you know young people?" He waved at his grandson, who turned the volume down on the portable CD player he had with him so he could hear his grandfather. "That's more like it. We want to keep what we have until it goes away...naturally."

Neil gave him a thumbs-up sign and resumed working on the fence. Eileen decided to prepare something to eat for the young men and suggested that Murray accompany her inside the house. As they went from the foyer and through the sitting and dining rooms into the kitchen, they heard when the volume of the music went up again.

"That boy," Murray said, shaking his head as he sat on a stool. "You should hear what it's like at the house."

"No thank you." Eileen laughed, as she began making sandwiches.

"Do you have any grandchildren?"

She nodded. "Eight," she replied. "Ranging from ages six to seventeen, so I understand what you go through."

She was acutely aware of his presence as she prepared the food. From her peripheral vision she could see him watching her every movement.

"I understand you're a widow." He saw the questioning look in her eyes. "I asked my son and he told me a little bit about you. I hope you don't mind me asking?"

"Oh no, no."

"I noticed all the family pictures," he pointed in the direction of the sitting room. 'You must be very happy."

She didn't respond as she finished preparing the sandwiches and side orders and took some fruits out of the fridge to blend into a juice. She carefully avoided his searching gaze. He seemed not to notice her reticence. "I'm a widower myself," he continued. "My wife died seven years ago. I have a son and two daughters. You met Neil. He's the eldest of my four grandchildren. I'm staying with my son, Craig, and his wife for a while until I get myself settled in."

She looked at him, surprised. "Settled in?"

"Mm-hmm. I lived in the States for over forty years. I've been thinking of coming back home ever since Amy's death." His eyes twinkled as he smiled at her. "I think now's as good a time as any, what d'you think, Eileen? May I call you Eileen?"

She felt her face growing warm as she quickly nodded and began blending the fruits. When she was through, she poured a drink for him after adding a few cubes of ice to the glass. As they left the kitchen and passed through the sitting room, he stopped.

"May I?" he asked, indicating his wish to look at the many photos more closely. She nodded and watched him surreptitiously as he went from one to the other, murmuring softly to himself. It had been so long since she had been alone with a man, excluding her sons and family physician, in the house or anywhere for that matter. He seemed to swallow up the spaciousness of whichever room he happened to be in.

She almost fainted when she came out of her reverie to discover that he had finished his survey and was looking at her looking at him. She was certain her face was ten shades of red.

"L-let's go out on the patio," she said in a too bright tone and wondered what was happening to her.

Once outside, they found out that Neil and Paul had almost finished the repairs. Eileen went to them and told them to take a break and invited them to come on the patio. There, she served them the meal she had prepared. As they ate, music blared from the CD player they had brought with them.

"What's that song?" Eileen asked. "I've heard my granddaughter playing it repeatedly whenever she's here."

"It's a song by Savage Garden," Paul replied. "Truly, madly, deeply."

"Savage Garden?" Murray looked skeptical.

"Is a love song, grandpa," Neil grinned. "The guy's singing 'bout his girl and he's describing his love for her. He's saying that he loves her truly, madly, deeply. That's the type of love he has for her."

The boys began to talk and joke about the song with Murray, who was trying to rationalise the name of the group. Eileen had noticed, though, that never once did he take his eyes off her during Neil's explanation.

When the boys had resumed their task once more, Eileen and Murray sat together on the patio watching them and sipping the fruit punch she had made.

"Would you like to come to my son's house tonight for dinner?" he asked suddenly.

Eileen almost choked on her drink, but managed to remain composed. He saw her look of alarm, nevertheless, and chuckled.

"Don't worry," he said reassuringly. "It's really a little soiree they're throwing for me, so there'll be just a few friends over. I'd be honoured if you would come as my guest."

She tried to breathe normally. Oh, how she felt like sixteen again when she had an army of suitors and eligible young admirers clamouring for her attention. She felt herself transported back to those happy, happy days when she had been so young and carefree and desirable. What was she thinking? Reality washed over her like a wave of ice cold water. She couldn't accept his invitation. Everything was happening far too fast. First, that encounter with the mysterious, young stranger – she still hadn't gotten over that. Then the truck crashing through her fence and botching her plans to - she tried not to think about that either, and now, meeting this wonderful, charming, attentive - oh, she could go on and on - gentleman. No, she couldn't do it. She had changed and too much had already happened for her to try and become that young girl in her dream.

"I'm sorry," she said stiffly, "but I won't be able to attend." She tried not to care when she saw the disappointment on his face. "I-I have other plans." She stood up. "Thank you again, Murray, for all you've done."

He rose to his feet slowly. "The pleasure's all mine, Eileen. And if you happen to be able to come at all," he spread his hands expansively, "please give me a call." He took a piece of paper out of the breast pocket of his shirt and began writing on it with a fountain pen that had also been in his pocket.

"You don't need to –," she began hastily.

"Oh, that's quite all right." He handed her the piece of paper.

She took it reluctantly and slipped it into the pocket of her dress. He smiled, gave her a half bow and descended the steps from the patio. She held the piece of paper tightly in her fist, still in her pocket, and felt her heart ache with each step that took him away from her.

"What do you mean you're not going?"

Helen's voice was shrill over the phone. Eileen held the handset away from her ear, and then brought it closer when she was certain her friend had calmed down.

"Helen, I can't go."

"Why not?" Helen's voice rose again. "If its Leonard you're thinking about, I can assure you that he's in no position to be of any concern. To anyone."

"Helen."

"Oh, stop being such a fuddy-duddy. Murray obviously likes you. You're an intelligent, beautiful woman. And a great cook. Why else would he invite you to dinner?"

"But I barely know the man."

"That's why you need to go to the dinner. Wear that lavender dress. It shows off your legs. You should show them off, y'know. Why, if I had legs like yours..." Eileen groaned inaudibly as she listened to the rambling voice on the other line.

Something woke her. She sat up in the bed, her eyes slowly adjusting to the shadowed room. Turning on the bedside lamp, she found her watch on the night table and saw that it was 5:45 p.m. She had slept for over two hours. She heard the muffled sound again coming from downstairs and tried to remember if she had locked the doors and windows. She remembered that she had decided to lie down for a while after talking to Helen, but she couldn't recall if she had locked up before doing so. Cautiously, she came off the bed and padded barefoot to the bedroom door, which was slightly ajar. She looked in the little basket in the corner of the room and noticed that Aurora was not in it. Slowly, she peeped outside. The corridor stretched before her gloomily. Timidly, she ventured out, all the while glancing about her. At the balcony, she gripped the railing tightly and peeped over. The sitting room below lay in dusky stillness. As she descended the stairs, praying that they wouldn't creak beneath her weight, she hugged the wall, her eyes trying to penetrate the gloom. The sitting room was vacant, so was the dining room and kitchen. She began to breathe more easily, especially when, on checking, she discovered that the front door was bolted.

She left the foyer, forgetting about the back door, and was about to ascend the stairs, when there was a piercing yowl and a warm body sailed past her almost causing her to trip and fall. Once she had regained her composure, her eyes detected a quivering ball huddled in a corner of the sitting room. She went over to it and bent down.

"Aurora." She reached out to pick up the obviously frightened creature. She never got a chance. The room suddenly exploded in a burst of stars as she felt a hard blow to the side of her head. Then there were no more stars.

She came to, and felt a wet sensation on her face. She tried opening her eyes and through a haze, saw the foot of a chair leg. There was a prickly object against her cheek and her head thudded dully. She discovered that the wetness was Aurora licking her face and that she was lying face down on the carpet. She tried to rise and felt a wave of dizziness overwhelm her, so she remained still for a while. After a few moments, she tried again. Nothing happened, so she slowly sat up.

She obviously had no broken bones, so she held on to a chair and cautiously stood up. The memory of what had happened gradually returned and fear flooded her. She wondered if the intruder was still inside. Everything seemed untouched, but it was hard to confirm, as she didn't know how much time had elapsed during her unconsciousness.

Her fear soared, making her feel dizzy all over again. She felt rooted to where she leaned against an armchair for support. She no longer felt safe in her own house. All that was once familiar now seemed alien. She pushed her hand into the pocket of her dress and felt a piece of paper in it. Withdrawing her hand, she saw that it was the same piece of paper Murray had given her earlier with his number on it. A sob of relief died in her throat as she shuffled as carefully as possible to the phone on the coffee table. With trembling fingers, she punched the numbers.

A woman answered on the fifth ring. "Good evening, Campbell residence."

Eileen's throat constricted.

"Hello? Hello?" the woman called. "Who's there?"

Eileen tried again and her voice came out in a croak. "H-hello."

"Yes, may I help you?"

"M-may I s-speak to Murray, please?" Eileen could feel herself falling apart. This last episode was the last straw in all that had happened to her.

The woman asked her to hold and there was a seemingly endless pause. Eileen felt as if her whole life had been put on hold.

"Hello?" said a familiar, rumbling bass voice suddenly.

Never before had she been so happy to hear someone's voice. "Murray," she said and stopped, unable to continue.

There was silence for a heartbeat and then he spoke. "Eileen, is that you?" Eileen began to weep quietly.

He arrived with Neil and a few other men a few minutes later. Eileen sobbed when she saw them.

"I've r-ruined your party," she wept as he held her, her face buried in his shirt. She raised a tear-stained face. "And I've ruined your shirt."

His body shook with uncontrollable laughter. "You're something else, Eileen Wainwright, d'you know that?"

Neil returned to them. "Look like the person came through the back door," he reported.

"It wasn't locked. Daddy an' the others checking out the rest of the place."

"Well you're not staying here," Murray stated matter-of-factly. "At least for tonight until everything is back to normal."

She sniffled. "Where will I stay? What if my family calls?" She looked flustered. "I should call them."

"I'll do all of that for you." He helped her to her feet from the sofa where that had been sitting. "Right now, you're coming with me. Where are your shoes?"

She pointed upstairs, trying to make sense of what was happening. Murray asked Neil to get them for her then turned his attention to her once more.

"You must be hungry. Cecile, that's my daughter-in-law, she cooked up a storm. You're gonna love her."

Neil reappeared shortly with her shoes and Murray helped her to put them on. He told Neil to tell the others that he would take her to their house.

Eileen looked behind her as he led her gently out to the patio. "But I'm not properly dressed. W-what about my things? What about the house?"

"You don't worry your pretty little head. We'll take care of everything. You can do everything up at the house. We've got more than enough space. Did anyone ever tell you that you're a beautiful woman? But I'm sure you've heard that a lot. By the way, I still can't get over the name of that group. Can you believe a name like that?"

Eileen relaxed as she listened to him and thought that she could do so for the rest of her life. But tonight, she might just dance, and smile, and dance again.

They Don't Have Wings

I walked past the fence enclosing the schoolyard, watching the children as they played. I observed their small bodies as they tumbled about, and heard their clear laughter is they shrieked at each other. At the end of the enclosure, there was a bench, so I went and sat on it. I was hungry, but I was determined to ignore the insistent rumblings of my stomach. Leaning forward, I took the little book I had with me out of my pocket and began to record in it. Soon, a little girl, about eight years old, came through a side gate in the enclosure crnd sat beside me. I felt her curious gaze, but continued with what I was doing. She took a sandwich out of her lunch box and unwrapped it.

"Would you like a half of my sandwich?" she asked.

I stopped reading and looked at her. "That's very kind of you." I smiled at her. "But you should eat your lunch." I resumed my task.

She continued to stare at me. Suddenly, my stomach rumbled audibly. The little girl giggled and held out half a sandwich to me. Slowly, I put my book down in my lap and took it from her. We ate in silence.

Out of the corner of my eye I could see a woman, obviously a teacher, crossing the schoolyard towards us. She called sharply to the little girl to come with her. Reluctantly, the little girl took up her things, waved goodbye to me and went to the woman, who glared at her and looked disdainfully at me. Then, taking the little girl by the hand, they both headed back to the school.

That evening, as I came to a bus shelter, I saw a crowd of people gathered on the sidewalk near to a taxi stand, making a loud commotion. On inquiring, I was told that a man had been involved in a hit-and-run accident. He lay bleeding profusely on the sidewalk. People hovered over him, their faces revealing that they expected the worst.

Suddenly, a taxi driver left the stand and began asking some of the people to help him put the injured man into his car so that he could take him to the nearest hospital. Some of the people gathered berated him for his actions, saying that he wasn't responsible and therefore shouldn't get involved, but others applauded his efforts. He drove off just as the bus arrived.

All the seats were filled on the bus. I was tired from all the walking I'd done and wished for an empty seat. A man standing beside me must have seen the expression on my face because he nudged the man seated in front of me.

"Yu can give di lady yu seat, boss?" he asked him. "She nuh look too well."

The man who was seated looked at us and hissed his teeth. The man beside me looked ready to argue with him, but I begged him not to. "I'm alright, really," I assured him.

A teenaged boy who was seated behind the boorish man touched me on my hand that was holding on to the back of the seat.

"Lady yu can tek my seat," he offered, as he stood up.

I told him thanks as I smiled at him and sat down.

As I came off at the stop that faced the entrance to a hospital, a car passed me, its blinkers flashing, as it rounded the corner into the hospital entrance at an alarming speed. I would have ignored it if I hadn't seen a familiar face in the back seat, her uniform soaked with blood. It was the little girl who had shared her lunch with me.

The doctors and nurses in the antiseptic, white room hovered over the little girl as they worked patiently. Outside, in the waiting room, her father held her weeping mother, as he himself struggled to remain composed.

Minutes elapsed as the operating physician deftly used his instruments. Finally, he removed an object that made a metallic sound as he dropped it into a basin held by a nurse beside him.

"That's it," he said to the others. "Send her to the recovery room."

In the waiting area, the same doctor spoke with the little girl's parents. They shook his hand, gratitude and joy on their faces. The woman began crying again, only this time with happiness.

In another room, a man lay attached to intravenous tubes. In a chair beside his bed sat a taxi driver, looking exhausted but relieved. A doctor entered the room and spoke to the driver, who stood up and shook her hand before leaving.

Outside the hospital, dusk had fallen. I walked, unseen, past the few people who were heading into the building. As I surveyed the still scene before me, I thought of all I had seen, especially during the earlier part of the day. As I took out the little book from my pocket and began transmitting information to it, I remembered the faces of those that had served their fellows and thought, how like us they are, except, they don't have wings because they don't need any.

My work finished, I closed the book and, with a flap of my own wings, I was gone.

MACHINE SHOP
BY RHONDA HARRISON
2006

Me, Sonny, Leroy, and Boxer could barely control our laughter, rocking from side to side slapping our thighs loudly. Boy that Biya sure know how to tell the wickedest stories and everybody that is anybody know that any story with Henry Lalasingh and crowd must mean joke.

"So what next, eh? Yuh sitting next to this chick that is the Indian version of Rita Hayworth and then..." encouraged Boxer.

"Dat bwoy Henry Lalasingh know how fi scent up a room," responded Biya loudly, "Tell yuh man, I in di front of the theatre and I never haffi look round fi tell when Henry Lalasingh walk in. Bwoy I tell you, some people man, some people." He said shaking his head in mock indignation.

Realizing that we were hanging on to his every word, he held the pause a little longer.

"And???"

"Tell you man, I just take this little chick in my arms and was just about to put my lips on har when, me hear 'Excuse me, excuse me' nuh Henry Lalasingh that pushing him way through my aisle cause the only empty seat that left in the theater is sida dis likkle chick?"

Squeals of delight echoed through the machine shop causing the other apprentices to look up.

"Hush before yuh mek Grayson come down pon we!" warned Leroy hissing his teeth.

"Alright, mek yuh so miserable?"

"And then what?" queried Boxer, "What the likkle chick do?"

"First she kinda ease off my chest, yuh know cause she don't really know if I know the fellar. Then I see har face start change; nose a wrinkle up and ting, then she start drift to my side asking me if I smell something funny."

By this time our laughter was becoming uncontrollable.

"Me like a fool nuh go answa. Lawd, Henry Lalasingh head flash round like a gig and him start call 'Ralph, Ralph, Ralph, ah yuh dat?' Me dere acting like ah don't hear a ting. What yuh tink happen nex?" asked Biya.

"Hope you boys over there welding that pipe and not just flying off you mouths" interjected the Supervisor Grayson.

A deafening 'Yes sir' placated Mr. Grayson who happily strolled off in the direction of his office to listen to the ten 'o clock race day preview.

"Yes, yes, yes and then what?" prodded Boxer, even more eager to hear the end of the tale.

"Then, Henry Lalasingh start stretch cross the chick face to touch me. The scent of him arm make the girl start..."

"WHAT????!!!!"

"What's up Lalasingh? Never see, hear, nor smell yuh a come."

"Bwoy, man ah late cause ah did have di rammie fi tie out fi Mama befoe a come." explained Henry Lalasingh. He paused, caught his breathe and continued, "Lawd a tired an ah not even start yet!"

"Look like is yuh a di rammie" mumbled Leroy under his breath.

Without missing a beat, Boxer chimed "So what tired yu so eh? Date out with the girls?"

"Cho, man. Tell yuh Boxer, ah go show go watch The Gladiator with Victor Mature last night an' come back late. See Ralph dere with a nice little chick, but him neva look like he was having a good time. Dat likkle chick vomit up on 'im new suede shoes."

The roar of laughter drowned Henry Lalasingh' s voice.

"Chups! Unno mus want Grayson come back!" snapped Leroy.

The whistle sounded for the morning break. We and all the other apprentices drifted out to the yard. The morning heat had begun to rise, making it look as if the tall stalks of cane were shivering and dancing in the distance. The wind stirred miniature whirlwinds across the factory yard and blew trash and dust onto shoes and clothes, and the occasional sandwich that was brought out. For the most part, the apprentices used the time to jostle, to splash water on their faces and to perhaps have a long drink.

But stop, who that coming up to the gate in that bright orange dress? Look at that figure, the heat and sun just making it dance and jump as it gliding up the road. The basket on her head elongating her figure made all the men and boys in the factory yard immobile. Lord, have mercy, that guardie mad?! A factory yard full a man and him a let her in!

The men moved against the shadows of the tanks and chimneys pulled as if magnetized by her every step.

"Biya, your chick did look anything like that last night?" rasped Sonny.

"Lawd have mercy no! If she did look so then even Victor Mature would come outta Gladiator!"

The girl walked toward the machine shop briskly. As she neared them, she slowed down and gave us a hard stare, it seemed as if her mouth was forming to ask a question when she paused, wrinkled her nose and stared on Henry Lalasingh. Poor Biya and the rest of us cut Henry such an evil look that him wilt and step off. With Henry Lalasingh gone, we felt sure she would stop, but just as it seemed possible, Bala Rao step up,

"Dottie!"

"I glad I find yuh so quick. Mama waiting for me by the main gate, we going to sell some lunch down by Alley market."

"What Ma cook?"

"Roti, dhal, curried kathar, and some banta choka." She said as she handed the basket of food to him, "I guess yuh'll find something to drink. Mi not staying. Later." She spun on her heels and headed toward the gate.

It seemed to the apprentices hanging outside the machine shop, that the girl sprinted away. It wasn't until we heard Supervisor Grayson that we were jolted back to action by his booming voice:

"Look how all of you are standing out here as if you haven't heard the kachi blowing. Get inside. You think that any of you are going to become class one welders by standing and staring at the gate?"

His stern tone acted as the whip to drive us back inside. He worked us so hard that it seemed as if it were a punishment for thinking about how the breeze blowing pushed the dress against the girl's body. The image of the roundness of her breasts and the revealing push the breeze gave as it forced the dress between her legs, showed her up. It's a miracle we never welded we fingers together.

At the ten thirty break the next day, all the apprentices rushed outside waiting to see if Dottie would come back. The push at the gate raised our heads. Lord we waiting to see who it is, but is only Henry Lalasingh. No Dottie, only Henry. We waited until Supervisor Grayson came and chided us. That day he drove us harder. This time, we concluded, it was Henry Lalasingh's fault.

Henry Lalasingh had few friends. Let me see, he had... come to think of it, who was Henry Lalasingh's friend? We never saw Henry Lalasingh with friends back in the school days. He never came to hosays and certainly not to any of the Hindu festivals because of his granny. You see, it's just because we know, but Henry Lalasingh was a half-Indian fellar. You couldn't really tell because he did really look like a full Indian. His father, according to my father, used to live across the street from us, but they say he never really owned Henry Lalasingh as his son although everybody did know that he was his father. As for Henry's mother, she left for Panama shortly after Henry was born; so that left Henry with his granny-Cong Ivy, his mother's mother. Cong Ivy was an Anglican and never really allowed Henry to come around to the hosays and such. It wasn't really her fault Henry Lalasingh stay the way he stay, it goes back to the time when Henry was a baby. They say that he got consumption before he was one and because of that, Cong Ivy practise tidying him instead of giving him regular baths. She would rub him up with eucalyptus oil and wrap him up so that he didn't get a draft and prevent the consumption from take him up worse. Maybe that's where it started, but all we know was that by the time Henry Lalasingh started school at seven, he hated water.

One of the sweetest school jokes that we ever got off him was at Class Three when teacher telling us about hygiene and Henry Lalasingh stand up and say "Well, Teacha, once my hand, foot and face clean, di whole of my body clean. Furthermore, I will catch up fresh cold if I expose my body to water and air." Lawd, the school nearly pop down with laughter.

You should have seen how we laughed when Teacher grab the strap and start put some licks on Henry. From that day, and all through school, we call Henry Lalasingh 'Soapie' cause him disappear every time water touch him back. You should see how we used to run up to Cong Ivy yard when we hear Henry Lalasingh bawling cause we know she trying to bathe him and him bucking like a mad bull. It looked so funny; that old-old woman running down that boy to bathe him. Although we visit his yard almost every week, we never considered him our friend; we use to him, but we not him friend.

Despite how him smell, Henry Lalasingh had the prettiest teeth, hand and foot that we ever see. Sometimes, when we in the machine shop and Grayson checking our nails, the rest of us would get sent outside, but not Henry Lalasingh because of his clean-clean nails. It just hurt us when Grayson would say, "Henry, works in the machine shop too, but look at his nails. Would it kill you to wash your hands and clean your nails?" It hurt us just as much as when he would show us how 'Henry Lalasingh's welding perfect' and suggest that Henry would make Class One welder before he finished his apprenticeship.

As for girlfriend, heh-heh, which girl in her right mind would want Henry Lalasingh? Well that's what we think until yesterday when Bala Rao come up to us with this story. His uncle wife sister, Chunnie, have a daughter that she want to marry off before she get too old and nobody don't want her. Bala wanted to know if any of us interested. We killing laughing — who going to marry some girl that they don't know?

"How you guys getting so, eh?" asked Bala.

"How you mean, we in the green stage of we life, marry now?!" asked Biya laughing.

"Anybody will do?" queried Leroy. We could see his eyes narrowing and realize that he must be thinking up a wicked plan.

"Ah guess, they wasn't too picky" shrugged Bala. "They just want a husband for this girl. Girl-child is too much trouble, you know that already." We all nodded in agreement.

"Well then, if that's the case," suggested Leroy slowly, "What you think bout him?"

We looked slowly in the direction he was focused and our gaze fell on Henry Lalasingh sitting on top of an old boiler eating his lunch.

"Yuh mad!!???" We chorused "HENRY LALASINGH?????!!!!!"

"Look man," explained Leroy "nobody want him, nobody want her — that sound like match to me."

Slowly we began to see the logic of Leroy's conclusion. After all, Henry's we friend, we have to take care of him.

Bala's uncle wife sister, Chunnie, agreed. All she concerned bout is that Henry can take care of the girl. Now we have to make Henry agree and agreeable to this unknown girl.

"So Henry, what you doing this weekend?" asked Boxer

"Nothing as usual."

"Well, Biya, Leroy, Bala, Manu and meself say we going to do some fishing by the river, bottom-side Laloo yard. We planning to cook some food and eat it with some of the fish that we catch. We was just wondering..."

"Bwoy, mi nuh really know, the river is not a place I like too much."

We held our breaths, then Biya chimed in "Henry, we going to the river not in it! If you want come you can come, but me not standing here begging you to come catch fish and eat food with me. Chups"

The shocked looks on our faces did not discourage Biya's sour faced expression. Lawd, what him do now?

Henry scratch his head back, "Just catch fish you say and eat food to?"

"Yes" said Biya softly.

"What you planning on cooking?"

I don't even remember what we tell him, we was just too glad that he would come.

The big kerosene pan was just beginning to boil when we see Henry Lalasingh tracing the footpath to the river. Everything was ready: the blue soap hidden under the root of the Poinciana tree, the washing brush and the soap powder tied up and hanging on the mango limb over our heads. We heard his whistle in the bush; Bala responded with a whistle from the star apple tree.

"Ah bring two poun' a flour" said Henry.

"Where you line and hook?" asked Boxer

"I don't really have any you know, but I was thinking that I would scale the fish."

"That alright" responded Leroy.

"Shhh, I think ah hook something!" exclaimed Biya excitedly. "Help me pull it in!"

We all grabbed on to Biya's waist and started pulling; somehow in the pulling we push Henry up front and SPLASH!

Poor Henry, start bawl out "Mi a drown, help me, help me..." as he thrashed around in the waist deep water. We couldn't help laughing.

"Look how unnu stand up dere laughing, quick grab di bwoy!" yelled Bala.

We dove in; Biya holding Henry's thrashing arms yelled, "Pull off him pants quick!"

Realising what was happening, Henry start buck and kick, now we know what Cong Ivy had to go through. Him wield and kick off Leroy with the pants;

"Hold on, nuh let him go yet! Him still have on him shirt!"

"Hold him foot? Hold him foot?"

Henry start let go some thump and buck. After him fling me off, I could see him bucking Biya, but lawd Boxer sure hold on. We regroup and hold Henry and take off the shirt.

"Run and put it in the kerosene tin" ordered Boxer. The water soon turned black with dirt and lice.

In the meantime, Me, Biya and Bala poured the coarse soap powder on to Henry's hair and scrubbed. Poor Henry, he was too outnumbered and tired to resist for long. When we had finished washing his hair and forcing him to bathe with the blue soap, we coaxed him out of the water to sit on the rock. Leroy had just finished washing his clothes and was in the process of hanging them out on the lower branches of the mango tree. I had turned in the meantime toward cooking the provisions that we had brought. I sort of felt sorry for Henry sitting on the rock, shivering in his underpants, but that was short-lived as Bala and the others soon let him in on the plan.

"You see Henry, there's this girl that like you, but she don't like how you keep you self. So we giving you a head start, you know to fix up and thing."

Henry trembled even more; I thought that he would fall off the rock, but he just sat there not saying a word. Bala began to praise the virtue of the girl's shape and culinary skills. Still no word from Henry; then Boxer chimed in,

"Ah did like her myself, but she say is you she want. Not even Biya impress her." Henry looked hard at Boxer; personally, I didn't think he was buying a word of it. Then he cleared his throat and said:

"Di lunch ready yet? Me can't think about no girl on an empty stomach."

We cheered loudly and shared the lunch. It was dusk by the time we leave the river side, poor Henry head full up a visions of this mystery girl. It look to me that him just floating along. When him get to Cong Ivy house, Bala gave him the last word,

"Just gwaan bathe and keep you self clean. I will carry you go meet her on Wednesday. See you at work on Monday."

Lawd the plan work good.

Grayson was in a bad mood Monday morning. We could tell by the way he made us undo everything we welded that morning. He seemed angry and kept us in during the regular break time. At lunch, he jumped in his car and raced through the gate. As we sat eating our lunch, Ivan Durrant came up to us:

"How come you guys never tell bout what happen to Soapie?"

"Soapie? Nutten nuh happen to him."

Ivan continued, "So unnu nuh know? Soapie gone to Lionel Town Hospital! Him granny say that him go river go bathe and pick up pneumonia!" He stared hard at us. "Him in the hospital from yesterday afternoon."

"Him was right to rathid, water and air would sick him!" exclaimed Boxer in surprise.

"Yesterday, Boxer uncle kill a goat and we were down there eating until late." Responded Biya guiltily.

The food turn brick in mi mouth. The rest of the day was a big blur. Henry Lalasingh spent two weeks in the hospital. The three times we visit him in the hospital, he was fast asleep so we never bother wake him. Grayson never let up on us for as long as Henry Lalasingh was away, it seem like the punishment that we deserved for bathing him.

But wait, who that? Must be a new guy. Look at how him hair slick back like him buy the real pomade for hair, not no coconut oil like the rest of us. And that white shirt, gleaming white; those pants seam look like they could cut iron; and what a boasty black pair of shoes. Who that? But wait, that look like… no man… stop… nuh Henry Lalasingh!!!

"Manu, man, mama tell me that you guys come look for me in the hospital. Sorry man, most of the first week I was sleeping. But as you can see, I get better man. So how I look?"

I just shook my head.

Henry continued, "My mother send a lot of clothes for me from New York. Never had any reason to wear them, but now I have a girl, I have to dress up and look good. The cologne I wearing, I had it for years, but this girl make this bottle half already. Is three time she visit me in the hospital, I tell you, this is love."

As you can well imagine, no work got done for the day, everybody just staring on this new Henry Lalasingh. Grayson so happy to have Henry back that he just left him to watch us while we welded; the world turn upside down.

Biya, Sonny, Leroy, Boxer and me well dress up to get to Henry Lalasingh's wedding. We've never gone inside an Anglican church so we couldn't stop staring at the cross, stained glass windows and laughing at how their priest dress. How could we miss this wedding, we want to see the girl that Bala uncle wife sister wanted to marry off. But, mainly we reach early to see Bala sister Dottie.

Henry Lalasingh look so nice in the white suit that him mother send from New York for him. Cong Ivy sitting up front in her nice lilac dress and big white hat; the organ start playing the wedding march, we stand.

"Any sight of Dottie yet?" whispered Biya,

"If I see her, the next wedding that you go to might be mine." Leroy chuckled.

This type of wedding excite us; is the first we seeing something like this. Look, look is time for Henry to kiss the bride; him gingerly lift the veil and smile; bwoy who teach that Henry to kiss. Look, the priest have to pull them apart heh heh heh. But who the girl? We still don't get a good look yet. See, they turning around; we lean forward to get a good look. We swallow hard and rub our eyes; look good again.

"Leroy," I said still staring at the happy couple, "look like Henry beat you to Dottie."

"Yuh coulda fool me, I think that Dottie was Bala sister."

COCONUT WATER

BY VERONE JOHNSTON

2004

No one ever listens to me. That's why I'm here, in the Barclay Psychiatric Unit. I'm not mad and I didn't try to kill myself. It was an accident. But they won't believe me. And if they think you tried to kill yourself, that means you're mad, and if you're mad they don't believe a word you say. Unless it's what they want to hear. It's so unfair.

But it's been the same all my short life. Like the time when I was about seven and I presented my maths homework that I'd worked really hard on. It was bound to please the teacher and get me a star or a team point, but no!

"Who did your homework for you?"

"I did it."

"Who did your homework for you?"

"I did it."

The teacher's voice rises to a crescendo, and the class falls silent.

"Who did your homework for you?!"

"Mummy," I mumble, looking at my toes.

"Then why did you lie? Why didn't you tell me the truth in the first place?!"

There follows a lecture and a scold about not letting parents do your homework for you, which I listen to in submissive silence, and slink back to my desk.

As if that wasn't bad enough, at the end of the day when I was looking forward to putting it all behind me, I ran up the playground for one quick go on the slide before home time. But it had been raining, so when I slid down I got my skirt wet, and when my mum came to collect me she wouldn't believe I hadn't wet myself. She wouldn't let me go to Linda Barr's party and I had to stand there in silence while she made up a lie to Linda's mother.

That sort of thing happens to me all the time. It's so unfair. Why am I always punished for things I didn't do? Usually 'cause my wretched brother is too clever to get caught and he always stitches me up. Sometimes though, it's just my rotten luck, like the slide thing. Somehow, the weight of evidence is always against me.

Now I'm here all because I drank a small cup of bleach. No one made me do it, it's true, but it was still an accident. How can I explain it, when my mother has always drummed the cry wolf story into my brain?

"If you tell lies all the time, when you're telling the truth no one will believe you!"

But I tell the truth and tell the truth and tell the truth and no one believes me, so I have to lie, just to be left alone.

The fat nurse plumps down on the end of the bed, making my pens roll towards her.

"Are you depressed about anything, Hannah?"

Of course I'm depressed, I'm a teenager!

All my friends are depressed or obsessed or repressed. Jo's anorexic, Neeta fantasises about older men and about killing her mother, Clare's evangelist boyfriend thinks she's a she-devil come to tempt him in the wilderness. Oh, and Anna's so paranoid about being laughed at that she constantly makes a fool of herself. These silly friends of mine call me up all the time to pour out their problems to faithful, boring Hannah.

In my family, nothing dramatic ever happens. It's forbidden.

"Eat your dinner or you get a lick, do you hear me?"

No room for anorexia there.

"What do you mean you're depressed? Don't be so ridiculous, get on with your homework."

You see what I mean? You can't even slam a door in our house. You're not allowed to be angry or upset. Reading and writing's encouraged, though, so I write down all my anger, thoughts and dreams, and let my imagination grow. It keeps me company, 'cause you see my life's really rather ordinary.

But the doctors aren't satisfied that nothing sinister lurks below. No dark family scandal, secret boyfriend, forced arranged marriage, child kidnapping or honour killing. The girl in the next bed told me that the Indian girls always get asked those kinds of questions. But I'm not Indian, we're from Nevis. I've said so, but they don't seem to take it in. Maybe they've never heard of Nevis, or they think it's a place in India.

They ask me the same questions every day:

"Do you love your parents?"

I hate my parents. But that's normal, isn't it?

I've been in here four weeks, and I think they're just coming to the conclusion that there really is nothing wrong with me. Then the unthinkable happens. They find my writing. My diaries, my letters and my stories. Delusions all, they call them.

"Do you know who you are?"

Of course I know who I am, and where I am, and what my name is, but that doesn't mean I have to like it!

"Do you have a boyfriend?"

They're trying to trick me. I wrote about my gorgeous boyfriend in an un-posted letter to my friend Neeta. If I say yes, it'll prove I can't separate fact from fiction. If I say no, they'll produce the letter and try to make me admit it's all made up, but why should I say that? He's real in my head and on the paper, but to tell them that would be courting disaster. Too wacky for them to understand.

My thoughts are my own, and they have no right to take them from me. It might not be real to anybody else, but it is to me. I mean to say, when they cry in sad films I don't barge in and turn the lights on and start capering about the room destroying the atmosphere and telling them that it's all just a story. I mean, how rude! But here they are trampling over my stories.

"Why do you write these things, Hannah?"

"Just bored, I guess."

That's the only reply I can think of that even comes close to the truth.

My mistake has been to write fiction with a ring of truth. But that's what they're always telling us at school. Write about what you know. I used to write fantastic stories of bloodshed and murder, but always got criticised and marked down. So I started to write about what I knew, but I'm hardly going to say, "Joe Benson down the road said good morning to us on his way to church. The End." So instead I wrote that Joe Benson was having an affair with the vicar's wife, and that she told me about it when I went to tea with her. I also wrote that she'd given me some love letters to post to him, and I bought a sheet of stamps from the post office and slipped it between the pages of my diary.

"If it's not true, then why did you buy those stamps?" they ask reasonably.

Their minds work on one plodding level only. I wasn't trying to trick anyone else, 'cause no one else was meant to see it but me. It's like when you watch a horror film with the lights off to make it more real to yourself.

But sadly, my reputation as a prankster (silly word) went before me and made sure I'd be convicted without a fair trial.

I've always been something of a practical joker. Phil next door is two years older than me, and last summer our craze was jokes and tricks. It started when he came round to show me his whoopee cushion. I just had to get one too. Between us we had everything: glow in the dark plastic eyeballs, Dracula teeth, black face soap (never get that by the way, it's completely pathetic). What else? Oh, the snapping chewing gum is the best! The only thing I don't like is insects and spiders.

My big brother's always putting fake spiders in the bath, which is really scary because quite often real spiders come in the bath, and you can't tell the difference. And the real ones always seem to appear when Dad's not in, so I have to accept any terms from my horrid brother before he'll remove them. 'Say that I'm the best brother in the world.' 'Say "I stink".' 'Say "I'm a silly spoilt little brat".' That's the sort of stuff I have to submit to when no one's around. Of course, Mum and Dad never believe me when I tell them, 'cause he's got this big Golden Boy smile, like butter wouldn't melt.

Plastic flies in your food – that's another favourite of his. And he always does these things when you least expect it. He's the kind of person who, if you win in a game of tag, two weeks later he'll come up and tap you on the back and say 'Got you back.' Stupid boy.

Billy's his name. Billy the Bastard. I don't dare call him that to his face, but it all goes down on paper. Three years older, he thinks he's too clever to be fooled by little me.

But I got him back last year:

Mum and Dad went through a phase of bringing home coconuts. I liked eating hunks of the dry white flesh, and Mum made delicious things like coconut drops and grater cake. I didn't like the water, though. Everyone else drank that. One day I was washing the dishes and noticed how similar the dishwater looked to coconut water. So I poured some in a glass and told Billy to drink it. He only took one sip before I stopped him. That's not so bad. It was a hot day and he could easily have glugged down the lot before realising. But I'm not that cruel. Funnily enough he took it in good part. One never knows whether he'll be nasty and kick up a fuss about something, or whether he'll just laugh. This time I think he admired me for actually thinking up something that worked.

I know he'll get me back some time when I think he's forgotten all about it. But I don't need to worry about that now. For the time being I can gloat over my own cunning victory.

Where was I? Oh yes, so that's what my life was like before the accident happened – I mean the accident with the bleach, not Billy's bike accident, although that wasn't my fault either. But I can see the blame in Mum's eyes – Dad's too. Anyway, I don't want to talk about that.

Uh oh, here comes the doctor with the enormous glasses. She looks like someone from a seventies soap opera. What does she want?

"Now Hannah, how are we feeling today?"

"I feel fine. Can I go home?"

"Is there anything you'd like to talk to me about?"

Didn't you hear? I said I was fine!

You see? I'm not crazy, but sometimes I think I'm invisible and no one can hear me. Hey, do you think I should say that to the doctor?!

"Doctor, I feel like no one can see me. I speak but no one seems to understand. I must be talking a foreign language – or tongues! Do you think that's it?"

She pushes her big glasses up her nose.

"Do you speak your parents' language? Urdu perhaps?" she asks hopefully, pen poised. She pronounces it 'Er-doo'.

What are you on about, you mad woman? My parents speak English!

Oh my God, maybe I'm not the only one who can't be understood. If all this time she thinks my parents have been speaking a different language, it's small wonder the whole lot of us haven't been declared insane and banged up.

There are several black boys on the ward opposite. They all seem perfectly normal to me, but the Asian girl in the next bed, who seems to know everything, said there are always lots of black kids in mental hospitals, because white people think we're all dangerous. She and another Asian girl were caught slipping over to the boys' ward one night. Their parents don't like them talking to boys, and as for black boys – heart attacks all round. So just to spite them they pick the biggest, baddest, blackest boys they can find.

Now the doctor is asking me why I'm always over there talking to them. Well, they're the same age as my older brother Billy, so I understand when they talk about football and stuff, and I like playing cards and listening to their conversations. There's Lester, who pretends to know nothing but patois when the doctors and nurses come round. He's soooo funny! He has us is stitches every day. Alvin fell off the bed, he was laughing so much; that earned him a double dose of Diazepam.

"How is it you understand their speech, Hannah? Do you have a West Indian boyfriend?"

"I've told you," I repeat wearily, "I'm West Indian too."

"Well you don't look like a West Indian."

Well you don't look like an English woman, you stupid fat bug-eyed alien!

"And you don't sound like one either."

We don't all talk like Bob Marley, you know!

"Is this another one of your stories, Hannah?"

Whatever.

I wish we could go back to Nevis. I wasn't born when we left, but everyone's always going on about the good old days, the year-round sunshine and the fresh fruit they used to pick. I'm the only one born here, so I'm left out of their conversations. And Billy always boasts about things he did or had in Nevis, though I'm sure he makes it all up, 'cause he was only a toddler when they left.

Everything's gone wrong here. Mum complains about the cold, and Dad's tired and grumpy when he comes home from work. I hear them talking in bed at night. Dad says stuff like, 'It would never have happened if we'd gone home before Hannah started school … before Billy's exams … before this, before that … ' and Mum just cries. When I talk to the boys in here, I pretend that I too can remember life in the islands, and they accept me and they laugh at my stories.

Now the Alien Doctor is asking me about my fantasies. That's easy to talk about with half a mouth. I'll tell her my Indian Princess one. That'll keep her pen busy for a while. What can I do if no one will take me seriously? Not my parents, not my self-centred friends and certainly not these idiot doctors who think just because I've got a long ponytail, I must be an Indian. I'd chop it off now, if I didn't think they'd interpret it as some psychotic form of self-harm, or a cry for help.

I remember Billy once locked my ponytail in the door when Mum and Dad were out, so that I had to spend the whole evening in the dark passage while he watched TV in the sitting room and made me miss all my favourite programmes.

It's not easy having a bully for an older brother who always gets you into trouble and then laughs behind your back. A bully who can't take a joke. If you put a fake snake in his bed, he puts a real one in yours. If you snap his finger in the trick chewing gum, he takes your whole hand off in a mouse trap.

But then, Billy died in a road accident six months ago. So he's not here anymore. He's gone…and he never did get me back for making him drink dishwater. I thought I'd be happy without him, but I'm not. It feels curious and wrong somehow that I should have the last laugh. He always gets his own back, much as I hate him for it. I'm not supposed to win.

He used to make me think I'd spontaneously combust. Maybe that would happen and he could laugh at me from beyond the grave. Or maybe he would haunt me – he'd like that. How would he punish me for riding his prized Chopper bicycle without permission? To be fair, I told him the brakes weren't working properly, but (surprise, surprise) he didn't believe me, and went riding all the same. But I didn't damage them deliberately. I was riding around the garage and it just happened.

After the tragedy, Mum started to work the day shift again. When we were little, she'd work nights and Dad days, so that there was always someone with us. But I'm older now, and I think she feels sad with just me in the house during the holidays.

When I'm alone I have to spend the whole day cleaning the bathroom and kitchen, so that Mum will let me go out later.

I'm doing the kitchen first. It's the easiest, and I can listen to the radio while I work. One annoying thing though is that Mum always buys enormous containers of stuff. She says it's better value, but it means I have to spend ages decanting gallon tubs of bleach into a dozen smaller jars, so that they'll fit into the cupboards. Such a waste of time.

I sigh and get on with it. Oh, and the coconuts are back. Dad won one at a shy at the local fair, and it revived the craze, so now we have four lined up on the kitchen worktop.

I pick one up and shake it, churning up the water inside. Actually, I've grown used to the taste of coconut water, and I quite like it now. I've got a glass of it here next to me. Cleaning is thirsty work, and I sip it from time to time.

I hardly have time to think about my brother. Housework keeps my hands busy, and my attention-magnet friends wrap their problems around my brain like candy floss. I'm like the calm eye of a storm, with madness all around me. Cyclone Hannah. Hannah 'the Cyclone' Adams. I sound like a boxer! Or maybe just a boring snooker player.

I slap on the hob polish with a swirling motion, round and round, scowling at my face distorted in the black ceramic surface.

Why do they always tell me their problems? Perhaps because I never have any of my own, so they can talk at me as much as they want and I'll listen and be sympathetic.

Well, I wanted problems and now I've got them. For real this time. Like sorting out my brother's games bit by bit. Mum can't bear to do it. She wants to give the whole lot to charity, but I don't want strangers playing with his stuff, particularly when he was so fussy about people touching his things and messing them up. I've taken the stretched Zebedee toy – I stretched it years ago. And the Thunderbirds car with Parker missing – my fault again. Oh, and I found my long lost Star Wars Frisbee under his bed, and a few other things I thought I'd lost. He had them all the time. Just as I thought.

Who's that on the phone? Neurotic Neeta, no doubt. The jars of bleach are full, and I just have one little bit left. Quickly, I finish pouring out the measure into the nearest thing to hand – a plastic cup. I hope it won't melt or anything. Then I rush for the phone. She chats endlessly about the Turkish kebab man she fancies, and how she wishes her mother dead – oh, it's not that shocking really, just her twisted Oedipal fantasies, like she's the first person in the world ever to have discovered Freud.

God, I hate being a teenager. I just listen to her like I always do, and when she's talked herself dry, she says goodbye without so much as a 'How are you, Hannah?' 'How are you coping with the death of your brother?'

I slam the phone down and stomp back down the hall. Typical, bloody typical, I mutter.

So how did I get from there to here, the Barclay Psychiatric Ward?

They think I blame myself for Billy's death, and that I tried to kill myself as some kind of self-punishment, or something. Neeta would say I'm a masochist. Utter rubbish.

So what did happen after I put the phone down?

Nothing. I flounced back into the kitchen and downed my coconut water. He said he'd get me back, and he did. That's all.

IN THIS WORLD
BY MICHAEL RECKORD
2006

Despite the sultriness of the mid-August night, the water in the slum's communal shower was chilly the next morning, and as she left her ramshackle board and zinc shack, Beverly welcomed the warmth of the sun on her skin. Her daughter, Lisa, was still sleeping, for it was just seven o'clock and a Saturday. School would begin in another fortnight and when it did, Lisa would have to be up by five-thirty every weekday morning.

As Beverly picked her way along the garbage-strewn dirt path past shacks like her own, the sun was the only thing that she felt pleased about. The news blaring from a dozen radios made her feel hopeless: three more murdered overnight; more Government corruption uncovered; sugar cane workers on strike over low wages and poor working conditions; dismal examination results again for the island's 50,000 school-leavers. From a score of tape recorders and CD players came dancehall lyrics which made her angry with their denigration of women and promotion of violence against "Babylon", police informers and homosexuals. She saw a connection between the violence of the lyrics and the violence in the country.

What was of most concern, though, was the thought of the request she'd have to make of Mrs. Teape that day.

On her way to the main road, Beverly greeted several persons on the path or at their doors: "Morning." "Morning, Miss B." "Morning." "Morning, Bigga." "How you daughter, Evelyn? Oh. I hope she get better quick." "Morning, sah."

Beverly felt superior to them all, but respect was a must. People got harassed, even killed, for "dissing" their neighbours. Beverly often told herself that Jesus knew what he was talking about when he told his disciples that though he and they were in this world, they were not of it. She certainly didn't consider herself a part of this world.

Reaching the gate in the zinc fence which hid the inner city community from the eyes of the road, Beverly felt her spirits lift. She always enjoyed stepping up the three concrete steps to the gate and out onto Barbican Road. It led to a number of Kingston's wealthy residential areas and much of the traffic on the road consisted of luxury cars and SUVs. One day, Beverly continually told herself and Lisa, they would live in one of the big houses in a good area and drive in a big car.

"But is you haffi tek us dere," she warned. "Me can't do it. Me is a domestic servant. You haffi go to university and study to be a doctor or lawyer. Or computer expert."

Lisa always answered confidently, "Yes, Mama."

A bright girl, she was starting high school in September, but she was only eleven and Beverly wasn't sure if she realised the difficulty of the challenge. It meant twelve or thirteen years of hard study and good grades before she got her degree, then she had to get a job that would pay millions of dollars. Houses and cars were expensive God knew what level the rapidly shrinking Jamaican dollar would have reached by then; it'd shrunk sixty percent in the last fifteen years.

Beverly herself faced a big challenge--to earn the money to keep Lisa in school until university graduation. That's what she had to speak to Mrs. Teape about.

It was late in the afternoon before the opportunity came. Washed, tidied and ready to go home, Beverly entered her employer's modern, well-equipped kitchen, which had more floor space than Beverly's rented shack. Mrs. Teape was making the last component of dinner, a vegetable salad. In various plastic and glass containers on the kitchen table were the ingredients: lettuce, tomatoes, carrots, melon, raisins, dressing. Also on the table were the cutting board, grater, bowls, knives and spoons which Mrs. Teape manipulated with quick, manicured fingers.

Waiting for Mrs. Teape to speak first, Beverly watched the well cared for hands with envy. Hers were rough and hard from doing her own housework, but she was thrilled again with the satisfaction of knowing that her hands were brown, while Mrs. Teape's were black. She strongly suspected that Mrs. Teape envied her complexion. Being brown was desirable in Jamaica.

It was a pity, Beverly often thought, that Lisa had inherited her father's dark complexion--not as black as Mrs. Teape's, though, thank God! Lisa was bright, and with a university education she should be all right; still, if only God had made her bright and brown, the big house and car would've been guaranteed.

"You ready, Beverly?"

"Yes'm."

Beverly didn't move and Mrs. Teape glanced at her, clearly puzzled.

"You want a drive down the hill?"

"No'm. Is not even six o'clock yet. It still light."

"Well, take care all the same. Remember what happened to Mrs. McFarlane's helper."

"Yes ma'am." Beverly moved toward the kitchen table. "Yu need any help, ma'am?"

"Oh no. This is mostly for me. The boys hate vegetables, but I'm trying to get as slim as you. I don't know how you do it."

"Easy. Hard work an' whole heap a worry."

"What do you have to worry about?"

Beverly sighed. "Aah, Mrs Teape, you wouldn't know."

"Tell me. Your daughter, your mother?"

"Lisa, ma'am."

Mrs Teape finished grating the carrots onto a plate and Beverly passed her a ceramic bowl into which she scraped the bright orange, pyramid shaped pile. Beverly dropped the discarded tin grater into the sink. "Well," said Mrs Teape as she began slicing the succulent, red tomatoes on the oval Lignum Vitae cutting board, "all of us mothers have that sort of worry. You know Frankie is in sixth form at Campion College, and I don't think that even after a year he's settled down... But you don't want to hear my troubles, you want to go home. Have a nice weekend."

"But ah coming tomorrow, ma'am."

"Tomorrow's Sunday. Your day off."

"Ah took a day off dis week a'ready, ma'am."

"Wednesday? You were ill."

"Yes, ma'am, but ah can't tek two day off in one week. Too much work to do." Beverly had spent the day dusting, sweeping, cob-webbing, mopping and vacuuming the house and had almost, but not quite, finished the cleaning. The house was a two-storey building with four bedrooms, three bathrooms, a study where Mr. Teape –an aircraft engineer with responsibility for the eastern Caribbean –did his work, a large dining room, a larger living room with the giant television and the music system, and a recreation room with wall-to-wall book shelves and a second television set. Beside the house was a smaller building containing a helper's quarters and the laundry. This building and the recreational room had been constructed about twenty years before, just after the Teape's first son, now at university, had been born, and they had easy-to-clean tile floors. The original house, though, was more than one hundred years old and had wooden floors.

Beverly liked to imagine that it had been build by Jamaicans who, some decades before, had been slaves. The thought gave her comfort. If her ancestors had been able to make the giant leap from slavery to freedom, she and Lisa could make the leap from poverty to wealth.

"Icy's coming back tomorrow," Mrs. Teape said, "and I'll pitch in and help if necessary." She laughed and the five extra pounds distributed around her waist and hips that she was concerned about jiggled.

"I do get some exercise from housework, too, you know, not only gardening."

Mrs. Teape worked for half-an-hour in the garden every morning, before the sun got too hot. She re-potted, picked, pruned and watered, leaving the really hard work for Clive, the gardener.

Beverly loved Mrs Teape's garden. Lining it was a hedge with two varieties of bougainvillea, one with dark red flowers, and the other with pink and white ones. Two rose beds with waist high red and yellow plants were in the centre of the crab grass lawn. Edging the front of the house were other beds, with a variety of flowers--Mexican blue bells; lantana, with their small red, purple and orange clusters; lilac-coloured plumbago; the multi-coloured impatience; and, close to the ground, the scarlet four-o-clocks, which opened in the bright daylight but closed in the early afternoon.

On the other side of the house was the patio with flowering plants in large and small clay pots--white and purple orchids, pink and yellow bird of paradise, yellow allamanda, red and pink ginger, and variously coloured gerberas and lilies.

Beverly had no garden. None of the residents in her community did. The few metres of ground that separated one shack from another was hard, bare earth in which nothing ever grew. There were three trees on the very edges of the property, one ackee, one mango and one coconut. All bore fruit seasonally, and all were picked young--too young to be of any use to the picker. Whether the reaping was done with the hope that the fruit was indeed edible or out of spite, to prevent anyone at all from benefiting, Beverly was not certain.

Starting to pick the leaves off a head of lettuce, Beverley asked,

"Don't you an' Missa Teape teking de children to de beach tomorrow?" She asked.

"For the morning, not all day. I'm sure that Icy and I can manage without you."

Beverly rinsed off the lettuce leaves.

"No, ma'am, ah have to come tomorrow. Missa Frankie clothes haffi iron and ah goin' haffi do de window dem--

"Icy did them."

"Never do dem good, ma'am."

Mrs Teape sighed. "Oh dear! Again?"

"Yes, ma'am. She sick, ma'am."

"I know. That's why you've been here for the week."

"Ah tink yu should mek it permanent, Mrs Teape." Beverly heard the unintended harshness in her voice and saw Mrs Teape frown.

"I don't need two full time helpers, Beverly," she said, "and Icy has been here for five years."

Weighing her words carefully, Beverly replied. "She not working properly, ma'am, I haffi follow up on what she do, an do it over."

"Only when her pressure's acting up. When she takes her medication regularly, she works fine."

"Lemme wash dose fah you, ma'am."

Beverly took the bag of raisins from Mrs. Teape, poured them into a strainer and held it under the tap, shaking it vigorously.

"Well," Beverly said after a moment, "She not teking de medicine regularly."

"That was only last week."

"No, ma'am."

"She told me. She ran a little short of money and didn't refill her prescription when she should have. I was really distressed that she hadn't told me, but I lent her the money."

"It happen before, ma'am."

"You sure?"

"Yes. She never want tell yu. How much raisins yu want?"

"That'll do."

Mrs Teape meant the half cup Beverly had poured into the bowl with the lettuce and carrots. Beverly had rinsed too much.

"Can have dese, ma'am?"

Beverly took the casual urgent wave of Mrs. Teape's hand as a yes and she emptied the raisins left in the strainer into her rough palm and tossed them into her mouth. Chewing, she said, "An' it will happen again. Den yu won't know until she faint like las' time. She's a proud woman. Poor but proud."

"But isn't her husband working?"

"On and off. Sometimes she have to support him."

"So you see why I have to keep her."

Beverly admired Mrs. Teape's generosity and loyalty. She was loyal to her husband, her two sons, her wider family and her friends and she often got into trouble when various persons within the groups fussed with each other. Fortunately, her gentle personality and training in psychology made her an ideal peacemaker. But, Beverly told herself, Mrs. Teape didn't live in the world that she did. In that jungle, it was eat or be eaten.

"Cause she poor, ma'am?" Beverly asked. "Me poor, too."

"But I can't afford two helpers. Not with the minimum wage so high."

"Cost a livin' higher. An me have a pickney to mind, an' no husban' to help me."

"Icy's sick. How could I fire her?"

"She sick an' can't do de work. I need de money to buy school uniform and books fah Lisa, an pay her school fees. Please, Mrs. Teape! She haffi do well in school and go to university. We haffi get outa de ghetto. Ah haffi work tomorrow."

Mrs Teape arranged the finished salad decoratively in the ceramic bowl and sighed.

"That means time-and-a-half. All right, work tomorrow."

"Tanks, ma'am. Yu want de dressing now?"

"Not yet. Thank you."

Beverly started loading the used implements into the sink. "What about a permanent job, ma'am?"

"No, Beverly. Just continue to come on the days Icilda is off." She paused, "She got you this job, Beverly, remember?"

"Yes, ma'am. But she is a old woman."

"Just past sixty one, not even eight years older than me."

"In de ghetto you age fast, ma'am. Is me doin' mos' of her work here, ma'am. Why yu tink me been leaving after six every day? De house big and tek time to clean, and it tek whole heap of energy to wash fah you and Mr. Teape and de children."

Beverly went to the sink and began washing up. Mrs. Teape sat at the kitchen table and watched her.

"How old is Lisa?" Mrs Teape asked,

"Eleven."

"So she can look after herself when she comes home from school and you're at work?"

"You can't leave a girl pickney in de house alone in de ghetto, ma'am. De idle boy in de area too dangerous. She stay up de lane wid Mama."

"Well, I'm sorry I can't help you. You'd better look somewhere else."

"Is two year me was lookin' before me get dis job, Mrs Teape."

"Two years without working? Doesn't Lisa's father help?"

"Him was helping...but a year ago him get shot."

"Dead?"

"Yes'm."

"I'm sorry. How did you live all this time – food, clothes, rent?"

Having loaded the draining rack by the sink, Beverly asked, "Leave dem, Mrs. Teape or dry dem?"

Mrs Teape drummed her fingers on the kitchen table. "You got help from you mother, didn't you? From Icy?"

Beverly's answer was a soft, exhaled, "Yes."

"And you want me to let her go? How could you be so heartless?"

"Is so life go, ma'am. If old people can't keep up wid de tribes dem get left behind. Just like how Mama did help me, me haffi help Lisa." Tears started streaming down her face, "Me can't help two a dem, ma'am."

Mrs. Teape ripped two squares from the paper towel roll by the sink and handed them to Beverly to dab her eyes. They were the thick reusable kind.

Beverly closed the gate, picked a red bougainvillea flower from the hedge and started walking down the hill to the bus stop. Six houses down was the McFarlane's house, where the helper had been abducted a week before by three men in a car as she was leaving one evening. Her body was found in a cane field in the adjoining parish two days later. She'd been raped and strangled. Beverly wiped her eyes again and looked longingly at the large, beautiful houses with their lovely gardens that she was passing. This was her world. She began praying for the quick deterioration of her mother's health. Inheriting her job was the first step toward getting one of the houses.

Mrs. Teape had said she would think about letting Icy go and taking Beverly on permanently. Beverly had said, "All right, ma'am," and left. She'd done all she could. Now it was up to God. He'd sacrificed His son. He would surely understand that Beverly had to sacrifice her mother.

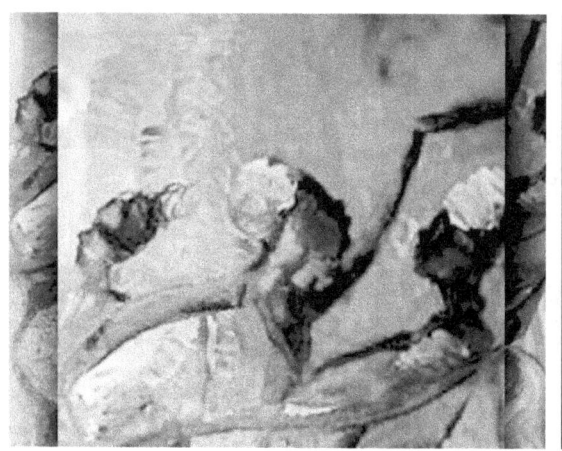

RHYTHMS OF LIFE
BY CARROLL EDWARDS
2004

The church seemed much smaller than I remembered. The altar, the pews, everything seemed to have shrunk in the years that I had been away. The magnificent pipe organ of my youth that only Teacher Rockwell had been permitted to play now stood neglected and disconcertingly dingy, its once-splendid mahogany façade obscured by the grillwork in which it was now encased.

The service had not yet started. Restless, I wandered outside, striving to identify familiar landmarks. The cotton tree, bane of my youth, spread a majestic shadow over the graves and I could still see the thick wooden pole protruding awkwardly from its side. Local folklore had it that the pole was the remnant of a shot fired by the French when they had landed at Carlisle Bay in an attempt to capture the island from the British. It had lodged in the tree trunk, saving the church from certain destruction. It was divine intervention, the local people said.

I strolled around the graveyard, examining the headstones: Sacred to the memory of John Jacob Beach, Esquire May 6, 1656 – January 31, 1683. Here was another one: *Here lyes the bodie of Mary Pierce Sunderland, Beloved daughter of Mary Ellen Sunderland, who died in 1695 at the age of 15. This tomb is erected by her disconsolate mother and relatives.*

An overwhelming sense of sadness engulfed my entire body. I felt a sense of kinship with that disconsolate mother. Had grief been any different in the seventeenth century, I wondered. How had she coped with the death of a child?

I realized that I had played among these graves, unappreciative of the chronicles of life revealed by the inscriptions. For me, the graves had been nothing more than a backdrop to the games we children played as we waited for services to begin or, a resting place as we waited after church for our mothers to finish their conversations so we could begin the long walk home. On Good Fridays, as pastor lead the congregation through the stages of the Cross during the three hour long service, Mother would send us outside just before we started to get really fidgety, with a bag full of bun and cheese to keep us quiet. One by one, the other children would join us, and we would race around the churchyard, using the gravestones as hurdles, all the while trying to stifle the inevitable laughter, so as not to disturb the service inside.

Mannis had been aghast the first time he saw us jumping over the graves. Normally, he didn't attend the Good Friday services, but for some reason that year, he had decided that he would ('out of respect," he told me). You can't take it so slight!" he had admonished us. "Bite you finger, bite you finger quick, so the duppy won't trouble you." It was then we realized that his anxiety had more to do with his fear of the dead in their graves, than any concern for our welfare or for that of the living sitting reverently in the pews inside.

But if you were so afraid of the dead, Mannis, why hasten to join them?

The church began to fill up as people arrived for the service. The whispering was deafening. I could see members of the congregation jostling to view the casket which had been placed just inside the tower, at the entrance to the church. Mannis' face had been left unscathed by the fire and the undertakers had skillfully positioned his body inside the coffin so that the rest of him was barely visible. Still, they crowded around the casket, some casting furtive, accusatory glances in my direction, others averting their eyes as they passed, pretending that they didn't want to view the remains. I knew better though. Nothing as exciting as this had happened in the village in years!

"Is who find him?"

"Nuh the daughter. Mi hear say she find him tie to the coconut tree at the back of the yard."

"Then nobody never see him?"

"Tie up and douse himself with kerosene. Burn up till him skin crackle! Is the grace of God that the house itself never burn down."

"Is because him is an Indian, you know. Mi hear say them don't wait to dead. As soon as them reach a certain age, them just burn up themself."

"Them shoulda watch him."

"Nobody never expect it, especially like how him live in this country so long."

"Shhhh! See she a come!"

The whispering stopped as I approached, replaced by appropriate expressions of grief.

"Good afternoon, Selby. Remember me? I'm so sorry to hear about your grandfather. Mannis was so good to all of us."

Old hypocrites! I dismissed the thought as quickly as it had appeared. In truth, some of them had gone to school with me. I had no doubt that in their own way they, too, shared in my grief. Yet I said a silent prayer as I looked at their faces, proof positive of what I might have become, if I, too, had remained in the village. I nodded in acknowledgement and swept past the group, determined that they would not see me cry.

The rest of the family was already seated in the two front rows, every head bowed, as if in silent acknowledgement of our corporate guilt: *Why had no one realized what Mannis was going to do? Had we ignored the signs?* Without warning, the service began. There would be no procession with the casket up to the altar. Earlier, Pastor had advised us in grave tones that Mannis' body could not be brought inside the hallowed walls of the church. He had taken his own life, thereby committing a mortal sin. For this, the Church would not forgive him.

****

Mannis had lived with us from as far back as I could remember. My first memory is of a small, wiry-looking Indian, silver grey hair peeking out from under a brightly coloured turban and a long hooked nose jutting out beneath piercing black eyes which twinkled out of his wrinkled, cocoa-brown face. In my mind, he's always dressed in khaki: frayed shirt buttoned half way up revealing a white merino underneath, sleeves rolled up to his elbows, slightly crushed pants, one leg caught up by a bicycle clip, revealing very skinny calves, feet thrust into brown leather sandals. My father said it was because he had worked on the sugar estate all his life and didn't know how to dress any differently.

Everyone said that Mannis had been a champion cane cutter. They boasted of his speed and dexterity with the cutlass in the days when sugar was king. To me, he was my grandfather, the one person in whom I could confide when my parents were too busy to listen. Every morning, rain or shine, we would leave the house promptly at seven to walk the three or so miles it took to arrive at the school gate for the start of classes at eight o'clock. He never wore a watch yet every afternoon, at exactly three o'clock when school ended, he would be there, waiting to walk me back home, along with all the children who lived near our house. Most times we competed for the bag of sweets which he always carried and would distribute readily, once we could answer his questions about our school work. Years later, I discovered that he himself was illiterate, yet he could always tell when the answer was incorrect.

Then of course there was the protection that he provided when we were passing the cotton tree. Mannis said that it was over 100 years old. It was an enormous tree, with a trunk that was solid and thick like the trucks that transported the sugar to and from the factory. At times, the branches spread out dark and impenetrable, extending all the way across the road, casting murky-looking shadows on to the ground.

We children would become increasingly quiet as we approached that section of the road. Mannis had warned that duppies lived at the foot of the cotton tree. "Always bite you finger and count one, two, out loud when you passin'," he hissed. "Duppy can't count pas' three, so they will stand there waiting for the 'three' and that will give you a chance to run and get 'way from them."

"After two: one, two!" he would shout. And we would run as one, determined not to be the one to be caught by the cotton tree duppy.

Once Teacher Rockwell passed as we were running by, and told my mother what we were doing. She had scolded Mannis roundly, embarrassed that he should hold her up to such public ridicule. "You think ah sending the child to school for you to be filling up her head with foolishness?" she fussed. Behind her back, he winked at me, and we shared a smile. She doesn't understand, we agreed silently.

****

Shortly after this, I was sent off to school in the city. The morning of my departure, I woke up early, unable to sleep. Outside, the cock crowed incessantly, as if heralding a major event. The trees were still shrouded in darkness although the early morning sun was beginning to touch their crowns. I raced through the front door and saw that Mannis was already up, feeding the pigeons.

I helped him for a while then we sat in companionable silence as the sun peeped around the corners of the house, hinting at the new day ahead.

"So, is your las' morning, Selby," Mannis finally said.

I laughed nervously.

"Promise you won' forget me."

I looked at him, uncertain. Suddenly, he seemed very frail.

"Come. Give me a hug and tell me goodbye."

Suddenly fighting back tears, I clutched him tight. "I don't want to go. Don't let me go, Mannis!"

But he only smiled. "Is so life go, child. You can't stay one place. Everybody have to move on."

****

Richard was sitting in the living room when Selby returned from the funeral. He watched in silence as she opened the grill, walked slowly over to the entrance table, and set down the car keys. The years had been kind to her, he thought. She had put on a little weight but still had that tall, athletic build which he had found so attractive in the early days.

He remembered their first meeting well. He had just returned from New York and his mother had insisted that he attend a play being put on by one of her charities. Richard had agreed reluctantly, prepared to be bored. As they entered the theatre, he had heard a woman laugh, a deep throated infectious sound that soared above the chatter. It turned out that she was a friend of the playwright's daughter and had been away in England. She was home for the holidays but would return at the end of the summer to finish up her law degree.

"So will you sue me when you graduate?" he had asked facetiously.

"Well that tie is definitely a crime," she had laughed. "Hi, I'm Selby Whittaker."

She was wearing blue: an off- the- shoulder blouse that emphasized her long, slender neck and the smooth, chocolate brown of her shoulders. Her calf length skirt swirled as she walked, emphasizing long, elegant legs. Richard tried to think of something else witty to say, but failed. She laughed again, fully aware of the effect she was having.

He had pursued her with a determination that had surprised even him. He found himself making excuses to call her at odd moments every day. He delighted in the sound of her voice, her laughter. They talked for hours on end, days passing into weeks as the summer sped by. "We're made for each other," he said, reaching over, caressing the dimple on her cheek.

"Get over it! It's summer, Richard," she laughed derisively. "I have another two years. I can't focus on that now."

"Timing means nothing. Marry me when you're through," he said, arms outstretched, as she caught the plane back to England.

"Oh! Richard! You are such a romantic!"

He smiled. "So you'll marry me?"

****

We had been married for five years when I became pregnant for the first time. We hadn't really planned it that way. I was busy establishing my law practice and Richard's consultancy was really taking off. There just didn't seem to be the time. As luck would have it, the pregnancy was uneventful so I was able to work right up until the time that Nathan was born. He was a delight - a cheerful baby who gurgled happily whenever anyone came into focus.

I returned to work when he was six months old, despite Richard's objections.

"It's not as if you have to work," he said.

"Richard! I love what I do, remember?"

"More than your son?"

"That's not fair. You're still working, aren't you?

"That's different."

****

The September that Nathan turned three, he caught two colds in quick succession. The months of July and August had been particularly hot, with temperatures reaching into the high nineties. The slight breeze that surfaced every now and again only made the situation worse, like a fan circulating hot air in a closed and windowless room.

Everywhere that Selby went, conversations turned inevitably to the heat, until she felt like screaming to the skies to let loose some rain, a hurricane even, anything that would cool things down and give people something else to talk about. In response, September dawned dank and dreary. Soon, it began to rain, a steady, unrelenting downpour that refused to let up, drenching everything, fraying nerves.

Nathan was increasingly fretful. He had suffered through the heat but now the rain seemed to be saturating his body, evidenced by the mucus that streamed incessantly from his nostrils. When he developed a cough, Richard insisted that they take him to the hospital. "No temperature. It's just a cold," the doctor told them. "It's normal at this time of year." He prescribed cough syrup and antibiotics. Behind their backs, he exchanged a smile with the nurse. New parents! He dealt with them all the time.

****

By Christmas, life had returned to normal and we decided to spend some time with Mannis and my parents in the country. Richard had negotiated a good deal with his business partners in Miami and called to say he would return home early to celebrate. My case was scheduled to end on the Tuesday before the holidays and we agreed that we would leave that same afternoon, so that we would arrive at my parent's house in time to put up the tree before Christmas Eve. I finished packing late Monday night then looked in on Nathan, hoping he would sleep long enough the next morning to allow me time to review my notes thoroughly before going off to court.

I was up by daybreak. From the doorway, I could see that Nathan was fast asleep. If he slept for another hour or so, I thought, I would have time to complete my final arguments. Some time later, the shrill sound of the telephone interrupted my thoughts, and I glanced at the clock, amazed at how much time had elapsed. I raced over to the phone. It was Richard. He had taken a taxi and so I wouldn't need to pick him up from the airport.

"How's Nathan?" he asked.

"He's fine" I answered breezily. But it suddenly dawned on me that the house was very quiet.

"Hold a second," I said, and ran upstairs.

The room was still dark so I pulled back the curtains to let the light in. We had spent a lot of time putting the room together. We had listened to the advice of the interior decorator who told us that a child's room was much more than a room. "It's a castle, a sailing ship, a rocket, an oasis of imagination, and a refuge" she had trilled. However, since Nathan was so young, Richard had argued that we needed to give him time to develop his own personality. In the end we had compromised, using colourful walls and bedding, investing in stackable furniture and keeping the layout simple so that he would have a large play area for his ever growing collection of toys.

"Come, pumpkin, time to get up!" I laughed. He looked so peaceful lying there, his arms tucked under his head, legs spread wide in that pose that I loved, the blanket a tangled mass beneath him. I reached down to the bed and lifted him out.

"Good morning, my darling!"

His skin felt cold and clammy.

"Nathan?"

His head lolled back, lifeless.

Later Richard would tell everyone that he had found me on the floor of Nathan's room motionless, curled up in a ball in a corner of the room. "She never came back to the phone. She never called a soul", he told them. "I had to rush them both to the hospital."

Everyone was struck by the horror of the situation.

In the days that followed, I tried to explain that I had been in shock, unable to react, that I was paralyzed because I realized that Nathan was already dead. But Richard was unyielding.

"Did you check on him when you got up?"

"I did. He was asleep!"

"How do you know that?

"He wasn't sniffling or anything."

"Did you touch him?"

'No."

"Did you check to see if he had a temperature?"

I was silent.

"But you finished working on your case, right?"

I stood, head bent, condemned.

****

"You're young, you'll have other children," Mannis said. But we didn't. It's not that we didn't try. I became pregnant on five different occasions over the next four years. Four ended in miscarriages. Dr. Metcalfe, my obstetrician, advised me to stop trying after pregnancy number four, a particularly difficult period which saw me lose the baby at six months, three weeks and two days. When I turned up four months later, pregnant again, he was appalled. He claimed that I wasn't giving my body a chance, that the pregnancies were affecting me physically and emotionally. He even appealed to Richard to be 'more responsible, more careful'. However, Richard merely shrugged his shoulders. "It's her choice," he said.

Dr. Metcalfe offered to refer me to a specialist, but I refused. In my heart I knew why no child could survive in my womb. Richard's bitterness about Nathan's death had so corroded our bodies that nothing could take root.

****

Selby threw herself even more deeply into her work, determined to be made a partner in the law firm. Richard's consultancy flourished. As time passed, they entertained frequently and attended all the major events on the social calendar. If either one noticed the absence of any real emotional involvement, neither one mentioned it. There was no time, no need for introspection. Occasionally, when a colleague celebrated the birthday of a child, Richard would remark in Selby's presence, that they were both wedded to their work, that children were not important to them. He said it with a smile, defying any contradiction, and they both agreed that children would not allow them the lifestyle that they enjoyed. At other times, when friends visited and commented on the elegance and quiet of their home, he would joke "That's why our marriage works. It's because we have no children."

The words cut deep, searing her very soul, but in time, Selby learned to ignore the pitying glances and laughed along with him. They had found a way to survive.

****

Richard coughed slightly, and Selby started.

"Oh! Richard! I hadn't realized you were here."

"Or, you wouldn't have come home just yet?"

A flicker of irritation crossed Selby's face.

Richard took a deep breath. We used to love each other, he thought.

"I'm tired, Richard. It's been a long day."

"I can imagine."

"How did you get in? I thought I had taken back the keys?"

He ignored the comment. "So how was the service?"

In times past, this would have been the cue for him to reach out and hold her close. She would have been hesitant at first. It was almost as if she feared that putting her thoughts into words would somehow prevent her from savouring the event to the fullest.

Richard had learned to wait. He would continue to hold her, stroking her shoulders slowly until she was perfectly relaxed. Then the words would come tumbling out as she described what had happened: the people, the setting, and her impressions of the event. Richard had loved those moments. Selby was an excellent raconteur and by the time she finished, oftentimes he would be rolling with laughter. Afterwards, her mood would change and it would be her turn to draw him close. The lovemaking then was phenomenal. What happened to us?

"So what do you want?" Selby started across the room. Her heel snagged on a crease in the carpet and she stumbled. Instinctively, Richard reached out and caught her hand. Their eyes met. Selby pulled away sharply. Richard could see that she, too, remembered. For a brief moment he toyed with a fantasy of pulling her down to the floor and his heart quickened in anticipation. He glanced across at Selby but her expression was cold. It reminded him of the purpose of the visit.

"What is it?"

"I want a divorce."

****

I have always loved this room. It was on the eastern side of the house, so it received the morning sun, but in the afternoons, it was very cool. Richard and I had spent months selecting the furniture to ensure that it was just right. I had wanted an area where I could unwind after work; he had wanted to listen to his music. We had selected cool blues and earth tones for the plumped up cushions which covered the wicker furniture. The huge sisal map on the floor had been made by an old man that Mannis knew. We had spent hours driving up into the Cockpit Country to find him. "I know where him live" Mannis had told us stubbornly, flatly refusing to ask for directions. In the end, though, the result had been well worth the effort.

I sank deeper into the cushions, trying to find some soothing music on the CD player, striving hard to conceal the consuming anger that filled my belly and made me want to slap Richard in his face. This room was created to promote harmony, I thought. Such disrespect! What on earth could have possessed him to bring this up now, in this room, after the funeral? My continued silence was making Richard uncomfortable. I could see him willing me to say something, anything, to become angry, so we would fall into our familiar pattern of recriminations, so that he could justify what he was doing.

"Who is she?"

I was proud of how coolly I asked the question. It came out offhandedly, as though it really didn't matter whether he answered or not.

"You don't know her. A business associate."

"Oh! A young girl!" God, my life is such a cliché, I thought.

He hesitated. "No. In fact she's about your age."

My stomach churned. I wouldn't even have the satisfaction of ridiculing his choice.

The plaintive sounds of a saxophone filled the room. Ace Cannon was playing "The End of the Road'. I turned to Richard. "Mannis is dead. Do you understand what that means to me, how it makes me feel?"

He had the grace to look embarrassed.

I was suddenly weary of the whole charade. What had Mannis said? It's a lesson of life. Everyone has to move on. I got up, picked up my bag and walked to the door.

"Let yourself out, OK?"

DEATHGRIP
BY RUDOLPH WALLACE
2004

Let me admit right away that I came to the grisly subject of murder as something of a dilettante; a teacher of Jamaican creative writing with two published articles on the murder-mystery genre. I cannot recall how I came to embrace the canard known as "the death grip"; the notion that dead people cling to objects till you have to pry their fingers loose. What I know is that it took a particularly bad experience to finally set me straight.

It was my fortieth birthday, more than two years ago, and I was rushing home in the hope of catching a short nap before joining my friends for a birthday drink. Hopie Barnwell and I shared a common birthday and, being both single, we had evolved an annual hell-raising routine in celebration of the day. She was nine years older than I, and darker of skin than the rest of our crowd, but she managed to fit in all the same. I had come within inches of making a pass at her last year, but she had been too drunk to notice. All week long I toyed with the notion of completing the job this year, if she so much as laid herself careless. My plans were by no means definite but I had asked Alton to bring along an extra Viagra just in case Hopie needed help to get me going. We had all arranged – nine or ten of us – to meet at a newly opened 'mature entertainment' bar at Red Gal Ring. I had viewed the place, outside and in, and it seemed the perfect spot – large enough to accommodate my boisterous posse, and with enough secluded nooks in the event one wished to go for the kill.

Hopie's humongous breasts were probably uppermost in my mind as I cut short my four o'clock lecture and made my way to the car park. All in all it was a great day to be forty. The sun peeked out from behind a pile of white, billowy clouds high in the western sky and glistened from the mirrors and chrome roof-racks of the duty-free SUV's which belonged to the administration bigwigs. I located my own, rather modest Hyundai, barely giving a thought to the young miss hurriedly approaching me on the bias. I recognized her right away as Tamika Macintosh, one of my first year hopefuls who never spoke in class. It was not unusual for the more insecure students to seek private audience in this fashion and I was ready to dispose of her with my usual 'Read the textbook' line. But these things do not always go as planned.

"Dr. Bell", she started off, "there's something I want to ask you. I don't know if you have the time."

"Not really. What is it?"

"Sorry…another time then."

She was already turning to go, and I feared I had been too harsh. I dug deep for a gentler tone.

"Tamika…what is it?"

She paused. Her frightened eyes held mine for a split second before she reached into her knapsack and took out a dog-eared document.

"I was wondering if you could please read this for me Sir, and tell me what you think."

"Sure," I said, grabbing the papers from her hand. "I'll be happy to."

I hustled into my car without further ado, relieved that she had not attempted to engage me further. As she walked away I sized her up for the very first time, and was distressed from this angle at her general state of impecuniousness. It was no secret that there were students on the campus who did not know where their next meal was coming from. Tamika, from all appearances, would have been hard pressed to remember when her last had come. Her hair was done up in the all-too-common low-maintenance braids that now perched on her head like a market woman's cotta. The faded blouse she had on seemed, now that I thought about it, like the only one she ever wore. I could not help thinking that a child in such dire circumstances would have been better off entering the job market directly after high school, or 'if she felt duty bound to improve herself,' embark on a crash course in home economics. Her physical structure was frail, like she would crumble under some good sex, but I could think offhand of several fellows who would have no difficulty retaining her services as a housekeeper or in some similar pseudo-domestic capacity.

It was one of life's tragedies that Tamika and thousands of starry-eyed girls like her had fallen under the spell of Mills and Boon and come to fancy themselves as writers. As I watched her waif-like frame disappear among the trees, I made a mental note to show mercy on the paper she had so diffidently offered up for my blessing.

The birthday bash was a bad scene from beginning to end. Alton casually pulled me aside the moment I arrived and informed me that, birthday or no, he had to deny my Viagra request. He was running low and no way was he going to dip into his emergency stock just so I could screw the insipid Hopie. Besides, I still owed him for two and it was becoming apparent that I could not afford to have sex on a lecturer's salary. Not to worry though, he and his brother Delbert would pick up the slack. And that was just the start. Edwina Skyers, a lanky Peace Corps worker, vomited on my shirt and, though I tried to wipe it off as best I could, the odour lingered stubbornly, contributing in all likelihood to the sudden and suspicious increase in my allotment of personal space. The object of my desire never made eye contact with me all the time we were there, and when I finally offered to go home to clean up, refused to ride with me - "for company?... as one guest of honour to another?" I drove out alone, promising to return soon but knowing in my heart that the night could not be salvaged.

My mind was hardly focused on Tamika's manuscript when I reached for it on the passenger seat where it had lain all evening. I was cruising along at twenty miles per hour or thereabouts, slowly coming to grips with the full extent of my desperation. To set my sights on an old fart like Hopie Barnwell was to hit rockbottom. To grovel before her in the presence of witnesses was to plumb new and unexplored subterranean depths. Alton's dictum came back to haunt me: "If you going to beg, beg for something worth the while." The man was no orator but he understood to a tee the intricate dynamics of sexual pursuit.

I glanced at my face in the rear view mirror. Not for the first time, I winced at the crow's feet that made me look closer to fifty than forty. It is true what they say: Red people do not age well.

Once inside my apartment, I threw myself on the bed, wallowing in my bitterness for a full fifteen minutes before it dawned on me that Tamika's manuscript was still in my hand. I switched on the light and glanced at the cover page: "Siblings – a short story". It was something of a relief to discover that the girl was an aspiring novelist. She had displayed all the trappings of a purveyor of god-awful poems and I had been bracing myself to do some vomiting of my own. In a sense, I was ahead of the game already.

The story held me right away, with an emotional time-bomb that ticked ominously from the opening exchanges. It told of a nineteen year-old Fletcher's Land girl in the grip of an unseemly admiration for her seventeen year-old brother, wrestling with feelings she was determined to express, yet knowing that when she did it would tear her family apart. This was Jerry Springer territory – no doubt about it – but the deft handling of the subject matter, juxtaposed against the raw and occasionally graphic dialogue, betrayed a level of insight and maturity that would have done credit to a seasoned author. The finely wrought characters burned their way one by one into my psyche and engaged me in a way few fictional characters had. When I had finished, I went back and read the entire piece again… and again. It seemed to improve with every reading. In due course, I had to set the manuscript aside because my vision was becoming blurred with tears. Tears, I must tell you, which were not all story-related.

Tamika's unbounded talent seemed to throw into sharp relief my own failings as a man and as a writer. Creative Writing, more than any other field of academic endeavour, exemplifies the old saying: "Those who can, do; those who can't, teach." I was respected by my peers as a trenchant critic, good at dissecting other people's work and in my constructive moments, quick to point out areas of possible improvement. The tragedy was that every year I came into contact with a new crop of facetious freshmen who wanted to know why, if I knew so 'effing' much, I did not have a bestseller – or any kind of novel come to think of it – to show for my efforts. I had by this concocted a few cleverly-worded stock answers to the question, all pointing to a certain indifference on my part. But the stark reality remained – there was no list of authors, however lowly or obscure, that had ever found space to accommodate the name of Albert Bell.

It had not been easy for me to confront the growing evidence that perhaps I could not write. Several years earlier, I had entered a prestigious literary competition in the hope of proving my true worth to the world. My submission took the form of an avant-garde short story which I had nursed along for many months and which I thought had now gelled into high art. I knew I was taking a risk in pitting my skills against an invisible army of amateurs, but reckoned that the anticipated victory would expose me to a popular audience and validate my standing on the campus itself. It was a ghastly mistake and, ironically, it was only the sheer ineptitude of the work that saved me from total humiliation. Had I not completely bombed – had I for instance been favoured with an Honourable Mention, the official stamp of mediocrity – my name would have made the Sunday papers and my reputation, such as it was, would have been severely compromised.

I awoke on the first day of my forty-first year with a splitting hangover and a startling revelation. It was amazing that I had not seen earlier what was so obvious now in the clear light of day. Tamika Macintosh could not have written that story if her sorry life depended on it. Spelling and grammatical errors had in all likelihood been planted to throw me off the scent; to disguise the fact that she had purloined the thing lock, stock and barrel from a senior writer. The only question was, why? Since this was not a class assignment, what did she stand to gain from this willful trickery?

I announced at the start of our next lecture that I wanted to meet with Tamika afterwards. She seemed to twitch at the public revelation of our deep and dark secret, and must have been surprised that none of her classmates – a usually inquisitive bunch – was curious enough to hang around the precincts during our meeting. They seemed to know instinctively what Tamika herself had not been able to grasp – that there was no chance of a sexual liaison between her and me; that while I was not a hunk in the classic sense of the term, my skin colour and faculty status gave me automatic access to a higher standard of student p***y than she would ever embody.

"Did you write this?" I pushed the folded manuscript across the desk.

She nodded vigorously. "You like it Sir?"

"I think it shows real talent. I wouldn't have expected someone like you, someone so young, to take on such a theme…Where did you get the idea?"

She shrugged and lowered her eyes, but said nothing. My mind was again warming to the idea that she may actually have authored the story. I could think of no established writer with the first-hand Fletcher's Land experience so vividly displayed in the work.

"Did anybody help you with it?"

"You're the first person I ever show it to Sir. I can't show nobody else."

"Surely you must have discussed it with your *friend?*"

"I don't really keep that kind of friend," she mumbled.

I reached for the manuscript again. Our eyes locked for several seconds as we stood there, each holding one end like we were posing for the camera.

"Let me take another look at it, and see what I can recommend."

She let go of the manuscript and smiled.

I headed home shortly before noon, reflecting on my encounter with Tamika. I had no more classes for the day and could easily have delved into the details of her story then and there. Why had I chosen not to do so? I searched what was left of my soul but could find no suitable explanation. Our situation was uncannily reminiscent of Deathtrap, the movie in which Michael Caine's character, a has-been playwright, plots to murder an unknown author, played by Christopher Reeve, to steal his masterpiece. It was a demeaning premise really; something no self-respecting writer would contemplate in his most desperate moments, yet, there was no getting away from the possibility that the Deathtrap plot lay somewhere at the back of my mind throughout our brief exchange. Why else would I have delved into matters of authorship, collaboration and the like?

I did not look at the manuscript for several days. During that time, I found myself chuckling aloud whenever I thought of the ludicrous notion that had wormed its way into my head. It all seemed so far away now. Siblings was good, to be sure, but not good enough to kill for. And however much I craved the recognition that had eluded me thus far, my pride would not allow me to plagiarize another's work, least of all an untrained child's.

Calabash Literary Festival was approaching and the organizers had put out a call for short stories. Tamika's manuscript was good enough to make the grade, and I decided to encourage her to submit it. I started to read it again, this time to correct whatever minor flaws existed. It seemed that Fate, in denying me the gift, had imposed on me the role of mentor to the gifted. As before, the story pulled me in, entangling me in its complex emotional web. I heard myself reading long passages aloud; saw myself holding forth at the Calabash podium as the audience clung to my every word. I sneered in my mind's eye at the homosexuals in the crowd who hugged each other openly, overcome by my moving paean to forbidden love. I reserved an extra dose of charm for the delectable 'brownings' who queued up to get an autographed copy of my short story collection. Their wide-eyed expressions said it all. With a Viagra or two under my belt, I could cut a swath through this group under cover of the Treasure Beach darkness, and be up with the crack of dawn to celebrate the latest African-American poetry sensation. (I would have preferred if Channer and Company had scheduled me earlier in the day, but not to worry. My silken cravat provided more than an adequate buffer against the evening chill.) I was now a famous author and, all in all, it was a hell of a thing.

I offered to meet with Tamika on the weekend to share a few thoughts about the work. It was important for both of us – though this was never voiced – that no one from the campus should see us out together and jump to the wrong conclusion. At first I thought of inviting her to my apartment, but quickly abandoned the idea. My neighbours knew me as a man of discriminating tastes; one look at Tamika in her distinctive lower-class getup would force them to revise their opinions. I settled instead on a river, three or four winding miles above Papine. It was a spot I had frequented in my salad days when my desire for privacy had a decidedly more sinful twist.

I bought two fast food lunches at a drive-through and picked her up at a bus stop at Matilda's Corner. Along the way I attempted to discover as judiciously as possible how much of the story was autobiographical. I raised the question of siblings; she grinned and looked the other way. Yes she had brothers, and no she was not in love with any of them. The inspiration for the story had come from a brother and sister in her community, now in their sixties, who had lived together all their lives. Neither had ever been seen with another member of the opposite sex and Tamika thought it only fair to assume that they were lovers.

"So your story is about this couple in their younger days?"

"I try to put meself in the woman position Sir…Suppose she was the first one feel the urge? How you tell your brother something like that?"

It was impossible, of course, for me to venture a response. Suffice it to say that once she started to talk the veil of shyness lifted and there seemed to be nothing she would not discuss. As regards her social circumstances, I soon discovered that I had been right on nearly every count. She was the eldest of her mother's six children, born and raised in Fletcher's Land where she still lived, and having only a passing acquaintance with her biological father. Her mother's affection towards the children was doled out in strict proportion to the assistance received from their six separate fathers and, as luck would have it, Tamika's sire was the stingiest and therefore the most despised of the bunch. There was a tremor in her voice as she observed that, even now, her mother rarely addressed her without reminding her of the lowliness of her bloodline. In the circumstances it was not surprising that the girl kept mostly to herself, finding what satisfaction she could in books and in her own fantasy world. I no longer had to wonder how, at nineteen, she had come by her precocious grasp of the human existence, nor why she had chosen to seek her catharsis in fiction.

The riverside was not as idyllic as I remembered it and we had to walk a long way downstream in search of a spot that was both secluded and free of garbage. Tamika, who was wearing a tube top and knee-length jeans, quickly took off her sandals and urged me to wade alongside her in the shallow water. She stretched out an arm, indicating that the offer included the holding of hands. I politely declined.

The narrow bank disappeared altogether in some places, making it difficult for me to retain my magisterial poise. I soldiered on for ten minutes until we located an acceptable picnic site, a large well-grassed area that sloped gently down to the water's edge. By then my shoes were soaked and I had to take them off in any case. This act of disrobing, small though it was, advanced the informality of the moment beyond what I could comfortably tolerate. I was grateful for her silence on the matter of my toes, which had been known to attract unfavourable comment in the past.

It was well past midday when we sat down to eat. As I watched Tamika methodically devour her meal, a KFC two-piece, I felt a surge of satisfaction not unlike what real philanthropists must feel, and instantly came to regret my decision not to splurge on a three-piece. I was half-inclined to offer her some of my fries but concluded, after some deliberation, that the sharing of food was an act of intimacy that would jeopardize, if not completely breach, the teacher-student divide.

She gathered up the boxes and the empty cups and went off to dispose of them, while I turned my attention to the manuscript. I was flipping through the pages, organizing my thoughts; when I heard her voice somewhere off to my left.

"Ow! The water cold!"

Her jeans were spread out on the bank and she was up to her knees in the fast-flowing stream, tube top still intact but festooned now by the skimpiest of panties. I remained unfazed. The poor child was probably used to bathing at a public standpipe. Who was I to hold her to uptown standards of modesty? (That you could cup her entire ass with one hand was not necessarily a bad thing. Her Fletcher's Land lover would probably need the other hand to hold his spliff or, in an emergency, reach for his 'nine'.)

"I thought we were here to discuss your story," I remarked, with an austere professionalism that communicated clearly my immunity to half-naked teenage girls.

"I want to bathe in the river first Sir. Is alright if I take off mi clothes?"

It was something of a trick question, but I was equal to it.

"It looks like you've already started. I don't suppose it matters; nobody is around here to see you."

Grinning playfully, she whipped the top off in one easy motion; then, without warning, tossed it to me. I failed to catch it as it soared over my head, being momentarily distracted by the jiggling 30-B's with their tiny, off-colour nipples.

I focused again on the manuscript, this time even more intently, knowing her eyes were fixed on me. I scrupulously ignored her intermittent squeals, supposedly in reaction to the cold water. I was too seasoned a campaigner to fall for such amateurish attempts at titillation. Should I decide to peek at the body, I would do so without her complicity and in my own good time.

"The water nice you know Sir; you should come take a dip."

I pretended not to hear.

"Sir! Sir!"

I still did not look up.

"Sir…Help me!"

I was suddenly aware of the edge of panic in her voice. My own panic set in when I looked up and did not see her. Then I glimpsed her hand, clutching, slipping and clutching again on a large rock twenty feet away.

"Tamika? What's happening?"

Her head bobbed up from behind the rock.

"The current drawing me way…Help me Sir!"

She was indeed in trouble, fighting desperately to hold on to the rock while the powerful swirling waters threatened to tear her loose.

"Sir!"

She was screaming her loudest now, as if hoping to summon assistance from Papine. I jumped to my feet and saw for the first time the churning expanse of water behind her. It was dark green – too dark for my liking – with none of the translucent sparkle I had come to admire. Also registering for the first time was the loud, hollow wail of the river as it crashed with fierce momentum around the bend some forty yards away. An involuntary shudder propelled me forward half a step and may well have filled the drowning girl with false hope. I, for one, knew I was going nowhere. The manuscript was in my hand, secure and dry. The Calabash podium loomed larger.

"Can you stand up?" I shouted.

"No, no…help me! I can't hold on no longer!"

"I…I can't swim," I explained.

It was not something I was proud of, but from the look of things – barring some kind of miracle – my secret would be safe.

"Si-i-ir!"…Now I knew what writers meant by a plaintive cry.

"Didn't you see the current before you went into the water? Honestly, I don't know what to tell you."

I could have told her of course that there was no point in the two of us drowning. I could have said that one of us at least had to remain alive if this gem, now firmly in my grasp, was not to be lost to the world. I could have said that the best person to preserve a work of this standard was the man with the credentials to take it to the next level.

"Sir…Please!"

It might seem unconscionable at first blush to weigh a short story against a human life, but this was an exceptional story, and hers was an unremarkable life.

"Dr. Bell! Help me!"

And what could one say about the body itself? The breasts were perky now, sure, but what would they look like thirty years from now if she did survive? Succulent naseberries do not mellow with age; they shrivel and rot. And nature is as hard on the female body as it is on fruits. For sheer durability, give me a good story every time. Was I being unduly callous? Probably. But I wasn't the one killing her. It wasn't like this was the Deathtrap scenario… Was it?

"I…I don't know what I can do Tamika…I'd love to help but -….Tell you what, I'll see if I can find a long stick."

With that, I hurried into the bushes, clutching the manuscript. Perhaps I am too sensitive, but young women's screams unsettle me at the best of times; and I knew this one would not go quietly. Sleep is hard enough to come by as it is; one does not need fodder for a whole slew of nightmares.

It was chilly in the bushes. I found myself a smooth rock where I sat down to ponder my options. Much as I would have loved to mourn the passing of one so young, this was neither the time nor the place. I drew instant comfort from the fact that no one of consequence had seen us out together, so I would be spared the need for elaborate explanations. More to the point, I was now free to establish my authorship of the story without having to suffer any pangs of false guilt. The story could not help her where she was going and, in view of the lurid subject matter, might even cost her a few spiritual credits. By changing the locale – where the hell was Fletcher's Land anyway? And adding my own distinct grammatical touch, it could be mine completely, copyrighted and everything, by Tuesday. Should another copy surface from her side at some later date, I would have to explain that the dear departed had taken it without my permission – a mere misdemeanour in comparison to the other crimes she must have committed with impunity as part of her everyday survival regimen in the ghetto. Calabash entries closed in a matter of days, but whatever happened from here on I could coast towards the deadline.

Twenty minutes passed before I emerged to retrieve my belongings. The containers from our meal would contain my fingerprints, but I saw no need to scrounge around for them. Assuming the body were ever found, it would be miles away from here and there was no way the police could identify the spot from which she was swept. I mumbled a silent word for the life of Tamika Macintosh, whose embryonic career had been snuffed out by a single act of stupidity.

Back in the clearing, I could not avoid a last furtive glance at the rock on which the brave girl had played her last parados. She could count herself lucky, I figured, bearing in mind the Bard's observation, 'The valiant never taste of death but once.' The rest of us would have to go through life with our fears and insecurities, dying many cowardly deaths before our time.

As I bent to pick up my folder, a twig snapped behind me and I almost soiled my Perma-Press Dockers.

"Sir?"

I spun around. She was reclining on the ground a few feet away, fully dressed.

"Tamika…you…you gave me quite a shock."

"I think you say you was going to get a stick."

"I…I couldn't find one…I'm glad you…How…?"

"You mean to say you really leave me there to drown Sir? I never know a big man like you coulda so coward. If anybody did ever tell me say-"

"Coward? That's a harsh word. Try practical. The water was rough. I was sure it would wash both of us away."

"You never have to come into the water at all. All you have to do was stretch out something for me to hold on to. But no. You run way leave me."

"You were ten feet from the bank – fifteen probably. The stick would have had to be at least that long…and extra sturdy too to withstand that terrible force…What was I supposed to do; cut down a tree with my teeth?…Look, I'm sorry."

"When I couldn't hold on no longer I just let go and pray…and the water toss me and pitch me…all the way past where you see the river bend. Next thing I know I find meself 'mongst some shallow stone, way down so."

"Thank God. Maybe if I had gone in to help you I would have been the one to drown. Everything has worked out for the best, when you think about it…Are you still in the mood to discuss this story? That's why we came here; remember?"

I smiled to ease the tension. It was a poorly timed smile, coming as it did on the heels of a premature suggestion. Tamika lost control.

"I don' wan' discuss no story!" she snatched the document from my hand. "To hell with this damn story. Me nearly drown to rahtid and all you can talk bout is story?"

She hurled the manuscript towards the river. It swirled around in the wind and landed near the bank, no more than five yards from where we were standing.

I sprang into action. "What you doing girl? You crazy?"

I grabbed her by the shoulders and shook her. Her head snapped back and forth, light and easy like a balloon on a stick. I had forgotten in my anger how frail she was. The horrified look on her face told me I had overreacted badly. Her eyes searched mine for a moment then slowly turned to the manuscript, still clearly visible beneath two inches of water. It had taken her a while to see the light, but it was blinding her now.

"Dr. Bell, you cold y'know."

"I take that to be some kind of moral judgment?"

My tone was just right and went a far way to restoring my image of detachment, I thought. If I could sustain my studied indifference for a few crucial seconds more I could stroll over to the water's edge and casually retrieve the document. I relaxed my hold on her – foolishly as it turned out – and she lunged for the papers again. I do not recall how I covered the ground so quickly. I only know that our bodies collided as she bent to pick up the soaking document, and the momentum sent her sprawling on her backside in two feet of water. More to the point, the manuscript was again submerged.

"It's my story, and if I want to destroy it you can't stop me."

Evidently she was yet to come to terms with the reality that a ninety-five pound weakling had no right messing with a big man's dream. She made to rip the papers and I pounced again, before her emaciated fingers could begin their fiendish work. My hand held on to her neck, and her head, offering little resistance, plunged beneath the surface of the water. She didn't thrash around; didn't fight back – perhaps it was a malnutrition thing. Her eyes stared at me from below the water like she didn't believe she was drowning; like there was some rule somewhere that said lecturers can't drown students; like I was bound to let her go any time soon. She seemed in a curious way to be studying my face. Who knows? Had I released her then and there she might well have come up with a good recommendation for treating crow's feet. We will never know. My instincts in that moment did not incline towards quick disengagement. I hadn't set out to kill her. She sort of died on her own, if you really want to know. A couple big bubbles followed by a few smaller ones and that was that.

If the death grip scenario has any validity, the girl – whatever her immediate problems – ought not to have let go of the manuscript. It is as simple as that. But there was no denying her astuteness, and perhaps she was astute enough to see, even as my tightening fingers extinguished her life, how by relaxing her fingers she could somehow diminish mine. It is futile to speculate at this stage. All I know for sure is that the flying leaves instantly mingled with the white foam, and disappeared among the rocks and the shadows. Dazed, I tossed her body into the vortex where it swirled around for a moment then took off, to reunite with our undiscovered masterpiece somewhere in ignoramus heaven.

Fame did not entirely elude Tamika Macintosh. Her picture adorned the television news for three days running – starting one week after our little outing – and again many weeks later, after a badly decomposed torso washed up on a beach in St Thomas. Nobody ever asked me about her and it is unlikely that they ever will. Every now and then I feel an occasional pang of remorse for what might have been, and I muse again on the idiotic concept of the death grip and the importance of always having a backup copy of one's work.

MY MAN MARCUS
BY CHARMAINE MORRIS
2001

Arrrrgggh! Miss Mingleton was going on again about Marcus Garvey. Couldn't this wait? Ten minutes to the end of the Easter term. Doesn't she know that I need to get home? I had things to do and clothes to pack. Me — in Miami for two weeks. Dad had given in — felt guilty over the break-up thing with Ma I supposed. But who cared? I'd gotten my trip and major bucks for spending.

I was lost in my head, as usual, and didn't hear Miss Mingleton speaking. "What? What was that Miss Mingleton?" I piped up doing by best to look as if I'd been concentrating all the time.

"Buela, you need to pay more attention – what's the matter with you child? she said. "Can you tell me the name of Marcus' fleet of ships?" She leaned back, more on one foot than the other, seemingly in a relaxed mood, waiting with the chalk poised in her hand. She didn't fool me. One wrong answer and she'd be all over my case. Just like she'd been all term. I cleared my throat and did a couple coughs. She shifted foot and waited. Some of the nonentities in class started giggling.

Well the joke's on them — I was the only one going away for the holiday. I looked at Miss Mingleton and squished up my brow. I knew the answer was in my book. If I could just flip the page. It was right there — him before a picture of a big ship. Black something. Then I heard Gary whispering beside me. Bless his pathetic little heart.

"Black Star Line!" I said and settled back in the chair, There. Take that to the bank you old bat.

She twisted her mouth to one side like she was trying to figure out what to do with whatever punishment she'd thought up for me that time. Sorry teach. Give it to the next dumb kid. This one is flying outta here in the morning on a yellow bird.

"I want 1500 words on Marcus Garvey done over the holidays." Miss Mingleton said looking at me.

Damn! When was I going to find the time. I shrugged my shoulders. I wasn't going to let that bother me.

****

That night, I was in a tizzy trying to decide what to pack. I had to take enough stuff to wear plus keep enough space for the ton load I would buy. All done, I sat propped up in bed waiting for the clock to alarm at four so we could get ready. When it did I was already dressed and pulling my bag through the bedroom door.

****

We exited the Miami airport and I took a deep breath. I loved that smell. It was a sense of something different; something new and clean. Everyone seemed so ready. Like something great was about to happen. Everyone was on-the-go. Everything sparkled in the bright sun light. I was with my cousin, Kelly, and her mom, Aunty Mac waiting for Uncle Mac who was circling because he didn't want to pay the parking fee.

Kelly and I literally grew up together, so we were like sisters. Since they migrated the year before, I only saw her once when they came back for Christmas. In between, we mainly e-mailed. We couldn't stop talking. She was telling me about her friends and shopping and I was telling her how glad I was to be out of school.

"But you know say you have to go school with Kelly next week — right Buela?" Aunty Mac said waving down their brand new F150.

School? How she mean school?

"Don't you guys get Easter holidays?" I said to Kelly.

"Not like home – dem people yah nuh believe in nutt'n sacred." The van stopped and Kelly hopped in. Her dad came around for a hug, but I was still boggled. How could I leave two weeks of no school to come all this way to more school? It was just the type of luck I had.

"You guys don't wear uniform do you?"

"No," both Kelly and her mother said.

Great, at least I could sport some clothes. Maybe it wouldn't be so bad. But still, two weeks of school!

Uncle Mac's F150 was fully loaded. I soon forgot my troubles when the custom fit TV came on and he turned up the sound so we could watch a dance DVD. They lived in a neighbourhood Kelly said was mostly white - but that didn't bother them.

"Caan bother with dem niggers." Uncle Mac said and I wondered who he was talking bout. "Especially fi wi own people. You woulda swear say dem no come from no way."

"You got that right Uncle Mac." I said. At least that I knew.

****

My mouth dropped when the pick-up swung into one of two garages. I mean we have big houses in Jamaica and even our own house was huge, but I never thought this was how Uncle Mac them was living. Ma never told me this part. And I would never have guessed — at home Uncle Mac managed a wholesale downtown and was always on hard times. I looked at Kelly and she smiled because she knew what I was thinking. We burst into laughter and bolted from the pick-up round to the side of the house to the pool out back.

"Jesus Kelly, you never tell mi say a so the house big! You even have swimming pool." She stood grinning at me like she thought I'd lost my mind. I ran around the pool saying 'damn' over and over. Inside, the house was on two levels. Everything was oversized. The living room smelt like an aromatherapy store. Candles were everywhere. Going back outside I was able to see the part of the garage that was closed off from the front protecting a spanking new black Bimmer. Kelly and her folks really had it good.

The weekend was a blast. We did the mall, movies, restaurant and Uncle Mac took us to the roller rink. By Sunday I was on an entertainment high – didn't know which side was up from down.

Easter Monday, I was in school with Kelly. It felt weird because if I were back home I'd be lazing around the house with my best friend the remote. But it wasn't my school and this was a temporary thing so I could cope. Plus, we were thrashed out in the best casual garb we could find. We sauntered in the school like we owned it and hooked up with Nina and some of Kelly's friends who I'd met on the weekend.

In class, Kelly's teacher made a big deal of welcoming me to the school. She asked the usual boring teacher questions about hobbies and the like. I humoured them all and flowed out my best. By Tuesday I had everyone saying 'irie' and 'yeah mon.' As if that's how we talk back home.

By the end of the week I was in the swing of things at Kelly's school and I was breezing. Friday morning during break we hung out by the side of the basketball court checking out the guys shooting hoops. My black denim low rise jeans were kept up with a wicked leather belt. I had on the hugger sleeveless rasta colored T-shirt Aunty Mac got me and my hair was braided with extensions, complements of Aunty Mac again. I gave no thought to the fact that Ma was going to make me take them out the minute I hit home, but lived with the fact that I looked cool. Kelly was in tennis shorts and an even 'wickeder' halter-back top that almost popped my eyes when I saw her that morning. As brave as I was, I wouldn't dare own or wear something like that. Even the platforms she had on her feet were off limits for me.

The boys were looking and we were showing. Nina and another girl joined up and we leaned against the fence planning for Friday night's sleep over at Kelly's when a group of white girls walked up.

"Well, well, if it isn't another drug smuggling African from Jamaica" one said staring at Kelly. I dropped my Jan Sport bag on the ground and stepped up to her face. I was ready for a fight but Kelly was telling me to back off and cool down. The girl gave us a sneer and walked away.

"What a sketel boo." I said. "What she really mean by that though?" I was brushing off my bag when Kelly told me that most of the people she met thought all of us lived in trees near the beach selling ganja.

"What the hell...! What? She never watch CNN. Which little back a wall world she live in? But the gal outaorder." I was ready to run her down and drop some ninja kung-fu kicks. No one diss my homeland like that. Girlfriend need to learn some manners. But Kelly, using better judgement, calmed me down. She told me not to worry about them because they were jealous. One of the guys came over to find out if everything was ok. "It is now." I said forgetting the ugly brat.

It was the last session of the day and I was watching the clock and tapping my feet. The guy I met on the court and his friend are hooking up with Kelly and I at the mall for a movie. I was scared at first but then Kelly checked with Aunty Mac and she said it was ok.

Immediately I wanted to live with the Macs. I would never have asked Ma to go out with a guy I'd just met and she didn't know from Adam. The Macs were cool.

"What was that?" I said. The teacher was talking to me but I hadn't heard. "Marcus Garvey? What about him?" I had no idea what she was saying. Sometimes it was hard to hear behind that yankee drawl she had. Kelly said she was an import. She said it the way Americans spoke about foreign cars. "But you get used to her after a while." Kelly said. Well, I guess 'a while' was more than a week because I really had to concentrate harder than I did in my life to hear what she was saying and when I had it figured out I couldn't believe my ears. She wanted me, as a Jamaican, to make a presentation on Marcus Garvey on Monday. What the hell! Couldn't I get away from this guy? Who cares what he did eons ago? He was now going to cut into my mall time. Damn! And it was my last full weekend too! Damn!

I saw the sketel who'd accosted us by the court grinning her big head off in the corner. I smiled politely and told Miss... (I'd forgotten her name) that I'd be delighted. Yeah right! How am I going to do this?

My man Marcus was really putting a damper on my act. All through the movie I kept wondering what I was going to do. Kevin (the guy I was with) kept whispering things in my ear but I wasn't listening because Marcus kept popping up. When they dropped us home, Kelly was "p-o'd" because she thought I didn't like the guy and that would affect her and his friend.

"No man. It's just this Marcus Garvey thing. Boy, I did tink I get way for the time being but is like the man haunting me."

"But you don't have to do it? What them gwein do – expel you?"

We both laughed at that because what Kelly said was true. But still it bothered me.

After Kelly went to bed, I went to the study to do a search for information on Marcus. There's no way I was going to spend Saturday morning doing that when we were to go shopping with Aunty Mac, and Kevin and his friend had invited us out again.

I didn't want to use Kelly's computer because she was a light sleeper and the slightest noise usually woke her. Also, the study was near the kitchen and I thought it was going to take forever to find any information on this character and I might need a snack to keep me going.

So I logged on to MSN Search and typed in Marcus Garvey. I looked at the count for the search result: *1-15 of 22,807 containing Marcus Garvey.* Wow! I never knew my man Marcus was so all over the web. I was even more surprised when I saw that the sites were well built — mainly by Americans though.

There were stories about the Black Star Liner; How Marcus was the first African-American leader in America – and the world – to organize masses of black people in a political movement. As if he was one of theirs.

There was a story about him wanting to take back Africa from the Europeans and how he believed in the Motto of the UNIA – "One God! One Aim! One Destiny!" The same words I heard echoed at festival time in Jamaica year after year but never paid attention to. Marcus even wrote poetry and the songs for the UNIA – there were over a hundred in all. I saw the full words to Africa for Africans and I was impressed. It made me feel good at ten past midnight to be reading on the world-wide-web about a Jamaican. Then I was sad because it suddenly occurred to me that Marcus Garvey is regarded more overseas than he is at home — typical.

I leaned back in the chair to study this black man. Black as night with his hat with the huge feather dangling above. I tried to think his thoughts at a time I couldn't imagine. He was such a proud man in such a hard time. He'd gone through so much and still remained true to his cause and people. It made me think for the first time about things I took for granted.

In the middle of my thoughts the MSN Messenger flashed. I clicked on it forgetting that I wasn't at home. It was a message from someone called Benny Boy:

Hey Mackie the thing go down today. Everything cool. When we going to share up?

This was Uncle Mac's message and I didn't want to be caught fassing. I was about to politely tell this guy he had made a mistake when the door opened behind me. "What you doing?" It was Uncle Mac. He had a look in his eyes that was a combination of fright and anger. I'd never seen him so uncomfortable and it made me afraid. I mumbled through an explanation about not wanting to wake Kelly and having to do research. His face changed and he told me it was alright —just that this was his private machine and Kelly knew to stay far from it. He didn't mean to scare me. I showed him the message and he asked me to give him a few minutes. I left him to get a drink from the kitchen and give him all the room he needed. After that look, I didn't want to get in Uncle Mac's way.

The next day Kelly, myself and Aunty Mac hit the stores. I had my list and Ma had given me another.

I was talking about the Marcus Garvey research when Aunty Mac said: "Your Uncle tells me you were using his computer last night. Maybe you should stay away from it from now on. You can use my laptop in the living room if you want." She gave this weird embarrassed look. Like how Ma looked when she was aplogising for Dad. I agreed. It didn't matter to me, but I was now curious about what Uncle Mac could have on his computer that was so secret. Then again some people are sensitive about their things – maybe he was one those.

We gave the bags to Aunty Mac and went to meet Kevin and his friend. I didn't have as much fun as I thought I would because I kept thinking about Uncle Mac and Marcus. I don't know why I compared them but I did. Maybe it was because Uncle Mac in a way resembled Marcus Garvey if you dimmed the lights and squinted your eyes. But the two were also so different. After three hours on the computer I wanted to know everything about the world that Marcus lived in. I wanted to know what it was like to grow up in all that oppression and come out so strong. Our lives paled in comparison to his.

I mumbled an excuse and told Kevin and Kelly that I needed to get home. She wanted to come with me but I saw the look on her face and knew she also wanted to stay. I told her it was ok. I'd catch a cab. Kevin was less than happy. But hey, sometimes that's life.

Back at the house in the living room, my two index fingers flew over the keyboard of the lap top. I'd made up my mind to do the project right. I'd present it at Kelly's school and then take it home for my own project on the life of Marcus Garvey. The house was still after Aunty Mac let me in and gave me the laptop. She had to go out for a while. Uncle Mac was in the study having a meeting and I wasn't to disturb him or go near the door – as if I would. Not after what happened the night before.

So I'm sitting plucking away at the keys when the door to the study opens. I more hear it than see and then I hear footsteps down the hall. A few minutes later some guy pushes his head round the door and begins to say hi but stops himself when he realised it wasn't Kelly. He was dressed in full black with a thick gold chain around his neck and smelt of some cologne that was too strong for indoors. He had on one of those stretch black tie-heads that Ma said was a waste of money because back in her day you'd use a stocking head to get the same effect. His hand, when he raised it, was a display of gold jewellery that glinted and sparkled under the glare of the dome lights. He had a scar from his ear to his mouth and I had the immediate thought that he was a crook. I said "Hello," winced at his gold teeth and quickly returned to work.

After another hour I got up to get some food. Nearing the study I stopped. I could make out Uncle Mac's voice because no matter how he tried, he could never manage a whisper. He had this deep hoarse voice that made you think he'd gotten a bad cold as a kid and never got rid of it. I heard other voices I didn't know but could make out pieces of phrases: shipment... drop... payment idiot... people... owe. I decided I'd heard enough. As I straightened to walk away the door opened. I moved quickly down the passage and could feel Uncle Mac's eyes staring at my back. A lot of things flew around my head when I was making the sandwich. I thought about what I'd just heard and what the girl at school had said — another drug dealer from Jamaica. I shook the thought from my head.

Nearing the study door, I stepped lightly but it was open. The meeting was over. Uncle Mac was sitting behind the big oak desk. He looked at me like he wanted to say something harsh but I gave him a quick nervous smile and hurried back to the dining room. I was afraid I wouldn't have been able to lie if he'd asked me what I'd been doing earlier.

At school on Monday I stepped before the class with Aunty Mac's laptop and a projector I burrowed from the science lab.

Kelly helped me set it up and I treated the class to a lesson on Jamaica and then a detailed presentation on My Man Marcus. At the end, I bowed to a round of applause. I looked at 'sketel boo' — her name is Wanda — and saw that she had a little smile on her lips. She wiped it off when she realized I was staring at her. Maybe if I had more time, we would actually have become friends. We were just two people from different parts of the world who'd judged each other wrongly. Kelly was impressed and the teacher, Mrs Beautilleaux, was going on and on about how informative and enjoyable the presentation was. She tried her hand at 'irie' and 'yeah mon' and we all roared with laughter!

I left the Mac's without saying anything to Kelly about what I'd heard. Me and Uncle Mac would never be the same. Aunty Mac kept asking what was wrong. But I could never tell her. I remembered the look on Uncle Mac's face and just said I missed Ma. And that was no lie.

On the plane I realized how much I like it at home. It'd been two weeks but it seemed like forever. So much had happened. When the plane landed, I was one of those clapping and grinning like an idiot. I don't know why they did it but for me it was the relief of arriving safely; happiness that I didn't have to deal with Kelly's life; a whole lot of love because I knew Ma was waiting for me, and pride that I was a Jamaican like Marcus.

****

Mrs Mingleton was surprised, maybe even shocked when I volunteered to go first because I'd never volunteered for anything before. I couldn't repeat the digital presentation because we didn't have the equipment at school. It was a pity because some of the others could learn a thing or two about their country. I took my place before the class and began... "Marcus Garvey is a Jamaican hero..."

END.

CONTRIBUTORS

CLAUDETTE BECKFORD-BRADY

An avid reader all her life, Claudette decided to try her hand at writing. She began by entering the JCDC Literary Arts competition where she achieved a number of gold medals and other awards. Her first novel, *Sweet Home, Jamaica* was published in the UK in 2007, and the sequel, *The Missing Years* in 2009. Not a writer by profession, she has turned a hobby into a paying concern.

MICHAEL RECKORD

Michael Reckord is an educator, writer and Minister of Religion. He started his career as a journalist more than 40 years ago and continues to write for the ***Gleaner*** as a critic of dance, music and drama. He has received numerous awards for his poems, plays and short stories on national and international levels.

CARROLL EDWARDS

Carroll Edwards is Head of Marketing & Communications at The University of the West Indies, Mona Campus in Kingston, Jamaica. Writing is a hobby and she has received gold, silver and bronze medal awards in the Jamaica Cultural Development Commission (JCDC) Creative Writing Competition. In 2006, she was named the JCDC Choice Writer in the Competition

CHARMAINE MORRIS

Charmaine Morris has won gold, silver and bronze at the JCDC Literary Arts competition and is published in Bookends and formerly the Gleaner. She is featured in two anthologies of the best of the Jamaica Observer fiction publications and placed in competitions opened to those published in the Literary Arts Magazine. Charmaine is the Human Resource Manager at Island Outpost.

A-DZIKO SIMBA

During her 40 year writing passion, Ms. Simba's work has been published locally, regionally and internationally and has attracted numerous awards. Her poetry, short stories and drama for stage, video, television and radio have been used by Ministries of Education and of Health and corporate clients and have featured on radio and television. She applauds JCDC's initiative in giving encouragement and recognition to writers working in an often disregarded area of the creative arts.

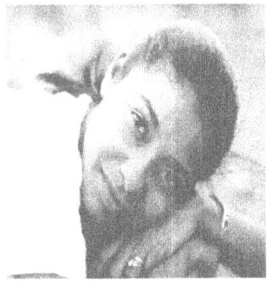

RHONDA HARRISON

Rhonda has won the JCDC overall writer's prize twice, 2006 and 2008. In addition, she has won nine medals for her creative writing.

NADINE TOMLINSON

Ms. Tomlinson aspires to be a published author of sophisticated fiction and poetry. She has entered literary competitions over the years, including the 2000 JCDC Short Story Competition, in which her entry placed first, and the Commonwealth Short Story Competition. An avid blogger, she is planning a spin-off of her blog, *Life, Unscripted, on the Rock*, as well as laying the groundwork for her first book. Her interests include yoga, travel, volunteerism, and reading. Her personal mantra - Rejoice and Relish Life!

DIONNE JACKSON MILLER

Dionne Jackson Miller is a journalist. For over ten years she's hosted a current affairs programme on radio, and also hosts a weekly current affairs programme on television. In addition, she recently qualified as an attorney-at-law and hopes to one day move into writing stories/books with a legal theme. She enjoys writing for children and is working on a children's book.

VERONE JOHNSTON

Verone Johnston is an editor, lecturer in adult education, and proud mother of a baby boy. In between teaching, writing, and looking after her son, she conducts genealogical research, and has traced her ancestors back to 1777 – so far. Although she lives in England, her roots are firm in her beloved homeland of Jamaica. Her Masters level research focused on 19th century Jamaican history, and was inspired by her historical novels, which she aims to publish soon.

RUDOLPH WALLACE

Rudolph Wallace has written for radio and the Jamaican stage for several years. His fiction has won gold and silver medals in the annual Jamaica Cultural Development Commission's Creative Writing competition, and he was selected as the overall winner of the competition in 2003. He currently divides his time between teaching and writing.